Ocean's Grave 1907

Sean Michael Malone

www.ten16press.com - Waukesha, WI

For information, please contact:

www.ten16press.com
Waukesha, WI

Edited by Lauren Blue
Cover design and illustrations by Teresa Carlson

For Ray and Debra

Often separated by distances small
or great, your love and support have
nonetheless remained ever present,
your character and wit an inspiration.

Prologue:
The Art of the Deal

Silas McGovern was not a man for fixing prices. As the experienced owner of a bookstore with an emphasis on the exceptionally rare, he objected to the practice and very notion of labeling his assorted books with a predetermined price. No "one charge fits all" as far as he was concerned. Every book on his shelves had one perfect customer, representing one perfect worth. Despite this conviction, if pressed, Silas would admit that at times he had been forced to settle for sales where he was not convinced of a seamless match. The flow of the capricious economy did not always enable Silas to hold out for the person who would surrender their heart's treasure for a piece of his collection. But tonight would be that occasion of auspicious thunder that caused the man to nearly salivate. Tonight, he would settle for nothing short of the best deal. He had found a perfect match.

The bookseller was assisted by his sole employee, Thaddeus Townsend. Thaddeus was the only clerk thus far to last more than a few months at McGovern's Rare Books, one of several such niche establishments in New York City. Silas was compelled to part with his previous assistants whenever business slowed, but he had not regretted those partings. Thaddeus, on the other hand, had proven a capable organizer and salesman and had demonstrated a general knack for the business. Thaddeus was also Silas's first Negro employee and did not request a comparable starting wage, which was no small benefit to his bookkeeping. Yet Silas acknowledged acumen when he saw it; after half a year's service, Thaddeus, a father of four in his late twenties, saw his salary raised higher than that of the rotating staff of McGovern's Rare Books. Silas hoped to retain the bright clerk as long as possible, a prospect that would be strengthened by the transaction he anticipated tonight.

Just under a dozen purchases had been made that day by the time regular business hours were winding down. Thaddeus had handled all but one of the exchanges; Silas insisted on always attending to the first patron of the day. Today it had been a red-cheeked errand boy for Charles Francis Murphy, or "Silent Charlie" to those who had lived in New York long enough to know the recently ascended influential leader of Tammany Hall. The lad had a list of several books on New York's political histories and a few memoirs, and Silas was all too happy to part with the niche editions with a non-aggressive negotiator.

Under most circumstances, Silas would have insisted on haggling personally with more customers, but he had been attempting to reserve his energy for his special customer later that night. The bookseller's quality of sleep had been disturbed of late; at night, he often woke to hear a strange clawing sound within the walls. It was a very gentle scratching, barely discernable to the point that the sound could eventually be overcome and the listener could return to slumber. Silas had reassured himself that the rats of New York City had not advanced into the brick structure of his home and business, but the mysterious noise that troubled his midnight waking was not completely absent from his thoughts even in the daylight. Worst of all, he believed that it had been getting louder.

"Mr. McGovern, I'm going home for the night," Thaddeus said, holding up his pocket watch to show 6:00 P.M. "I'm leaving the front unlocked, as you said."

"Wonderful, my good man. What is Augusta cooking tonight?"

Thaddeus paused with a thoughtful expression. "Pork chops with her special seasoning, baked potatoes, and green beans—the last fresh ones for the season I'd reckon."

Silas nodded to his clerk in farewell and now savored the first small moment of quiet in having the space to himself until the arrival of his expected patron. The pangs of the late autumnal sunlight filtered through the windows that looked to the street. Silas moved over to rest his hand where the last reddened sunbeams touched the smooth wooden countertop. He smiled as he felt its warmth and frowned when he observed the dust on his fingertips, then withdrew down a hallway that divided the central, inner wall that led all the way through the building to the back alley. A door separated this hallway from the storefront, and from here one could access additional inventory space, the back door, or the upstairs. Silas's destination was the back room, although in truth, he had two: one was for his general inventory, but there also existed a second, secret room underneath the staircase that led up to his apartment on the second floor. This small chamber was concealed by a section of wall capable of pivoting open. A handle, which operated the concealed hinges, hid in plain sight as a decorative flourish on the side of an adjacent bookshelf.

The secret room contained Silas's rarest and most valuable pieces. Not even Thaddeus was permitted to enter this sanctum. Indeed, Silas believed that he had kept its very existence a secret, even from his dear employee. It was a low space, barely large enough for a person to take two steps inside and hunch without kneeling down. The chamber was kept mostly clear, save for two felt-lined chests with separate keys. Taking out one of the prized books to examine and caress was a solitary therapy that Silas often enjoyed at the end of the workday. He would relish some final time with the strange text on the night of its sale.

"Mr. McGovern?" Thaddeus's voice called out, muffled and distant, and for a moment Silas had trouble discerning if his clerk's voice was the product of some paracusia.

"Damn it, man, what is it?" Silas yelled back all the same, turning his head in jolted alarm toward the direction of the voice to overcome the muting effect of the small space.

"You have a caller, uh, a professor—a client," Thaddeus said apologetically, the words trailing nearer, indicating that he was coming back in, past the main counter.

He's early, Silas thought in instant panic. *And Thaddeus is coming! Everything is wrong.* His premier client had arrived three hours ahead of time, and in Silas's experience, when someone arrived that far off the agreed appointment, it was never a good indication. Worse yet would be the awkward encounter with Thaddeus discovering his superior in such compromising fashion. Silas backed out quickly, taking care not to bump his head in the low space. He stowed the book and gently closed and locked the chest, fumbling with the nearby lever to rotate the wall back into position. He then closed the outer door and noticed another layer of dust on his shoulders. Upon inspecting the powder, he saw flakes of plaster and perhaps mortar, as if the foundations of the building had been disturbed recently. *It has been too long since the place has been properly cleaned. I'll have to get Thaddeus on it. Heavens, I may need to consult the surveyor about the foundation if that doesn't banish these fresh coatings of dust.*

Silas brushed the uneven gray patches off his black suede jacket and composed himself as he strode back to the front room. His buyer had communicated a certain formidability in his correspondence, and now that the moment had come, the bookseller found his breath short and his mind troubled by vague trepidations. He stepped through the hall into the front room, and the familiar sight at the front counter made him breathe easy.

The man standing in front of him was not his buyer. Silas had met the man once before at an academic conference at Princeton. He was Professor Henry Armitage, a well-spoken but, as Silas decided, thoroughly irritating man. He looked a touch over fifty, but had an apparently infinite reservoir of enthusiasm in acquiring new items for Miskatonic University's library. Armitage was also undaunted in sharing his cautionary expertise on the ownership of certain occult books, which was undoubtedly why he was standing in Silas's shop at this very moment. Everything about the man had a silvery aura, from the crystalline glitter of his whiskers and combed hair, the green-gray glint of his eyes, to the finely-pressed fabric of his clothing. "I am very glad to have caught you, Mr. McGovern," he said with a graceful nod as he removed his hat. "I understand that I am trespassing at the end of your business hours, but I can promise that it is for your express benefit."

"Mr. McGovern?" Thaddeus asked, unsure.

"It's fine, Thaddeus, go ahead," Silas said. He watched as his clerk strolled away, looking back once before going home to his family and dinner. "You're damned persistent, aren't you?" Silas quipped to Armitage.

"I don't object to either adjective," Professor Armitage replied calmly. "But for all of my traits, I only wish that I were more persuasive." He began shifting his hat around in his hands, giving cursory glances around the room and bookshelves. "But I wouldn't have returned if I did not harbor hope, even if it is motivated by a most foolish optimism."

Silas shifted his weight between his feet, causing the

floor to creak beneath. "I have nothing new to say, Professor, either from our last meeting at Princeton or from your incessant correspondence. I am not showing particular favoritism here; were you to offer a figure greater than your competing buyer, I would of course sell the item to you. But only under those conditions, as I have already arranged for the sale in good faith." Silas was growing angry as it seemed he already had lost Armitage's attention. The professor had produced something of a journal and had been scribbling things into it. Armitage cocked his head to the side, as if noting observations made earlier in the day. "Am I losing you, Professor?" Silas asked, almost as loudly as he had shouted to Thaddeus from the back room.

"No, but whenever one prattles on about money, I become appallingly distracted . . . and unintentionally rude," he added, catching his choice of words. "It is regrettable that I am of more humble means than your intended buyer. It is even more regrettable that my arguments to persuade you otherwise remain mostly the same: that you would be donating the rare book to a carefully managed university library, that you would avoid consorting with a man who has committed atrocious evil, and that you would have surer reward than whatever is being offered." He paused to clear his throat. "My presence here is because I have obtained one new insight, and on this alone, I have made the trip to New York for a final appeal."

Silas had already made up his mind before this surprise visit, but there was something in the delicate orchestration of Armitage's speech that gave a moment's pause. At the very least, it had sparked curiosity, and curiosity was crucial to Silas's craft. "Well, I won't deny you the chance to elaborate. You did make the trip after all," he said, retreating his tone slightly.

"That is good," the professor replied, for the first time showing a conservative smile. "Perhaps we could sit at your consulting desk that I spy over there?" He pointed, and Silas nodded.

Upon being seated, Henry Armitage again opened his satchel, this time producing a folder. He had assembled a file on an incident that occurred on November 13th of last year, 1905. The first item that he slid across the table was a newspaper clipping from the *Boston Herald* about the suspected arson of a bookstore in Salem, Massachusetts.

"The Essex Street Collection, a well-established fixture of the historic district, was lost to a sudden, blazing inferno in the late hours of yesterday evening, November the twelfth. The owner of the store, Alistair Ragland, is presumed to have perished in the fire pending positive identification of the sole recovered body by the medical examiner. The source of the fire is under investigation by the Massachusetts State Police and has not officially been declared arson as of today's edition. In addition to the loss of life, it is feared that one of New England's finest independent collections of early colonial religious and occult studies—as many as four hundred volumes—are now lost. Mr. Ragland is survived by his sister Anita Somerset and her family."

"I've spoken with and have come to call Anita Somerset a friend," Professor Armitage began. "And Alistair Ragland's story played out eerily similar to the bidding process that you find yourself in. Anita and I became personally convinced of the identity of the perpetrator, whether it is genuine or an alias. Our conclusion is founded on this," he said dramatically, placing a brown, tattered strip of paper on the table. "It was found at the scene of the crime and somehow spared the ravages of the consuming fire. Please do not ask how I came to possess this evidence, but again, I place my hope that the cost of acquiring it was well worth it, in this case."

The slip of charred paper was such a delicate scrap that even Silas, a professional in handling such material, lifted the note with trepidation between his index fingers. After a moment's squinting, he perceived slightly darker letters among the black, burnt, and brittle paper: *7:30 Appointment: Reginald Linden.*

"The note, clearly taken from an itinerary book, was of little help to the police investigation, as clues only indicating a name often are," Armitage expounded. "By this time, the name Reginald Linden was linked uselessly to a missing professor of tiny Carroll College in Waukesha, Wisconsin. I have a contact near there who has confirmed that this is a dangerous and unhinged man, but exceptionally cunning. However, with no address and no assurances that Reginald Linden still lives, or that the arsonist and murderer implicated in this note actually is the missing scholar, the investigation could not proceed in that direction without regional cooperation of law enforcement." This long-winded sentence caused a short breath from Armitage, who leaned forward towards Silas. "But you aren't obligated to believe that the identity is authentic. I'm *telling* you that regardless of the name employed, this is the same party that you will encounter tonight. Please, Mr. McGovern . . . do not make the same mistake of Mr. Ragland. Sell me the book and promptly take some time, some days at least, away from your store, perhaps also holding your more precious inventory with you. The colored gentleman, Thaddeus I believe you called him, should do the same. No one and nothing will escape the perilous attention that you have now drawn here. It's not too late now, but it soon will be." Armitage leaned back in his chair, and to Silas now looked rather tired.

"A newspaper clipping and a burnt scrap of paper," Silas announced with crushing disinterest. In truth, he found Armitage's words oddly interesting, perhaps disturbing. While he had not yet decided as to the soundness of the advice, Silas was unable to resist pouncing on the thin evidence that implied a certain arrogance from Armitage. "I also recall, Mr. Armitage, our first meeting where you spouted out those incredible tales of devilish magic and unseen entities. The more I think on it, while you did make a retreat of such nonsense in our subsequent discussions, once again you have revealed yourself like one of those crazed street prophets predicting the Day of Judgment—it's as if you are unsatisfied with a more grounded existence carrying on. But I, Professor, am precisely one of those individuals, and don't have the luxury of entertaining such fantasies, no matter how much your own conviction might sway others. Now it is I that must infringe on rudeness and insist that you do not visit, inquire, or otherwise message me on the issue further. In fact, it would be better if you no longer contacted me on any matter; there are other stores that may serve you, certainly."

Armitage had the most shifting gleam in his eyes, a new and dangerous look for the mild scholar. While the man's lips remained closed and his jaw locked, the intensity in his pupils threatened that the middle-aged gentleman was on the brink of violently seizing the bookseller or thrashing through the store to find the book and be gone with it. He did none of these things. Armitage relaxed, gave something of a deep sigh that was aborted by a throat-clearing cough, and solemnly nodded while also rising from his chair. "I am sorry to have troubled you. I wish you and your business nothing but the best and will abide by your request." Armitage carefully reaffixed his hat, delegating how much of his silvering hair would be scrunched under the brim, and turned his back and left.

The silence that resumed inside of the shop seemed deeper than Silas was accustomed to, and he reminded himself to keep breathing. He was proud that he had stood his ground in face of the dramatic show of tactics, but found that he was not relieved by the departure of Armitage. The danger and implications of Armitage's tale increasingly nagged at him in the remaining hours of silent waiting that faced him. The owner of McGovern's Rare Books convinced himself that he merely required some liquid courage to settle his nerves.

With a visit to his pantry upstairs, Silas returned to the storefront to eat a cold dinner—he felt compelled to maintain a view of the street. He mixed some water and Scotch in his drinking glass, which quickly alleviated much of his unease. Silas reclined in his chair at the consulting desk while listening to the low murmur of activity in the street. He watched the lampposts come on one by one, and each beacon represented a small increase in comfort. During this time, he attended to the lighting within the store as well, which made a noted improvement in his general uneasiness. *Rather childish thing, fearing a client as some warlock or pyromancer hearkening to my doom.* Silas attended to a final work matter, preparing a shipment of all twelve volumes of Isidore Singer's *The Jewish Encyclopedia* for a buyer in San Francisco. He scribbled a note for Thaddeus regarding the Post Office Department and checked his watch to observe the time as 8:56 P.M., high time for him to retrieve the book before his guest arrived. Silas glanced at the doorway out of impulse after stowing the pocket watch.

An outline haunted the doorway—a figure that cascaded a perfect blackness with its shadow that somehow managed to escape the illumination of both streetlamps and the lights within the shop. Silas had not heard any knocking, nor the door open, indeed he had heard no footsteps, yet here was his invited guest, punctual by several minutes. "Mr. Linden, welcome," Silas rasped, finding that his voice had been deflated by the surprise. "Please make yourself comfortable and have a seat. I shall procure your book," he said more clearly, although he avoided looking at Linden and already moved away with unctuous, almost bowing motions against his intent but spurred by strange instinct. Something about Linden's presence cast an aura that demanded appeasement. "I am at your disposal," Silas added clumsily, a final impulse, while he spirited to his concealed room. It may as well have been a phantom that stood there, for Silas had waited for no response nor truly regarded the arrived guest. He grabbed the book from the secret back room and decided to resolve the transaction as swiftly as possible.

The bookseller returned to the front room to find his buyer sitting calmly at the consulting table, his features now visible. Reginald Linden was tall, that much could be seen even while he was seated, as well as slender, with an uncomfortably upright posture. His face had a very handsome bone structure as if modeled from a statue cast, and was nearly as pale as the Italian sculptures residing in the Museo Barracco. It was very difficult to estimate the man's age; Linden was certainly not old, but had become *aged* as if some daily Herculean exertion weighed heavily on him. He wore a single-breasted frock coat of black, as well as gloves, and his head was bare to reveal long black hair, touched with silver in many places, brought back into a ponytail. His right hand rested on the table and seemed to instinctually curl into itself, perhaps from some condition, while in his left hand, he held a bundle wrapped in cloth.

"I've always found the phrase so appealing, for someone to be at my disposal," Linden began with a casual and pleasant air, picking up where Silas had left off. "Almost always they don't know how right they are, for indeed, I intend to dispose of them—*with* them," he corrected. "Mr. McGovern, I refer to avoiding the common rabble's foolish discourse in mundane conversation, you understand?"

"Ah, right," Silas responded, not believing the placation. Nonetheless, he placed the book, packaged in leather, delicately on the table. "If it's all the same to you, Mr. Linden, I'd like to seize on your preference of concluding our business speedily this eve; I haven't been sleeping well."

"Certainly. Your payment . . ." he muttered, placing the wrapped bundle in front of Silas. The bookseller unwrapped it, revealing two bars of solid gold. The cast of the bars was unusual; there were small imperfections as was typical, but they lacked the usual inscription of the caster and weight information. As Silas squinted and tried to estimate their weight, which was at least four kilograms each, he saw that they were not entirely without engraving, but possessed subtle and strange characters that at first he deemed Arabic, but then decided were quite unknown to him. The bars of gold had a pallid, otherworldly glow alongside the element's typical luster in the store's gentle light. "These may even run a handsome dollar over our agreed-upon price in valuation, but I am inclined to generosity and also understand you may have a chore in redeeming them for their proper value."

"Very good, Professor Linden. I am of course quite

satisfied and trust that you are as well?" Silas asked, shocked at what little satisfaction the prospect of the glittering hunks brought him. He watched as Linden took a moment to examine the interior pages of the book and a small smile formed on his lips. Silas could not read Latin, but clearly Linden could, who muttered the name *Olaus* and a few other inaudible reactions while his eyes scanned the pages. Silas knew the book was called by a number of curious names, most often the *Necronomicon*, and he had acquired it from an old Frenchman in 1888 who had seemed relieved to part with it. After two decades of possessing the strange volume, he found he was more unsure than ever of its proper worth. Linden's aura suffocated any coherent thought; Silas only wished for the man to leave.

Linden gently closed the book. "Partially satisfied, verily, the book is what I wanted, but now that you've given me a taste of your hospitality, I wonder . . . since I have made a considerable journey, I must request that you show me to the rest of what must be an extraordinary collection. Nothing of your shelves in here," he gestured around him, "but your *truly* esoteric texts. I am prepared to further compensate you appropriately, no, *generously*, in the same manner as for this volume."

"Perhaps another time, Professor. The hour is growing late, and I don't think I'm of right mind to introduce such negotiations. I have been exhausted of late," Silas repeated while dreading the prospect of more time in Linden's company.

"You don't appreciate the opportunity you have here, McGovern," Linden warned through a more confrontational tone. His right hand began twitching, and Silas thought that he might have been trying to open those fingers more—it appeared that he was slowly succeeding. Linden noticed the staring. "I may only possess one good hand, but I won't be treated like some fool. I've contended with far worse than you, bookseller, and there are insights that don't deserve to be hoarded away here—sold off to some subliterate dunce or democrat that fancies himself a collector!"

"I apologize, Professor Linden, but I must insist that you leave. I won't be addressed this way in my own establishment," Silas blistered, attempting to straighten himself to the same commanding rigidness of Linden. "My business is the most respectable of its kind in all of New York City. You can't go about threatening me!"

Reginald Linden cackled at that. "No? You are not without some spine, I'll say that. But my patience with this type of discourse expired years ago." He bolted from his chair, seizing the book off the table and kicking up the desk at the stunned Silas while the gold bars thudded heavily onto the oak-paneled floor. By the time Silas had braced himself from the upended counter, which crashed to the side, Reginald had whipped around him and tightened his arm over Silas's neck. Reginald was much stronger than his wiry frame suggested, and although Silas threw his elbow and free fists back into the ribs of his attacker, the hold was not broken.

While he gasped, through watery eyes Silas perceived that

another man had arrived in the doorway holding a shotgun. "Take your hands off him!" Thaddeus shouted. "Keep them raised above your head, or you'll have buckshot in your back! You understand me?!"

"Yes, there's no need to get so excited," Reginald replied calmly, releasing Silas and turning to see the man who threatened him. He partially ignored the warning by wiping his sweating brow with the back of his hand and pushing falling strands of his hair to the side, which prompted Thaddeus to club him with the barrel then cautiously take a step back. Reginald endured the blow with astonishing stoicism, yet appeared more convinced of Thaddeus's intentions and raised his hands in submission. "I did render payment, however, and shall leave with my book," Linden insisted as a streak of blood moved down his forehead.

"Not a chance in hell!" Thaddeus barked, flanking quickly behind Linden and pressing the barrel of the gun into his back. "Out!"

The two went out into the street without further exchanges while Silas stayed in the shop and recovered. Both the book and the bars of gold remained, and Silas was unsure how much time passed as he panted and sat on the floor, his back to a bookshelf. Eventually he brought himself to his feet and began tidying up the front room. Silas began to worry about his clerk, who he realized might be his most dependable friend. At last, a tired-looking Thaddeus returned.

"Thaddeus, thank God . . . thank God," Silas remarked. "While I was meeting with Linden, you ought to have been unwinding at your home, digesting your pork chop and baked potatoes. I'm not sure what would have become of me if you hadn't appeared in that moment!"

"No, Mr. McGovern, hell no!" Thaddeus replied vehemently. "The more I thought about it, I'd have been mad to let you fend for yourself after that other professor came around here with his warnings. I hadn't decided who I needed to be warier of, but this second man was far worse!"

"Might have had some words with Armitage himself, did you?" Silas asked. "Where did you end up taking Linden?"

"Yes I did, beg your pardon, Mr. McGovern. I couldn't help but hang around for a spell after closing, and Armitage seemed rather happy to find me in the street and repeat his concerns. I resolved to come back here after dinner; I recalled your appointment time. As for Linden, I took him down to the nearest station house. At first, the officers were more inclined to Linden's account than mine, despite me telling them about the assault. One of the officers there, you know, Jim Donovan? Well, he knows us, of course, but he didn't say a damn thing! The more I saw their faces, their gaping jaws . . . I realized that I had made a mistake. I don't deny it must have been a sight—a Negro bringing in a well-dressed gentleman with a shotgun at his back. Before I was the one in the holding cell, the scene caught the attention of a detective there when he heard me mention the name Linden. That fellow's name was Chester Higgins, and he remains quite interested in that Salem case that Armitage was talking about and has been in touch with the authorities up in Boston. Him being there made all the difference," Thaddeus admitted, shaking his head. "I'm sorry it took so long, Mr. McGovern."

"Well, I'm damned glad you stayed around, and I do owe Armitage an apology. I count myself as very fortunate to have encountered that horrid man and remain unharmed . . . although not unshaken." A moment's pause transpired as both men searched for the next words to say. "I'll be glad to sell the book to Armitage instead . . . as I should have done in the first instance. In fact, here," Silas handed the book to Thaddeus, again secured in the small satchel along with one of the gold bars. "Let's get the book away from the shop, and that bar is yours to keep. We'll be getting that volume into Armitage's hands at no charge—no further bartering is worth the trouble that sodding book has already caused."

Thaddeus looked in wonder at the hunk of precious metal and the mysterious book, which he held reverently. "With any luck, Mr. McGovern, we'll be able to track him down before he's returned to Arkham. It might be a little bit crowded, but you're welcome to spend the night under our roof, sir." Thaddeus paused as he formed a weary smile at his awkward invitation. "I've already agitated my poor wife because of my tardiness to dinner tonight, so I'm in the doghouse for the day as it is."

"Thaddeus, no, I couldn't possibly impress on you and your family for that. I'm sure Linden has been deterred from any dramatic attempt and hopefully will remain detained for the next few days."

"Then I could stay the night here, sleep in the front room to keep an eye—"

"Go home and get some rest," Silas ordered, not ungratefully. "There will be work enough tomorrow, wires to send, and perhaps some general store policy adjustments as well."

Once he had assured Thaddeus countless times that he would be alright, Silas locked and dead-bolted both of the sturdy doors that granted entry to the building. That was enough to convince himself that he would at least hear a considerable disturbance should a forced entry be attempted. Silas had an old cavalry saber that he had accepted as payment from a visiting Englishman a few years back; he kept the weapon on an upper shelf in his closet and tonight moved it just beside him on the bed with the blade pointing away. The bookseller spent the better part of the next hour or two lying in bed and being aware of his thumping heart and his tightening muscles at each little creak and sound. But even this miserable vigil of paranoia became tiring after a while, and eventually, Silas slept.

The bookseller woke at a sudden noise, amplified to a thunderous disturbance in his dreaming. His instinct was to grab the sword, which he wielded in his dreams alongside Wellington at Waterloo, but he instead knocked it off the bed, sending it to clang on the wooden floor of his bedroom. Silas bolted upright, expecting to hear creaking footsteps or the harsh chiming of broken glass. Instead, as had been the case for several nights, the infernal and sporadic clawing noise emitted from the wall behind his headboard and seemed to be what had awoken him. Silas's earlier suspicions that the sound had been growing louder were now undoubtedly confirmed. Angrily, he got up and pressed himself to the wall, crouching in his nightgown to listen. The scraping sounds continued, and on a whim, he rapped at the wall with his fist, as if the action would stop the noise or perhaps startle whatever vermin had invaded his place of rest. Instead, his fist punched through the wall, sending bits of crumbled plaster tumbling down. His bedroom wall had become paper-thin, gnawed at and corroded from the other side.

A rush of cold, stale air discharged from the new opening, suggesting a chute of untold depth had been bored through building, street, sewer, and earth. In the dark space was something of a tangled network of vines, or perhaps roots, that coiled upwards from the delving void. As Silas squinted, he became aware of a second scent—a waft of humid rot radiated from the branching roots. He gagged at the smell, which exponentially became more pungent with each passing moment. Silas further noticed a sallow film that lined the walls of the hollowed shaft. It was the kind of nightmarish infestation he never thought he would face with waking eyes. The air of his room felt very close now, as if it had been deprived of all oxygen, and Silas crossed over to recover his sword.

The stench from the unearthly roots inspired a kind of hatred. Silas, still unsure of his reality in his half-woken state, turned the sword handle to bash through more sections of the weakened wall. Now with adequate space, he began hacking at the roots that had advanced the furthest. He was determined to rid himself of this conjured nightmare, at last exposed for him to strike back. In minutes, he was sweating heavily through his nightgown from the labor of dozens of sword slashes against the thick roots. The cathartic satisfaction of his savage attacks was diminished in that only seldom would the keen sword cut through the powerful carapace with a single strike, often taking three or more well-aimed swings before a burst of yellow ichor at last indicated that he had cut through and severed one of the roots. The bookseller grew faint from the exertion as he watched yet another section of vine tumble back into the void. He realized that it was a folly; there were too many clusters creeping up the hollow for him to deal with on his own. Alarmed, Silas became acutely aware that the noxious air was affecting him, numbing his muscles and mind, and he took ungainly steps towards his bedroom door. The cavalry saber dropped from his hand as he braced himself against the wall to buy an extra step. He fell forward, his arm slumped against the door just beneath the knob. He could barely lift his forearm and failed to secure his grip on the handle. Only a tinge of pain registered from his body slamming against the wooden floor. Silas was unable to rouse himself, and the last action he could do was turn his head ever so slightly.

He did not return to sleep, indeed he no longer blinked, but he remained conscious of his surroundings as long hours passed. In his peripheral vision, he could see the roots stretching out from the breach, never moving perceptibly but nonetheless slowly creeping towards his body. He could feel nothing, but his vision revealed that his body had been borne up from the floor, the roots coiling around his wrists and ankles. *How many hours has it been? Was this some grand design of Linden? Could he truly orchestrate such madness?* Silas wondered. *Is it morning? Thaddeus will find me! He must find me!* Through bloodshot eyes, Silas watched as he was lifted out of his bedroom and lowered into the hollowed shaft. His sensations partially returned in the form of piercing pain that assailed him in a growing number of spots across his body; Silas felt his flesh tearing off while the roots dug into him with hidden maws. Continually he descended, his dim sight always directed downwards into the void. In that blackness, he could begin to discern a larger figure, perhaps the size of a man, or that of a giant. It was impossible to tell without knowing the vastness of the cavern. It waited, silently. Silas desperately wished for his spirit to leap away from his body, yet only a choked and broken scream came out.

Part One:

City of Ghosts

1

San Francisco had once been called the Paris of the West, but it had become the city of ghosts. The picturesque polis of cable and electric street cars running up and down avenues overlooking the Bay had been transformed to a quiet desolation. It was now February 1907, but the city was far from silent when the great earthquake struck on April 18th of last year. Yet even then, the various shouts and screams had lasted only a short while and were followed by a crushing silence that signaled the many dead, a feeling that still prevailed and hung over the city. For survivors, to remember the frantic voices also reminded of the groans of crumbling structures which terrified their victims as walls, ceilings, and floors gave way in claustrophobic panic. But even deadlier was the fire that spread in the aftermath, consigning trapped residents to a scorching hell in their final moments. How many had died? It was difficult to say, as official figures were never even given for certain districts, such as Chinatown. But one man had survived, and despite his own expectations, had done better for himself from the disaster. His name was Mitchell Bernheim.

Mitchell Bernheim operated and co-owned an antique business on Van Ness Street called Bernheim & Hughes Antiques. Roland Hughes was Mitchell's partner. Mitchell had never actually met the man in person; apart from helping Mitchell by proxy with the investment to open the storefront in 1901, Hughes had no involvement with business operations. Mitchell had only directly interacted with Hughes's lawyer, J.R. Longstreet, though he had exchanged a number of letters with his partner, who wrote in a strong hand with courteous and lucid writing. Five years passed in this manner until the earthquake struck. Mitchell was having his morning coffee in his apartment directly above the store when the tremors began. A picture of his mother was among the first objects sent flying off of shelves and clattering to the floor. Yet apart from some minor building damages and insurance claims on damaged antiques, B&H Antiques survived, and Mitchell had been largely aloof from the pain and loss of that day. He regarded himself as more observer than victim, and it was hard not to feel guilty at that reality.

There was nothing but to try and return to business as usual. Mitchell had routinely sent his partner his share of the revenues, but the earthquake had interrupted this arrangement. Hughes's mailing address proved unresponsive, having been one of the many buildings in the city ravaged by the earthquake. Mitchell was eventually able to track down J.R. Longstreet, who had become awash in a sea of legal nightmares for his respective clients. After a long wait outside the office door of the new location of Longstreet's practice, Mitchell was admitted to a stuffy room stacked with papers on every flat surface, including the dusty floor. J.R. Longstreet's head had an extraordinary squareness to it, and it amused Mitchell to imagine one of the numerous stacks of paper atop the lawyer's head above his cropped hairline. Longstreet was a large man, over six feet tall, with a broad build to match. Yet any imposing qualities of the lawyer were softened by a good-natured face, suggesting the temperament of a kindly father or young grandfather, perhaps. The office's two windows were wide open, but this had not allayed the overwhelming crowdedness of the space.

"Ah, Mr. Bernheim, yes . . . oh, thank you for your patience, very gracious," Longstreet mumbled with fragmented thoughts. "Um, Roland Hughes! Oh, now I understand, let us track him down, shall we?" He moved two piles of documents to the side and brought another to the forefront. "Once, I must have had . . . a secondary address for him. The only question is, where? Oh, Good Christ, um . . . Mr. Bernheim, I'm afraid I will have to get back to you on this issue; it's no good for you to spend even more time here while I probe through my materials. Perhaps for now you can simply continue on with your records and set

Mr. Hughes's share of the revenue aside? Once I've either been contacted by Mr. Hughes or have tracked down a bank account or new destination for his share, I shall send a wire, a letter . . . I will reach you."

And in this manner, Mitchell played the waiting game while carrying on as best he could. Bernheim & Hughes Antiques had been spared from the earthquake, remaining structurally sound. It also had escaped the ensuing fire, being on the west side of Van Ness Street just outside of the dynamite line instituted by city authorities to contain the spreading fire. This deliberate demolition could hardly have been called a success; the fire was ultimately contained, but most city dwellers that you asked insisted that the explosives had leveled a good share of viable buildings not threatened by the fire or compromised by the quake. Mitchell had wandered close to the rubble and persistent fires the following days, joining a throng of onlookers as the city's civil resources, fire brigade, and police department executed desperate strategies to stop the inferno's spread. It was then that Mitchell made a new acquaintance: a soot-covered journalist out of Chicago, who singled out Mitchell as a resident as he approached.

"This utter devastation . . . my God," the man remarked, shaking his head. The journalist was about six feet tall, or just under, clean-shaven, with combed brown hair swept to the side and a certain keenness in his eyes that suggested both intelligence and a haunted listlessness. "In the past, those in my noble profession would have been hard-pressed to describe such loss, but now there's this," he said as he put away his box camera, apparently finished with his photographs for the day. "It's a finicky thing, this contraption, but by God does it sell newspapers. It gives such . . . blunt precision to things." Mitchell nodded at him and folded his arms, and the man continued. "The *Chronicle* has also been kind enough to share some of their photographs, and I'll need to be back on the train to Chicago tomorrow morning, provided I can find room. Serviceable trains are very tight right now, as you can imagine . . ." He then paused and shook his head. "Forgive my blathering. Your home, sir . . . am I to assume it was lost to the fire?"

"No, I was more fortunate," Mitchell responded. "I run an antique and curiosities store on Van Ness; all told, I've been remarkably well-off. I worry what this stroke of luck will cost me in the long run, however."

"I don't think there's evidence for anything such as karma," the journalist responded. "Antiques?" he added with an intrigued air. "I don't suppose you're open today?"

"I—I hadn't necessarily intended on it, but now that it comes to it, I wouldn't mind showing you around," Mitchell offered, deciding that his first patron after the disaster would help him rapidly readjust to something of normalcy. No streetcars were in operation that day, but it was not a far walk to Mitchell's home and business. The journalist did not hide his appreciation at the respite as the two entered the establishment. Once past the threshold, the man introduced himself as Roger Merrick for the *Chicago Tribune*. Although he did not purchase anything, for every item that caught his eye, he asked at least two questions about it. Mitchell was more than happy to accommodate his curiosity, although he didn't always have an answer. This discourse in turn led to pleasant discussions and speculation, usually drifting towards historical topics, and conversations from Chang'an to Constantinople kindled as the daylight dwindled. The two ended up talking late into the night; Roger became both Mitchell's dinner and overnight guest, as available accommodations were practically nonexistent in the aftermath. The two decided to retire just after midnight, and Mitchell asked Roger once more if he had been made comfortable. He had set up the journalist in the den, which had a leather sofa and heavy curtains to block out light and noise from the street. That night was more silent than normal, though occasional shouting or work by the fire department could be discerned in the distance.

"Much more comfortable than I had hoped for earlier today," Roger responded, smiling. The journalist looked over to a silver menorah on the top of a cabinet. "Lovely craftsmanship," he offered.

"I may not be as pious as my father wishes," Mitchell replied, "but I am more or less astute in observing the holidays, and that piece is a Bernheim heirloom."

"You hail from a particularly orthodox household?" Roger asked.

"Well, my parents, certainly," Mitchell began. "But my brother Isaac and I are perpetual sources of disappointment to my father, the rabbi. It's not a terrible strain, but he calls us *Cain* and *Tubal-cain* when he's feeling feistier or offering a lecture about our laxer attitudes. Most of the time it's clearly in good humor, but each year I sense rising bitterness in it."

"Does he practice in the city?"

"No, he resides in Los Angeles, thank God for that, but I don't thank God for His seeming indifference to the destruction of most of our city's synagogues . . . Russ and New Geary Streets, even Emanu-el on Sutter." After Mitchell mentioned this, Roger offered a conciliatory muttering about the building's beautiful spires, now lost. "What about you? What faith do you keep, Roger, or perhaps you are even more Nietzschean than I?"

"I am . . . *I remain* a steadfast Lutheran you could say, despite some great tests to my faith of late," Roger said after a momentary but intense internal deliberation. "It's strange, I've had such a profound cycle of doubt that I've oscillated back to a somehow firmer faith than before."

"That response was so strained that there must be quite a story attached with it," Mitchell offered.

"And because I sense that we both value the prospect of sleep, I must reserve that as a story for another time, my friend," Roger said tiredly, and Mitchell pressed him no further that night. The next day, Roger left, bound for Chicago. He expressed his gratitude as well as a desire to meet again, and Mitchell believed that Roger must have found an available train that morning, as he had not seen him since. He did hope to hear the journalist's full story someday.

On the whole, the period since the great quake proved

30

a good time to be in the antique business, and Mitchell was not oblivious to his general success amidst hard times in the city. He received reminders that he was the only one aware of the disparity, alongside warnings that his Jewish identity was not unknown; the B&H façade upon Van Ness had been vandalized three times in the span of ten months. The damages varied from panes of smashed glass to one incident of graffiti with the words "We Won't Passover Disaster Profiteers" inscribed in white paint. Mitchell's parents, Elazar and Miriam, had emigrated from France in the spring of 1870 when Mitchell was a baby, just before the onset of the Franco-Prussian War. Mitchell's birth name was Michel, but his youth in America had rendered the name inconvenient, especially among boys his age who had difficulty with the French name or regarded it as feminine. Elazar, who was now sixty-three, remained insistent that things were still much better in the United States than in the old country. He had become particularly fascinated with the new American Jewish Committee and often suggested that Mitchell set aside some of his profits for donation.

Mitchell had further consideration for what to do with his steady income when he finally heard back from J.R. Longstreet. Longstreet had news of Mitchell's mysterious business partner; Roland Hughes had been officially declared missing. He was uncertain as to the details—the man may have been a victim of the earthquake, fire, or related calamity. The net result of any of these outcomes being true was the offer for Mitchell to buy out the remaining share

31

of the business. Roland had already prepared exactly such a contingency before his disappearance. The buyout price was comparably humble, and as Mitchell gladly signed the paperwork in Longstreet's office, he wondered how he had managed to endear himself so much to Mr. Hughes, but did not overburden himself with the thought.

That is how, by February of 1907, Mitchell had become sole owner of B&H Antiques. Both out of caution that Mr. Hughes may resurface and out of a general respect, Mitchell did not intend to alter the business's name for another year or so, if at all. When he rendered payment to the Hughes estate through Mr. Longstreet, he discovered that he still had a good amount of cash available. Mitchell entertained a donation to the American Jewish Committee, but this initiative became derailed when he received an advertisement for a special auction of antiques.

It was impossible for anyone but a retired gentleman to attend every auction in San Francisco these days, even for Mitchell, who relied in part on acquiring new inventory through such channels. As a result, he was obligated to keep his ear to the ground only for events and selections of note. At other times, he simply took a stroll to any of the few that operated in the city to catch the occasional late-evening session or on a particularly slow day at the shop. However, on the morning of Monday, February 11th, Mitchell discovered a letter in his business mailbox outside the store. It was from the Butterfield and Butterfield Auction House, inviting him to a special sale of Chinese antiquities advertised as the largest

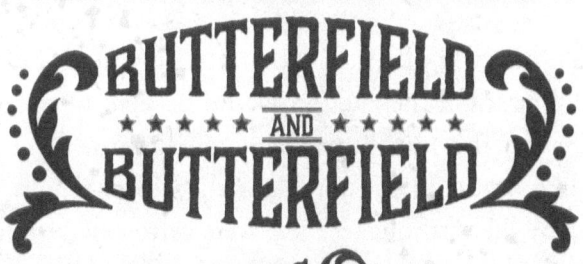

BUTTERFIELD ★★★★★ AND ★★★★★ BUTTERFIELD

THE TREASURES OF ANCIENT CHINA

ONE DAY AUCTION!

440 Sutter Street
PROXY BIDDERS ARE WELCOME.

FEBRUARY 13TH 1:00 PM

TRINKETS AND TOMB GUARDIANS

FROM THE BLOODY REBELLION OF AN LUSHAN!

single sale of its kind held in the city, spanning multiple Imperial dynasties. The auction would be held in two days on Wednesday the 13th. Butterfield and Butterfield Auction House, like others in the Bay Area, had been temporarily paralyzed by the earthquake; there were extremely few places of business as unaffected as B&H Antiques. In a remarkable reverse of misfortune, a subsequent flood of goods from both verifiable and unscrupulous sources established a bumper selling season among collectors. These days, Mitchell vended not only antiques, but a wide assortment of items that he hoped to make a profit on as he waded through countless offerings from desperate or opportunistic patrons. The auction, however, promised much more distinguished prospects.

Advertising was not unheard of for auction houses and had grown more common due to the stronger market that had emerged out of the earthquake. Despite this, Mitchell deduced that this flyer must have represented an event of special magnificence in its evocative descriptions and was precisely the sort that the dealer wished to catch. Two days later, Mitchell nodded to the doorman, who smiled beneath a thick silver mustache, as he passed through the double doors of polished glass into the building. He exchanged greetings with a few acquaintances and joined them in finding the way to the main auction hall. Mitchell secured a seat towards the back of the well-lit room adorned by proud crystal chandeliers and soft-fitted carpeting. He recognized a few more faces from the wider community that frequented such sales. Some were competing business owners, but most were personal collectors or their proxies. None of those present were the sort that Mitchell would call a friend. On the whole, he was on good terms with his competitors, but his friends tended to be those outside of the industry. Of these, some had perished and more had moved since the earthquake while Mitchell remained in the city of ghosts, tied to his business. Unfortunately, there was one distinguished enemy present, Louis Malcom. Louis Malcom was an insurance agent, a member of one of the great San Francisco families: a veritable spawning pool of other "Malcoms" that comprised the Malcom Insurance Company.

Bernheim & Hughes had thrived in spite of attempted sabotage and constant inquiries made by Malcom Insurance. The first great affront was Mitchell's polite refusal of any type of comprehensive coverage of a Malcom policy—either on his inventory or on the brick and mortar of his business. What followed was a series of continued appeals by the tireless Louis Malcom and subsequent denials by Mitchell. Infrequent criminal activity against the antiques store punctuated these gaps at an increasing rate. Mitchell became convinced that a handful of thefts, smashed vases, even one arson attempt were all done by proxy agents at the behest of Louis Malcom. What had stopped these activities was the confession of the attempted arsonist during the police investigation. The man, whose name Mitchell had forgotten, plainly informed the authorities that he had been contracted by Louis Malcom for the very act. Nonetheless, Louis was able to successfully (even impressively) distance his company from the allegation and prevent escalation to criminal charges. Yet the debacle had done enough to hurt their reputation and increase the visibility of law enforcement that it had bought a reprieve from such subterfuge that had persisted for over a year.

Mitchell did not need to speculate on the reasons for Louis's presence at the auction; the insurance agent would make note of the authenticity, auction value, and destination of the more interesting antiquities for the company's records. Malcom Insurance sold policies to some of Mitchell's competitors, and the information acquired here would enable Louis Malcom to set the highest adjustments to existing premiums possible, or conversely provide solid ground for him to establish the lowest possible claims values in the case of theft or destruction. In the wake of the earthquake, many households became woefully destitute from not having insurance, but just as many regional insurance companies were failing or had gone bankrupt in turn. Mitchell suspected that even a clever operation like Malcom Insurance would be hurting or on the back foot, and he would need to be on even higher guard than normal against the designs of the business. As Mitchell espied the listless agent a few rows away, he tried to turn his head so that Louis would not spot him. The furtive gesture failed, and to Mitchell's discomfort, the agent decided to relocate his seat next to the flustered man. "I see this chair isn't taken—good afternoon, Mitchell," Louis greeted him, always using his first name.

"And to you, Mr. Malcom," Mitchell replied, always using the man's surname.

"I'm glad to see that you are taking advantage of the bullish market," he said through a curled grin beneath a thin moustache. It is too often described of someone looking like a weasel, and Louis Malcom didn't quite match that, but perhaps crossed with a serpent. "The more I reflect on it, your establishment really was *inordinately* fortunate, surviving the disaster! I envy you, Mitchell. To be believing Noah with your ark of valuables amidst a sea of calamity and want. What's more, I understand congratulations are in order for the sole owner of Bernheim Antiques! Now is the perfect time to consider a new, nuanced policy as you have full sovereignty, Mr. Boss Man!"

"I see no piece of news escapes your notice," Mitchell replied in equal measure of suspicion and weariness. "I suppose it won't help to notify you that I haven't changed insurance providers?"

"I don't know why you pledge your business to the INA, those Philadelphia crooks," Louis Malcom dismissed, always sounding personally wounded by the rebuttal.

"According to the *Chronicle,* they've been paying out all of the earthquake claims and still haven't shut their doors, so I daresay they are doing something right," Mitchell offered. "As I have told you infinite times, Mr. Malcom, the policy was established along with the business itself—it's a closed book."

"And closed books are good for nothing but kindling," Louis responded acridly, but could offer no further discourse as the hall was quieted by the staff.

The auction began and proceeded with the usual assortment of items. Chinatown in particular had been ravaged of many heirlooms of apparent historical craftmanship, both from the desperate populace needing to barter for their next meal and countless thefts by opportunists and criminals. The first hour of the auction produced a grand parade of such trinkets and more substantial curiosities. Large bronze din vessels, which were Chinese cooking pots, were hauled up for display along with much smaller, fragile figurines or horses or soldiers made of clay or jade. Woodblock prints with authentic or dubious ties to classical artists went quickly in either case.

It was at this point that Mitchell won his first item of the day: a marvelous reproduction of the celebrated frontispiece of the *Diamond Sutra*. The discovered woodblock of the *Sutra* was now recognized by scholars as the earliest known printed book in the world, uncovered earlier in the decade by a Daoist priest, Wang Yuanlu. While not of use for business, it would provide an outstanding decoration, perhaps to be hung directly behind the main counter.

Almost everyone who had initially assembled remained keen on staying for the auction's whole duration, as the auctioneer continually reminded the attendees that some larger sculptures would comprise the finale. There was some murmuring as the auction reached the halfway point, which would signal a noteworthy piece. The auction master, far from being perturbed by the activity, smiled and allowed the anticipation to build for a moment. Mitchell looked up interestedly, as most of his bidding budget remained available.

"Next, we have a small earthenware statuette, the very one rendered on our pamphlet, authenticated as a Tang dynasty tomb guardian!" The auctioneer ceremoniously raised a small letter, his eyes peering over the tops of his lowered glasses. "From our consultant historian, Professor Hastings:

This figure is instantly recognizable as a Tang-era piece, and its humble first impression is quickly dispelled. Arguably the most unique tomb guardian for its miniature size, it possesses a particularly colorful and imaginative blend of the trademark demi-humanoid appearance. In this piece, man, squid, and bat are represented in unsurpassed symmetry and inspiration. The ceramic glaze of the figure remains in excellent condition, possibly the best extant example of its kind. But the most extraordinary characteristic of all is its dating; this bears an inscription denoting the short-lived Yan dynasty, a house of rebellion shattering the Tang hegemony, circa 755 A.D. and the start of the An Lushan rebellion. It must be noted that this rebellion is now calculated to have caused more deaths than any known conflict in the world, save for perhaps the Three Kingdoms War."

The auctioneer lowered the letter to finish the quotation, and with the exposition concluded, his more energetic tone resumed. "A lovely piece for a study, loft, perhaps even an outdoor garden, minding the humidity or precipitation for such a rare item, especially for our guests travelling from harsher climes." His voice had nearly given out, and he paused to cough. "We would be remiss to start the bidding for this very special piece at anything less than fifty dollars. Who shall I say at fifty?"

A man wearing a tie and a top hat sat in the very front row just to the right of the podium. He instantly shot up his arm at the invitation and just as quickly regretted the outburst as he timidly lowered it once his bid had been counted. With trepidation, he turned his head to scan the room behind him, then in turn seemed to regret this display, and to salvage his growing series of miscues, he turned to look forward again, giving an unconvincing impression that he was perfectly content. Mitchell got the bemused idea of a young heir or posturing fool who didn't know exactly what to do with his money. Difficult as it was, Mitchell resigned himself to losing the statuette to one such bidder who could massively outbid him.

In less than two minutes, the price had gone up to ninety-five dollars from about nine distinct bidders throughout the rows of chairs. If the artifact was genuine, it was indeed worth at least twice that amount—especially to the right buyer. Mitchell raised his arm to place a bid at a square one hundred dollars, evoking a look of interest from his unpleasant companion, Louis Malcom, still seated next to him. Mitchell knew that he would be outbid, but a strange part of him felt that he would have left wholly unsatisfied if he had not at least contested the curious tomb guardian while it still was within the realm of his budget. A few more beats and bids passed, and then the first great pause occurred. To think that the tomb guardian would only go for one hundred and fifteen dollars suddenly stung like a great affront to Mitchell—not only to the worth of the artifact but to his perceptions as an antiquarian. "One hundred and twenty," he shouted for the express purpose of protecting the dignity of the figurine.

"And I have one hundred and twenty to you, sir," the auctioneer said between pointing stabs that rotated between the three most recent bidders. "And do I have one hundred and twenty-five? Ah yes, very good to you, sir," he gestured back to the man with the top hat. Mitchell could live with the prospect of the item selling for that price. He relaxed back in his seat, bringing his hands behind his head and locking his fingers together to support it. Exquisite care was taken by the antiquarian to remain motionless and thus give no indication of further interest in bidding, and the price continued to rise without Mitchell's involvement.

For a heartbeat, Mitchell wondered if Louis would attempt some mischief and jab or prod Mitchell's elbow or arm upwards, but the fear quickly passed. Mitchell acknowledged that his adversary was interested in far more crippling maneuvers. When the price reached one hundred seventy-five dollars, the man with the top hat became quite agitated that he remained in contention with only one other stubborn bidder since Mitchell had cast his bid of one hundred twenty. When the wealthy speculator turned to get a good look at his adversary, his eyes widened and his mouth opened just a little bit, in the same way that Mitchell imagined a man would react while being stabbed in the stomach. Yet even in surprise, there was something gratuitous or ungenuine about his expression. Mitchell thought he read more cleverness, or perhaps pride in that face, but it was only a vessel of dumbfounded surprise at the moment.

"I, I am terribly sorry, good Mr. Suchy, but in my zeal . . . my excitement, I have overextended my credit," the man with the top hat said, practically swooning. "I am afraid that I must withdraw my last bid—I do understand what this means for my standing here with the auction house, of course. Good afternoon," he added abruptly as he checked his pocket watch without properly looking at its face. He rose from his chair and paced down the center aisle to leave the room. Auctioneer Suchy bristled at that, but he gave no protest and even indicated toleration toward the taboo behavior with a slight nod, seemingly out of respect to the man's authority.

It was an incredibly unusual display. A thought occurred to Mitchell that the man was perhaps an agent of the auction house, yet such a brazen tactic had such risk that he discredited the idea. "Mr. Malcom, perhaps you could be useful and tell me who that man is," Mitchell whispered.

"I wish I did know, so I could refuse you out of spite," Louis hissed back. That was enough to convince Mitchell, who could not believe that Louis Malcom would pass on tormenting or extorting him. A few beats passed, and Auctioneer Suchy struck down his gavel, ending the bidding.

"Then it is one hundred and seventy-five to . . . wait, I've seen your face before," Auctioneer Suchy said, as if only now properly noticing the leading bidder for the first time and withdrawing from his quick-reflexed scanning of the room. It wasn't entirely Suchy's fault; the bidder had been wearing a wide-brimmed hat, but now removed it to bask in the moment. "Who the hell let this man in here?" Suchy asked with arresting indignation. The auction house filled with murmurs, and the laborers that were responsible for hauling the heavier sale items sprang into action. Apparently they doubled as enforcers, and the auction master swiftly directed them to remove the bidder from the building.

The man laughed with relish, as if he ultimately expected the ejection, but complied when his arms were taken by the laborers. As he stood and turned, Mitchell finally could get a look at his face. The man was of Asian ancestry, and Mitchell assumed he was a Chinatown resident. Indeed, he now was almost certain he had seen his face in a sketch in the newspaper recently, although he could not recall in what context. The man's black hair came down to his shoulders and was styled in an ornate tie behind his neck. He broke from his silent escort just before leaving the main room; he suddenly turned and spat what sounded like truly venomous words at Auctioneer Suchy in Chinese. The belligerent Chinaman then turned to Mitchell, tilting his head up and offering a mock smile, as if marking him as his future quarry.

"My distinguished guests, I apologize! That Chinaman was to be barred from this place but slipped through all the same," Auctioneer Suchy proclaimed, his voice slightly trembling. "This is surely the greatest circus of an auction I've presided over in some time," he sighed, cleaning the lenses of his glasses. Once finished, he looked around hesitantly. "Then of course, it was . . . why yes, it was you, sir." He grinned as he placed Mitchell amongst the brown and gray suits in the room. "Your bid was one hundred and twenty dollars, which is now the winning bid! I trust that you are most pleased by this?"

"Well, I—" Mitchell stammered and hopelessly grasped for an excuse, finding that he now wanted nothing to do with the Yan tomb guardian.

"My God, does anyone mean what they declare at auction these days?" the auctioneer hissed, his face turning bright red. His patience had run out at Mitchell, who held no special status or notoriety here. "My apologies, but I won't have it, sir! You are the remaining highest bidder, unless someone else here now wishes to supersede you?" He briefly glanced upward to a silent and subdued room. "Sold! It's yours now, for one hundred and twenty dollars!"

Apart from the auctioneer, the other party most pleased by Mitchell's acquisition of the item was Louis Malcom. "You already have my contact information. I expect to be hearing from you soon," he quipped with a wicked smile, grasping Mitchell's shoulder firmly before excusing himself.

Mitchell spent the walk back to the store looking over his shoulder but was confident that he was not followed. He cradled the bundle in his right arm and carried his large print in his left, making for an awkward shuffle. The tomb guardian was far heavier than he expected it to be; Mitchell reckoned the dense figurine could shatter a window if thrown. When he reached his front door, he looked around, still seeing no suspicious activity or familiar faces. The shop could have reopened for a couple more hours that day, but Mitchell decided against it. He went inside and carried his purchases to the front desk, then immediately unwrapped the statuette. It truly was a marvelous and skillful craft, but now that he could take a long look at it up-close, he could not call it *handsome*; there was something decidedly unappealing in the figurine's features. The inside of B&H Antiques was not humid, yet there was a layer of condensation on the tomb guardian as well as a small ring of moisture on the table that he had placed it on. Mitchell knew at once that this would not be one of his "sentimental pieces" and he would be glad of parting with it at the first opportunity of moderate profit. *What the hell are you supposed to be anyway? An octopus-man with wings?*

After a light dinner of braised fish, Mitchell set the piece down on a small writing desk in his bedroom, nestling the object between his reading glasses and a pile of his most recent distractions: Phylos the Thibetan's *A Dweller on Two Planets*, Albert Schweitzer's *The Quest of the Historical Jesus*, and the first two volumes of George Santayana's ponderous *The Life of Reason*. He had not intended to place the figurine in the bedroom, but found that he was holding it as he was about to lie down to sleep. Deliberately, he set the tomb guardian to face away from him, towards the wall. Minutes later, feeling ashamed at the resurgence of childish fearfulness, he sighed and got up, then turned the figurine to look directly at him. "I can stare right back at you too, you know." He spoke with a soft smugness to the silent watcher, then laughed to himself. He lay back down in his bed, feeling decidedly better in his self-affirmed courage. The hanging dread had been banished for the moment, and he slept.

2

Mitchell could see himself sleeping—not in the figure of speech imagining a pleasant rest—he could *see* himself sleeping, his eyes detached from his body. He recognized his bedroom, which was dark, just how it had been when he had drifted off to sleep moments . . . *however* long ago it was. But things weren't right. Mitchell juggled puzzlement and alarm as to how precisely his perspective had been transplanted to a dark corner of the room. Unlike remembering a dream when one's thoughts, actions, and movement often seem so detached and fluid, his cognition was as secure as waking. Therefore, he began by piecing out where exactly his sight was now projecting from. As Mitchell could not quite see the door to the room, but had an excellent view of the length of his bed, he understood that he was looking from the small writing desk just to the left of his wardrobe, underneath his window. Furthermore, he was raised slightly from it, otherwise his view would be parallel to the bedside and unable to see over the hanging sheets draped over the bedside to espy his face. *The figurine. I'm looking straight out of the eyes of the figurine*, he realized.

Upon this revelation, Mitchell became aware that he could still feel the sensation of his heart thumping as not one, but four dark figures shambled in silently through the open doorway, crowding over his bed. *Who are these specters? Am I to witness my own death? Have I already died? Is this simply a nightmare? What awaits my spirit?* Mitchell could not cry out, for he had no mouth. He found that his viewpoint was locked. While he could not move, he could look around to a degree, and upon looking down to view his new body, he saw only the stubby physique of the statue. Attempts to exert his muscles, even to the point of pain, could produce no movement. One of the intruder's faces was now recognizable—the ejected bidder from the auction house. From the folds of his robed jacket, the man produced a cleaver with a wicked edge, the weapon glittering from a stab of moonlight admitted through the window. Inscribed Chinese characters were in the chromatic side of the blade, and in horror, Mitchell could only look on as the man suddenly raked the weapon's edge across the sleeping man's, *his* neck, in one violent motion. While a fountain of red began soaking through the pillow and sheets, a sharp and unrelenting pain formed where Mitchell thought his throat should be . . . and the men all turned now to the statue. A greedy hand grew to tremendous size as it reached out to seize the figure and turned all to blackness.

Mitchell gasped, if any such word could describe the hysterical croaking that seized him as he shot up in his bed, covered in sweat. His hand swiftly rested on the phantom pain in his neck. The disheveled man arose from the bed, and Mitchell inspected himself in a standing mirror. He was foremost relieved to see that it was himself in the reflection, and without a slashed throat. Yet he observed a new scar, coinciding with his dream, in a faint brown line that ran across his neck. Mitchell knew he had no such wound previously, and he rubbed his eyes in an attempt to dispel the sight. With no success, and a heightened sense of pain that seemed to come from just regarding the scar, he ceased this activity and paced his room.

The night terror would not depart from Mitchell, and he thought to open the window in an attempt to root himself again in the waking world. He looked out his window out to the street and searched for signs of familiarity: a night patrolman, a passing streetcar, another open window spilling illumination to the street. The avenue was empty; there was no one, just a false, hanging peace which suggested his ordeals were not finished. He then regarded the statue, still upon the desk and profiled in the same manner as he recalled from the visionary dream. *A warning? A dream of an impending future? Has time rewound itself for my benefit?* Mitchell decided to entertain all of these possibilities with equal respect and dressed himself fully. He grabbed the figurine, which was slick with moisture, and secured it in a large pocket in an old jacket, his only accoutrement that could fit the item. The new acquisition was hardly an irreplaceable treasure to Mitchell, but since it seemed so valued by dangerous men, he would try to keep it safe.

No sooner had he done this, he heard a curious scraping coming from downstairs. Mitchell crept to the staircase leading down to the storefront; from the top of the stairs, he was afforded a narrow view of the front door to the street, which had an arched glass window near the top. Through this small opening, Mitchell perceived shadowy figures hunched down in the exterior doorway. The brass doorknob gave sporadic half-turns, and the proprietor of B&H Antiques wasted not another moment in hurrying down the steps. The back door represented Mitchell's best chance of escape, and he reached it before his front lock had been successfully picked. Unlike the front door, he had no way of surveilling the other side into the alley. Should he encounter someone, he would be weaponless, yet as he again heard the clicking noises from the storefront behind him, he removed the figure from his pocket and raised it up in his right hand. He unlocked the door with his free hand.

Mitchell pulled the handle with a rushing sweep, and sure enough, there was a man on the other side. It was another Chinaman, standing laxly as a lookout, who clearly had been expecting to be granted entry, but not by the building's lawful resident. Mitchell didn't think, but instead followed instinct and struck the man in the forehead with the statuette's base. Regret instantly seized Mitchell on account of the precious figure. But to his astonishment, it did not shatter or crack; the tomb guardian showed no signs of damage at all. The same could not be said of the man, who had folded to the ground, streaks of blood running down his face. Mitchell stepped over the incapacitated sentry and disappeared into the alley. His steps echoed, and he took fretted breaths as he ran down the derelict backstreet. After running for several minutes—it was difficult to say how long exactly—Mitchell determined that he had avoided being spotted by the invading party.

Twenty minutes later, he returned with two officers of the San Francisco Police Department. By the time they returned, the gang of intruders had fled, the front door was ajar, and the valuable inventory of antiques was scattered about. Mitchell provided two descriptions for the officers, the distinctive man from the auction house (the very one he had witnessed slash his throat in the dream) as well as the man he struck with the statue when fleeing through the back alley. "I believe I've made note of all the missing items. The most valuable theft from what I can see is my Ming ewer. They also had a run at my dynastic coin drawer, but it looks like they only risked smashing one of the glass panels," Mitchell reported tiredly to the officers, who looked just alert enough to not appear discourteous.

"Well, Mr. Bernheim, if the insurance company contests any of your claims, we can share our report from this evening," Officer Timothy Madden, the younger of the two, offered. His ill-fitting glasses often caused him to fidget and realign them. "From our examination of your lock, the mechanism appears intact, just a clever bit of picking from the intruders. Now, can you think of any reason why you would be targeted in this manner?"

Mitchell was always inclined to suspect Louis Malcom, but this instinct did not spring up in this instance. "Oh, I certainly can! That first Chinaman I described to you, I think he's the gang leader and has a special fascination with the little statue I acquired. The same man from the newspaper sketch! I don't understand why he wants the damn thing so much . . . do you know his history, officer?"

Officer Madden shook his head and turned to the older officer, who had a great golden beard touched with gray. The senior officer, whose badge said "Wells," sighed, hesitated, then nodded. "His name is Zhang Yong, or Yong Zhang in the manner that we order given and surnames." Officer Wells' voice was touched by years of heavy drinking, smoking, or both. "If there's one man the SFPD would like to get into a holding cell and throw away the key, he would be high on the list." He crossed his arms and became silent in recollection. "Even in Chinatown, he's something of a polarizing fellow, but those in his gang and who are 'for' him are fanatical about it. On record, we don't have any murder charges on him . . . although we've got him for a whole docket of other things, and that's just from what's been reported. That's quite a coup he pulled, going to a public auction," Wells added, smiling as if in admiration of Yong's daring. "I don't expect we'll have another chance like that to nab him for years to come!"

"But he was escorted out—the auction house's staff could have detained him for you," Mitchell rebutted disappointedly. "They should have detained him!"

"Ah, we were called over, yes, but he had slipped away

before we could arrest him. I had heard at the station that the auction house orderlies were intimidated to release him just minutes after they had removed him. A bribe's just as likely," he added, removing his hat to scratch his scalp before reaffixing it. "I would guess he'll lie low in Chinatown for a while, but I'll be frank . . . if you now have a quarrel with this man, you can never, you *must* never be at ease until you either move away or give him what he wants, or until he's locked away or dead."

"Can't you organize a manhunt?" Mitchell asked worriedly. "Surely there's enough manpower to do a sweep. Mobilize the Chinatown Squad!"

Officer Wells shrugged. "We've tried that once before. They hid him away, maybe had him bouncing from home to home, or managed to slip him out of the city for a spell. As for organizing another search . . . I don't make those kinds of calls; take it up with the chief or the mayor. We are kept rather busy these days even with the boys from the military helping around, but I'll make sure a patrol comes by to check your storefront a couple of times each night for the next week or so. It's an easy stop on Van Ness, after all."

The incident had convinced Mitchell of two things. The first was that the Yan tomb guardian was much more valuable than the moderate sum he had won it for at auction. The second was that he would not rely on the police for his current troubles. The associated trouble that had begun since acquiring the tomb guardian may not have been worth it, but at the very least, Mitchell was obligated to further research the item to arrive at its true worth and purpose. Often he reflected on the surreal dream, doubting his reality and what exactly had happened to him, but he became convinced that the tomb guardian was at the center of it all. Mitchell decided that it would be best if he could arrange a meeting with the scholar who had provided the verification for the tomb guardian itself. He found the name referenced at Butterfield's among the faculty directory of St. Ignatius College, which possessed the most well-established history department in the Bay Area. After a series of exchanged messages on the wire and redirecting to an updated street address, Mitchell secured an appointment with Professor Nelson Hastings at four o'clock in the afternoon on Monday, February 18th.

In the interim days of waiting, Mitchell began conducting his own research on China's Tang period near the time of the An Lushan rebellion. The Tang dynasty was considered a golden age in China up until the rebellion. Indeed, the Chinese state at the time was undoubtedly the strongest in the early medieval period on a global scale, rivaled perhaps only by the Byzantine Empire. It would even recover from such a catastrophe to a lesser degree, and its greatest pride was its glorious capital of Chang'an, in modern day Xi'an. A marvel of city planning, it boasted a neat grid of broad avenues; entertainment, commercial, and religious districts; a place of peace; impressive commerce; and a melting pot of faiths and philosophies travelling in from the Silk Road.

Mitchell focused his study on the society's religious beliefs, burial practices, and sculptures, which very quickly revealed a diverse and cosmopolitan assortment. Yet his efforts were hamstrung by the fact that the San Francisco Public Library had lost 140,000 volumes, eighty percent of its collection, to the earthquake of the previous year. As such, Mitchell was able to track down one copy of a general survey of Chinese history up through the Japanese annexation of Taiwan, but it was hardly the specialized knowledge that he sought and had only two chapters on the whole of the Tang period.

These days of research passed with visits from the enthusiastic, young Officer Madden and without any more break-in attempts from Zhang Yong's gang. Mitchell liked to believe that the increased police presence had convinced the rogue that the tomb guardian wasn't worth further attempts for the time being. This thought hadn't improved the quality of Mitchell's sleep, however. His dreams had become troubled, returning to the locked perspective of the tomb guardian. Yet rather than observing his own bedroom, the setting of his dreams took on new and bizarre surroundings; they always oscillated between two distinct locales. Sometimes Mitchell would dream he was in a cramped earthen hollow, a tomb or burial chamber that sloped down toward its center, where the ceiling was low. Inside the tomb, a ring of similarly crafted tomb guardians occupied the space in alcoves, all facing towards a sarcophagus in the center and lowest point. There was no obvious light source in the entombed room, and the fact that Mitchell could perceive anything at all was remarkable, even for a dream. Consequently, the rock-cut reliefs of the cave and other details of the sarcophagus were rendered vague and indiscernible in the darkness.

The other location was conversely vast and open and either was underwater or in the most spectacular haze of dense fog. A layer of sickly blue-green covered everything and suffused one's senses with rot, drowning, and suffocation. Towering shadows loomed in every direction, and Mitchell thought that they must be seamounts: gigantic mountains that rise up from the great depths of the ocean floor but do not crest their proud heads above the sea's level. Unlike the dim tomb, he could move freely here, although his unwieldy, weightless walking didn't ever seem to get him very far as the shadowy monoliths always remained distant, yet terribly near. The longer Mitchell spent pondering their sight, he increasingly regarded their sharp, unusual contours as that of structures, proud citadels and strongholds of nameless and forgotten beings. But a hidden presence there, more massive and foreboding than any of the visible ruins, made its presence known with a building pressure that oppressed him, body and soul. The presence consistently expelled Mitchell's mind from lingering there too long, and he was grateful for this.

Monday the 18th arrived as a dim day of blowing rain which had not dissipated by the afternoon. The St. Ignatius faculty offices, once a quick stroll down the road from B&H Antiques, had been destroyed in the fire following the earthquake. Mitchell held his umbrella close and double-checked that he had indeed come to the right place. The college had been relocated further west to a building that looked more like a manufacturing plant than a college. After walking in on a rehearsal of Chekov's *The Cherry Orchard* in an open corridor in the building, Mitchell at last discovered a door to a very small room, labeled *Nelson Hastings: History, Chinese Language, and Oriental Literature.* Mitchell was late to the appointment by ten minutes, which had not endeared his introduction to the professor, who seemed to already be agitated by the day's events.

"You must be Mr. Bernheim. Do have a seat," Professor Hastings offered breathily as he reached for his handkerchief and blew his nose. He looked to be in his early sixties and had a full head of silvering hair that retained a slight trace of blond color. The skin under the point of his nose had been rendered raw and red, and Hastings took a look at the tissue before setting it aside. He then folded his hands and leaned forward slightly, blinking.

"Yes, I'm Mitchell Bernheim, Bernheim & Hughes Antiques," Mitchell offered with a half-wave and aborted handshake. "Thank you for agreeing to see me, Professor . . . sorry you're not feeling well. I had a little difficulty finding your office, I apologize."

"Oh, this isn't so bad. I've heard that the Golden Gate University faculty are still working in tents." He chuckled, interpreting Mitchell's apology as a reference to the professor's humble surroundings and not his appointment's tardiness. "They likely have moved on somewhere by now, managing as we have been. It has certainly not been easy for any college to maintain its *modus operandi* after 1906."

"Ah," Mitchell mouthed, and it seemed that redirecting Hastings to compare his misery with the new rival institution had already energized him. "I'll get right to the point. I won a Tang, more specifically, a Yan tomb figurine at auction and have been trying to learn more of it, as a great many people seem to value it more than just for its apparent historic value or rarity. As I understand, you are already familiar with the item."

Professor Hastings' eyes widened as Mitchell unwrapped the statuette, then he chuckled again. "Of course—that odd Yan dynasty piece? I remember providing the consultation and verification! Butterfield and Butterfield, right?"

"That's right," Mitchell replied, already feeling a sense of relief that Hastings would have the answers he sought.

"Well, I can't say I expected to have another chance to look at this! You see, they pay me modestly for the services I provide them," he explained, lifting the tomb guardian up in his hands, "but I was hoping that they would have the good sense to ensure some specimens arrive in responsible ownership—museums or colleges. A little wet, isn't it?" he asked idly as he took his handkerchief and wiped it down. He frowned as a very fine coat of moisture seemed to remain on its surface despite his best efforts, and he set it back down on the desk. "Also, the color seems to have faded, not quite that same tri-color radiance as I recalled. You haven't left it outside, have you?" Before Mitchell could answer, Hastings shrugged, dismissing the question. "No, in truth, I am partially relieved that it has come into the ownership of an antiquarian. You'll at least take proper care of the thing, until you find a new buyer, I suppose. What did you wish to know of it? Hopefully you recall the little description of mine that I'm sure Victor Suchy shared at auction."

"I would like to know . . . as much as possible," Mitchell pleaded. "In particular, if the superstitions at the time would associate any curses or *magic* with such artifacts," he postured, expecting to be laughed at, but Hastings continued to regard him silently. "You identified it from the Yan dynasty, from the tomb of this An Lushan character, so I should like to know as much about him, I suppose."

"I'll latch onto that as a starting point," Professor Hastings interrupted, not unkindly. "An Lushan was not an ethnic Han Chinese, but from Central Asia, Göktürk in origin. But by the year 750, China's territory had expanded to the point that the Tang government became perpetually in need of capable soldiers to defend the ever-expanding northwestern frontier into Central Asia. The dynasty was surrounded by competing Göktürk kingdoms, Mongol tribes, Tibet, and Kashmir. All of these border states were looking for opportunities to raid or annex patches of territory—" Professor Hastings stopped to sneeze.

"It reminds me of the Roman Empire, in a way," Mitchell offered to allow the unwell man a reprieve. "It could only expand so far before it became too difficult to maintain against raiding border states. Threatened by the Picts, Germania, the Sassanians, the legions could only be spread so thin . . ."

Hastings nodded vigorously, indicating he was ready to resume. "The Tang, in their prosperity, increasingly relied on military governors, sometimes of foreign birth, to rule with near-absolute authority to respond quickly to border raids and trouble, especially on the frontier. The process bypassed running every order through the capital, and An Lushan was one of those military governors. He was gifted as a soldier and eventually was invited to appear in the imperial court at Chang'an. He proved cunning and became something of a favorite of Emperor Xuanzong and his chancellor Li Linfu. As he rose, his soldiers became more loyal to their general Lushan than to the emperor and any notions of the state. After preparations, and when the time was fortuitous, the ambitious Lushan led a successful rebellion and overthrew Emperor Illustrious August, as Xuanzong was called. Thus, the An Lushan Rebellion ended the Tang golden age and interrupted the dynasty." Professor Hastings again blew his nose and poured a drink of whiskey, taking a large swig.

"What of his spiritual beliefs . . . or, I should say, what is known of the twilight of his life, if you don't mind?" Mitchell asked.

"An Lushan did not follow Buddhism, nor the Chinese folk religion. He loved another god, one of whom nothing is currently known. His last days were not kind to him. It depends on your sources, of course, but one account famously stated that the old soldier's eyes grew murky and his pupils grew so large that you could no longer see his irises. Deep-set boils set in his cheeks. Inertia and weight gain coupled with his failing vision, and rumors circulated that webbing was forming between his toes and fingers. The overall impression was that his head looked like that of a fish, and he grew more sequestered and violent—even with his favored servants and courtiers."

"Was some kind of curse set on him?" Mitchell asked. "In the chronicles, I mean."

Professor Hastings had a labored laugh at that through his congestion. "Well, Mr. Bernheim, you must understand that these descriptions were almost certainly apocryphal, various smears against him—out of spite by latter Han writers." Hastings hesitated, then leaned forward intently. "There are some who put more stock in these accounts. I have one such source, eccentric, but tremendously knowledgeable, who insists that the account does indicate fabrication, and furthermore goes on to say that the affliction was derived from An Lushan's own spiritual practices."

"So the implication is that the cult beliefs he adopted in his later years contributed to his death?" Mitchell asked, trying to follow. "I suppose he was foreign, but I'm not sure I understand why he replaced the prevalent Buddhism of his day with such esotericism?"

"Pah! I am no expert as we have now ventured into the realm of the extremely obscure, but from what I understand, the observed changes in Lushan's physiology were not regarded in his inner circle as a deterioration of health, but rather an *ascendancy* to a higher life form." Hastings wavered as he regarded his whiskey glass, but then decided against further indulgence. "Since we have left normal conversation," he began again, his tone becoming touched with a bemused abandonment, "let me ask if you have ever heard the term 'Deep One'? I encounter it seldomly, and almost exclusively from my solitary source . . . but when I do, such symptoms are emblematic of their shadowy identity."

"I have not, but I assume that is the culmination of this . . . fringe theory?" Mitchell replied, for the moment suspending disbelief, captivated that a man in Hastings' position would touch on such matters. "That An Lushan and a select few were becoming Deep Ones and pleasing their new god?"

"Precisely, and, among other reasons, this unacceptable religious practice served as one of the many impetuses for the upstart's assassination a mere two years after he had overthrown the emperor. There were many faiths tolerated in China at that time—in addition to the folk religion and predominant Buddhism, there were Daoists, Zoroastrians, Nestorian Christians—so much was tolerated that the faith that An Lushan and his inner circle espoused must have been especially perverse to have gained the dark reputation assigned by contemporaries. As to why he became a convert, that question may only be answered with speculation. Why do converts adopt their beliefs? An Lushan had usurped power from a well-established dynasty; there must have been something tempting or reassuring in the whispered and blasphemous promises that inspired conversion. Remember, he was always sundered, at least in part, from Han culture and customs. At the end of the day, he was a usurper general looking for a new method to secure his precarious throne, and such cult promises often are most appealing to the ambitious."

"Little good it seemed to do for him," Mitchell interjected, allowing the professor to catch his breath.

"After Lushan's death, the imperial mantle passed to Lushan's son An Qinxu, who likely played a role in the plot against his father. Qinxu either had not been initiated into the new cult or thought that gaining the throne was worth some infighting within the family and the ranks of the faithful, and no further emperors were associated as Deep Ones. More plotting and betrayals followed, this time with An Lushan's lifelong friend Shi Siming, who executed Qinxu and was in turn murdered by his own son. . . Chaoyi, was that his name?" Hastings waved his hand in dismissal. "The Yan dynasty, if you can call such a disorganized cabal a dynasty, collapsed after less than a decade to be resumed by a weakened Tang, and the cult did not survive beyond that spell, at least in China. But who knows? It is recorded that Shi Siming buried Lushan in a humble manner, so you can imagine the surprise of the academic community to discover anything turning up such as the sculpture that you brought here today. Perhaps there are yet more artifacts, evidence, even a shrine somewhere near the ruins of the Yan palace in Luoyang?"

"You're not suggesting that I need to go to mainland China to gain closure with this tomb guardian of mine?" Mitchell asked, anticipating the answer with dread.

"If you seek conclusive answers—most certainly, Mr. Bernheim! What better method is there than to go to the source? The only other recourse I could suggest would be to track down the inestimable J.J.M. de Groot at Leiden University, to whom I am indebted in much of my research. Of course, the Netherlands is also no small distance from here."

"Perhaps you should just have this for your office," Mitchell offered generously through a small nod to the figurine on the table.

"No, thank you!" Professor Hastings replied without hesitation. "I may have had a charmed opinion of the object a month ago, but now that its ownership is obtainable, I fear I would not offer you a fair price."

"Then let it be a donation," Mitchell remarked with no signs of enthusiasm.

"Whatever your regrets are for possessing the object, you'd be best served depositing it in a garden in Chinatown, if you've become that frivolous," Professor Hastings said, frowning disapprovingly. "I'd love to entertain you further, but it is now four thirty, and you'll have to excuse me to other engagements."

Mitchell thanked the professor and was granted one final piece of information: further details of Hastings' unofficial source who spoke of Deep Ones, the mysterious contact known simply as "Old Han." Old Han was a resident of Chinatown, although Hastings had never actually met in person with him; correspondence had been sufficient for their relations up to that point, and Hastings would not surrender any of the letters, nor show them. *Much like my relationship with Roland Hughes*, Mitchell thought to himself with amusement. As a conciliatory measure, the professor expressed that Mitchell could likely secure a meeting if he simply invoked the name of Nelson Hastings in arranging it with one of Han's associates.

In the following days, Mitchell augmented his sleeping arrangements to escape from his previous experiences of the great sunken city or the stifling, dark tomb. The first measure he took was removing the tomb guardian from his bedroom and storing it down in the storefront with the other items. At first, this helped; Mitchell was afforded a pair of restful nights of dreamless sleep. During the daytime, he regained his industriousness in managing his business, and the shadow of Zhang Yong and the feverish dreams retreated. He thought of who could possibly help him with such confounding new problems and sent out a wire to a friend that came to mind. Days went by without reply, and Mitchell cursed at the ill luck that perhaps all of his remaining friends' employments or residences had changed in the specter of the great quake.

As for Old Han, he was proving elusive. Mitchell tracked down a few of the newsboys who delivered editions to Chinatown and the adjacent neighborhoods, who themselves were usually Chinese but spoke just enough functional English. He paid them to ask around about Old Han in exchange for quarters, or even a dollar if the lead proved true. This resulted largely in the loss of a score of quarters for Mitchell, but within a few days, he received a visitor at the storefront. The day had started with the long-anticipated arrival of a parcel from McGovern's Rare Books in New York City, which he opened to reveal the complete edition of *The Jewish Encyclopedia*. A note was enclosed, informing Mitchell that the business was under the new ownership of a Thaddeus Townsend following the sudden and unexpected passing of Silas McGovern. As the antiquarian pondered the news from New York, a hulking man entered through the front door. He was Chinese, with short-cut hair, broad shoulders, and a broader belly, and wore a loose-fitting shirt of long sleeves. The man approached the front desk and rested his massive hands on the table, then idly caressed the wooden surface in a brooding silence, not regarding Mitchell.

The first thought that occurred to Mitchell was that the man could be one of Zhang Yong's gang. He dispelled the notion as quickly as it surfaced, concluding that Yong would have sent more men, and not in broad daylight. Yet as he looked up at the imposing patron, Mitchell did not doubt that there would be little he could do to resist any theft or assault, and the businessman cleared his throat. "Welcome. What may I assist you with today?"

"Where-did-you-hear-the-name-Old-Han?" The man asked the question in a slow cant, with halting, but well-memorized phonetics.

"Oh, well I should say . . . Nelson Hastings mentioned the name to me."

The man listened opaquely, but gave a grunt and a

slight nod at the mention of Nelson Hastings and pulled out a folded piece of paper. He set it on the desk in front of Mitchell, glanced down at it, then back to Mitchell, who nodded back at him, and then promptly left. When the man had gone, Mitchell opened the piece of paper to see writing in a florid script: *Saturday 7PM, Lucky Li's Club, say 'Equal Fields' to the doorman.* The message was a clear invitation, and Saturday was two nights from the current evening of Thursday the 21st. It was possibly a trap, as Mitchell had to trust the brute's rough indication that he was a representative of the mysterious Old Han. Mitchell was prepared to take the chance all the same; his plagued dreams had returned and drained him, rotating between the tomb and the city on the ocean floor. It now made no difference where he stored the statue in the building. The dreams always returned, and sometimes he would awaken out of his bed, finding himself in some lonely and dark corner of a storeroom or in an open hallway. Mitchell had never known himself to sleepwalk, and if he could take no rest at night, he would be unable to continue on. He needed answers, and he needed for Old Han to have them.

3

The following day also brought an unexpected visitor. Just past eleven thirty on Friday morning, Roger Merrick stood in Mitchell's doorway, notably cleaner and more refreshed than last time, bearing a suitcase in each hand. "I received your wire!" he offered in greeting. "I arrived very early this morning via the Southern Pacific train that pulled into the Oakland Long Wharf," the journalist explained as he removed his coat. "It appears that I made it in before lunchtime! Is that French onion soup that I smell?"

In fact, it was precisely that, but Mitchell had not been the one to prepare it. Nor did he employ a servant or chef; the pleasant aroma that had been trickling down from the upstairs was from the recipe of Wanda Silverman, Mitchell's occasional houseguest and lover. Wanda was a plain-spoken woman who Mitchell had discovered was much cleverer than she gave off. Her light-brown hair always displayed immaculate shine, although her disposition was more than a bit jaded; she had suffered a number of social setbacks, and Mitchell understood that he was not the only man who financially supported the charming socialite. Nevertheless,

Mitchell enjoyed the whimsical and unpredictable nature of her visits. Wanda was difficult to get a hold of but always knew where to find Mitchell, and he had learned to accept the arrangement as Wanda set it.

The two complemented each other in one sense as divorcées of earlier marriages that had turned to misery. Divorce had been no easy arrangement in the U.S. legal system, despite certain "havens" existing based on state laws—the closest regional hub was in Reno, Nevada. Jewish divorces did not require court decrees but merely the delivery of a get, a sort of in-house divorce document from the husband to the wife within the confines of the Jewish faith. The get was a one-way street of privilege, sometimes leading to the misery of wives in cases where their husbands denied any divorce initiatives, either for vindictive reasons or in genuine attempts to preserve the union. This had not happened in Wanda's or Mitchell's cases. However, Mitchell's failed marriage remained a source of disappointment to his family. Though it hadn't been his intention, he had resigned himself to something of a wilderness of morality to enjoy some of its benefits. This bittersweet freedom had not insulated him from the prospect of his parents discovering the relationship and, thus, more grounds for criticism.

"Your nose doesn't betray you," Mitchell replied. "And Wanda always makes enough portions for three or more, though I may begrudge you for not having leftovers on this occasion," he warned gently.

"Oh, only if you don't mind," Roger spoke without true

conviction, his eyes fixed on the staircase to the upstairs. He noticed Mitchell's amusement and offered "I really am quite hungry" as an apology. Mitchell showed him to the coat hooks, but Roger interrupted their movement toward the stairs. "The last time I was your guest, I had no suitable gift to offer my unexpected host." He opened one of his suitcases on a tabletop and reached inside. "Naturally, I made sure that mistake would not be repeated." He presented Mitchell with a small golden coin in a felt-lined case.

Mitchell perceived an imperial portrait on the heads side and a signal of victory on the reverse. Latin characters encircled the rim of both sides, but Mitchell spied a *globus cruciger* clutched in one hand of the personified victory. "This must be Byzantine," he remarked confidently.

"You know your numismatics! That is a tremissis of Anastasius I, from the fifth and sixth centuries AD," Roger said slowly, recalling the vocabulary. "I have something of a source in Chicago, and I understand that these may sell for a good sum to the right buyer—"

"I suspect I shall keep it instead!" Mitchell responded warmly.

"Then we must dispose of the second gift together," Roger added, producing a bottle of Jack Daniel's whiskey. "Maybe with some coffee?"

The two made plans for the bottle and then proceeded upstairs after Mitchell turned his sign at the front door and locked it. They joined Wanda, who was wearing a blue bib front apron, for lunch at the circular table in Mitchell's kitchen. Roger made very polite conversation. Despite Mitchell not yet having the opportunity to explain the nature of his relationship with Wanda, nor the reason for summoning Roger by wire, his friend did not press him on either issue but simply offered brief and sincere praise of the quality of the food and hospitality. After a few minutes of undisturbed enjoyment of the meal, Wanda turned toward Roger, her eyes scanning him, and broke the silence. "So, you are a *Tribune* reporter, Mr. Merrick? Please, what are some of the interesting stories you have covered?"

"Roger, call me Roger," the journalist replied tersely, minimizing the interruption from his soup bowl.

"Roger, it is then," Wanda replied, smiling.

Roger set down his spoon. "Regarding stories, well, let's see, which dramatic ones . . . there was Mr. Roosevelt's reelection in '04, no . . . not *reelection*, first election I suppose I should say. I did a bit on that canal of his and that teamsters' strike in Chicago. I tell you, that was a hot ticket item back home. I suppose that was about a year before the earthquake over here. Oh, and I did have the pleasure of an interview with Mr. Sinclair, the author of *The Jungle*, that all-too-candid look at our meat packing plants in Chicago. Please believe me, that conversation is best saved when we are not having a meal." The three shared a laugh at that. Wanda appeared spellbound and continually nodded at all of the mentions. "Of course, my first breakthrough story was on those murders in Waukesha, Wisconsin, to which I was a witness," Roger added more seriously.

"Funny word that . . . how did you say it? Waah-kesh-ahh? An Indian word?" Wanda asked.

"Indeed, there are scores of such town and village names in the state, and all the better for it," Roger replied. "There are enough Springfields and Washingtons."

"I can't believe it, but I remember that story now that you mention it," Mitchell said airily. "But I had not associated you with it until now. To think that you hadn't discussed such things at all the last time you were here!"

"Last time?" Wanda asked, eyebrows raised. "Mitchell, why do you keep such a charming friend a secret from me? How long have you been carrying on with this Chicagoan?"

"We've only been briefly acquainted," Roger offered in defense of Mitchell. "He was kind enough to offer me his hospitality in the aftermath of the earthquake. We have more than a little catching up to do."

"Then I won't keep the men from their fraternizing. I have quite a schedule to keep myself," Wanda replied, not to be outdone. She gathered her jacket, finished her coffee, and nodded at the dishes to which Mitchell would have to tend to himself as she left to meet with her girlfriends. Mitchell offered to close the shop for the day, but Roger insisted that he should take up whatever patrons the day might bring while Roger rested for a bit in "his" spot in the den.

When the business day ended, Mitchell prepared the suggested cocktails of mixing the whiskey with coffee. Roger commended the concoctions as he sipped approvingly. They sat in the den, the bottle of Jack Daniel's and the tomb guardian standing next to each other on the coffee table.

"Wanda seems nice . . . a very . . . *refined* woman?" Roger ventured.

"She is, and too nice to be held down by just one man," Mitchell replied.

"I'm surprised you're comfortable with such an arrangement—"

"I don't . . . *prefer* things this way, but the quality of our time together overcomes any misgivings or jealousies I might form. Sometimes I'll be instructed to secure tickets for the South San Francisco Opera House, other evenings I'll return home to see the trace of her body halfway underneath the sheets of my bed. If one thing, she is refreshingly whimsical."

"I see," Roger replied, still frowning. "Just don't sell yourself short, Mitchell. You have a great deal to offer to the right woman."

"So I've been told, but to turn the subject back to you, friend, there was something about that Waukesha article that seemed funny to me. I didn't quite understand how the narrative all fit together; I remembered that there were two crime scenes where the murders took place, a Fountain Spring House and a field . . . outside a cottage, I think. I was surprised as to why the drifters hadn't limited their altercation to one location."

"And as to that, I am now ready to share with you the unabridged account of those October nights, which I was not prepared for in the early hours of my last visit," Roger said, rubbing his forehead. "I have not shared the account of the Spring City Terror for a few years now."

It was then that Roger held nothing back from Mitchell. He wove a tale of Haunchyville, of Thalmak the Whispering Root, of the dark powers of the former professor of Carroll College, Reginald Linden, and of stabbing skirmishes in fluorescent lichen-lit grotto pools and burning abominations in polluted waterways. At several points, Mitchell asked questions and Roger provided further answers to complete the picture of the predawn horror on the outskirts of that quaint Wisconsin town. "I've been unfortunate in some things," Roger explained, showing Mitchell his scarred hand that had been scorched by Linden. "It almost always throbs, some days worse than others. I'm never as sure of my nerves in that hand. However, the single greatest boon that Providence has afforded me is that I met my wife Lucy through the ordeal." He showed the antiquarian a photograph he kept in his wallet. "Secondly, I have not yet been outed as a madman or sent to a lunatic asylum. I've walked a delicate line, a good thing to practice in my line of work. I've had some awkward conversations with well-intentioned authorities, but only a small number know the full truth. But I implore you, don't offer your agreement just for the sake of politeness. Perhaps I am quite mad, and no one has had the heart to tell me yet."

"Not at all," Mitchell replied as he refreshed their glasses. "I would say it is my turn to surprise you, but now I see that is no longer likely. Had you shared this tale two weeks ago, I think you would have guessed me right. But I too have been troubled by things I do not fully understand and am not so foolish to balk at strange accounts from others."

And once Mitchell shared his description of the cursed statue and bizarre dreams, the two were fully briefed on their otherworldly troubles and encounters, past and present. "It's no wonder you invited me here. I'm glad to offer what help that I can," Roger said. "I can't say I've ever quite experienced a prescient vision such as you described in that dream, and sure enough, there is the scar," he noted with wonder, leaning forward as he inspected Mitchell's neck. "There clearly is something more to that tomb guardian." He shifted back in his chair, thinking. "So in your quest to find 'Old Han,' you've arranged a meeting for tomorrow night. My timing seems to have been adequate, although at the same time I would have preferred a day or two of leisure before joining you on dark missions." This evoked a small laugh from Mitchell. "I hope you weren't instructed to come alone?" Mitchell shook his head in response. "I recalled Chinatown being wholly devastated by the great earthquake and fire. I also recall the infamous bubonic plague quarantine five years ago. Yes . . . I put it down as something like a *squalid hell of want and disease* in my coverage for the *Tribune*."

"From what I understand, that description still holds some merit," Mitchell replied, rubbing his neck. "But whatever answers may be found there, whatever risks we incur from this meeting with Old Han, I must venture a try. This damned statue weighs on me much like your Haunchyville dagger that you smartly deposited away. Yet unlike the curious weapon that Eugene Shepard entrusted to you, this tomb guardian is being sought, and I know there is something more to it that must be discovered."

More than half of the whiskey bottle had been finished, and the two spoke no more that night of grim portents and slept late into Saturday morning. Roger had left earlier in the day, although he returned by noon with a stack of papers. "I had to look further into this Chinatown outbreak while I still had the opportunity," he explained as the two took their lunch. "It appears to have begun with the arrival of a cargo ship in 1900, with infected rats carrying the bubonic plague, and we owe much of our knowledge of the bacteria to a man named Alexandre Yersin, who studied another incident in Hong Kong a little more than a decade ago."

"That Chinatown quarantine was nasty business," Mitchell commented, remembering the descriptions and photographs of the *Chronicle*.

"Indeed it was, and it appears to have been mismanaged. A connection was guessed by the authorities that the proximity of buried victims would spread the contamination. Inner-city cemeteries were closed, and many of the Chinese were denied the right to bury their dead in their familial grave plots—inadequate, extra cemeteries popped up outside of town," Roger added. "I'm sure it's quite safe to venture in now, although I still would be glad to have a surgical mask or something to cover my mouth and nostrils."

"I don't think that can be helped, much like my breaking of the Sabbath this night," Mitchell responded. "We would stick out even more than we already will. We don't want to spook our contact upon first sight."

The two agreed that they would have to trust in their own constitutions in Chinatown that night. Lucky Li's Club was not difficult to find in the evening's twilight, as it was situated west across Montgomery Street towards Portsmouth Square and the looming ruin of the Hall of Justice, the short-lived headquarters for the San Francisco Police Department. The collapsed spire at the top of the central tower, which still stood despite losing two of its own walls, evoked something of a haunted citadel in an old European countryside. The ruin was still visible in the distance when they reached the much more modest structure of Lucky Li's. A proud and garish sign, swaying in a strong westerly breeze, displayed the Chinese characters above the English title. A doorman raised his eyebrows at Mitchell and Roger, but yielded the way at the password of "equal fields," and even gave them a polite nod as they entered.

The two were the only Westerners in the establishment, but Mitchell found the overall impression of the club rather pleasant, and the atmosphere dispelled the dark necessities of the approaching meeting. The floor was of polished tile, and shoots of plants formed neat terraces along walls and in dividing planters at various areas. Incense and aromatic drinks contributed to a pleasing aroma, and musicians plucked stringed instruments at the far end of the club.

The surrounding misery of the district was banished by those who came to the club, and their undaunted cheer was inspiring. The massive man who had visited Mitchell at his shop flagged him down and led the Westerners to one of the club's corner booths, past tables of chatting patrons and one of mahjong players where a few stacks of quarters indicated the stakes of the game. He gave a friendly smile to Mitchell, surprising him. Mitchell offered a polite nod in return.

At the corner booth was an old man wearing a black, collared shirt and billowing pants, who sat placidly with his hands folded, taking little notice of the Europeans. Next to him was a woman of mixed European and Chinese ancestry, perhaps in her late twenties, wearing a traditional Chinese red dress with a golden floral pattern that ran in flowing spirals across the fabric. Her hair was styled upward into an ornate bun, and Mitchell was unsure if he would be able to stay focused at the meeting without being too hopelessly distracted by the beauty who he assumed to be Old Han's translator. Once they were seated, the bald enforcer stood as a guardian at the booth's entrance. "Mitchell Bernheim, and my associate, Roger Merrick," Mitchell said, bowing his head to the old man. "Perhaps I may order us some drinks?" he suggested, which was answered by an affirmative grunt from the elder.

A server was summoned, and the younger woman ordered yellow wine, *Huangjiu*, while the elder, who Mitchell presumed must be Old Han, ordered a *Baijiu*, a stronger drink. In courtesy to Roger and Mitchell, the server informed them that they also served local beer and they had just obtained their first case from the Anchor Brewing Company, which had recently resumed production since the earthquake. Mitchell and Roger both opted for that, and once the beverages were distributed and Mitchell had rendered payment, he resumed his discourse. "Now, Mr. Han, how shall I address you?" he asked with respect, his eyes wavering between the old man and the young woman. While he had no other name for his contact other than 'Old Han,' Mitchell did not want to stir offense in the man who may not embrace such a nickname.

"Old Han is perfectly acceptable. It's fitting, after all," the woman offered in impeccable English, who then whispered Chinese into the ear of the man, who nodded and gave an affirmative *ah*.

"Very well," Mitchell responded, clearing his throat after having a large pull from his beer. "Old Han, I have been told that your knowledge of the Tang dynasty is extensive. Furthermore, I understand you may have insight into the obscure practices of the cult of Deep Ones that influenced the usurper An Lushan in the twilight of his life." Mitchell then produced the tomb guardian from his large inner jacket pocket, placing it on the table. "I've come to understand that this statuette is connected to this cult, and I must be rid of it! It casts a cloud of ill magic . . . chakras," he added, unsure of the best descriptor. "I must learn all that I can about it and prevent its evil from spreading." *Evil* and *magic* were not Mitchell's typical bywords in formal conversation, but he invoked them without a shred of hesitation. Indeed, he already felt a small pang of relief in so openly proclaiming his woes and seeking solidarity.

The woman seemed taken aback by the speech, hesitating, and Mitchell began apologizing and offering to start over, but she shook her head. "No, Mitchell Bernheim, I understood what you said. I simply pondered your words. They are weighty and grim, as is that statue, but it is for the best that it came into your possession and was not acquired by the associates of Zhang Yong. And best of all, you found your way here with it. I will be able to help you in these matters—it is not too late."

"You mean to say . . . you're Old Han?" Mitchell asked with amazement.

The woman smiled and nodded. "I am called Han Yumei . . . Old Han, Young Yumei, whichever one suits the moment," she replied smoothly. "Han is a family name, and it *is* an old one, maybe the oldest?" she mused, rapping her delicately painted fingernails along the table's surface while sipping from her wineglass.

"Ah, forgive me then, perhaps you can understand my prior confusion?" a relieved Mitchell asked with an air of dismissal.

"And why should you be confused?" she asked, her face souring. "I am a woman and cannot correspond with American intellectuals? You truly know little if you think I should use an unconcealed name with the knowledge . . . the *enemies* I have. Zhang Yong is one such enemy, unless you think his activities are trifling?"

"Do you?" Roger suddenly asked, defending his friend. "You're the one who chooses to operate under an alias, and once you're finished trying to embarrass my friend, we can stop wasting time."

Old Han smiled. "Fair enough," she said with all sincerity. "But I'm afraid I must allow myself such indulgences. The opportunities are rare, and your friend has a very . . . attractive quality when he's flustered," she added, contributing more warmth to Mitchell's complexion. "Since it seems we are to become allies in such dangerous matters, you may refer to me as Yumei."

"You said that you can help me, Yumei . . . the statue, what should be done with it?" Mitchell asked, leaning forward. "Just tell me what to do, and it will be done!"

"I cannot," she answered swiftly, turning her head to the side. "That is, I cannot say with *certainty*. Such esoterica are dangerous to study too closely, but I know of one man who has mastered it, and he is in Chinatown this very hour!" Mitchell looked to the old man who still sat next to Yumei, maintaining his aloof grin. "No, not Uncle Mao," she said, laughing. "Bei Yun is the man you are looking for, but he remains a prisoner of Zhang Yong's gang. He may not even be alive at this point, but even then might provide answers."

"How do you mean?" Mitchell asked, amazed at what he was hearing and unsure of what Yumei meant from such an assertion. *Does she mean he will have a note or revealing item in his personal effects? Does she fancy that this Bei Yun can be contacted from beyond the grave?"* Mitchell's world now seemed to spring forth with unknowable mysteries, and he wondered if she would offer an even more fantastical account or claim than Roger had the previous night. As for Roger, he was frowning with arms crossed but had uttered nothing since his one interjection.

Yumei hesitated and looked down at the table. "We must simply hope that Bei Yun lives. But even if we are too late, whatever more you wish to discover about your tomb guardians, we will need to locate his whereabouts first. I believe that Zhang Yong is a member of the New Anshi Cult, named after An Lushan, which worships some ancient and forgotten god foreign to China, to the Pacific, to the world. They believe that this god has made its dwelling somewhere in the South Pacific, and pockets of its crazed believers are known to me. I have heard his name mentioned in passing whispers in Chinatown but will not burden you with that knowledge unless you wish to invest yourself as heavily as I."

"I plan to . . . invest myself as far as it takes to get my life back, you could say," Mitchell replied, unsure of himself.

"Then let us take the next step. Finish your drinks, and then I will have something to show you." Once they had done so, they rose from their seats, and Yumei took Mitchell's arm to lead him and Roger on, with the large bodyguard also following. They left the smiling Uncle Mao at the booth while Yumei took them to the back room of Lucky Li's, which was around a privacy screen and another vigilant staff member. She opened the door to reveal a man bound with ropes around his waist, tying him to a chair. A single hanging lightbulb cast harsh illumination on his face and revealed a large bruise on his forehead.

"I know this man!" Mitchell proclaimed at once. "This is one of Zhang Yong's gang who tried to steal the statue from me! I gave him that bruise!" he added with satisfaction.

"Yes," Yumei replied knowingly. "And I needed to allow enough time for his interrogation before inviting you here. He does not speak or understand English, so we may speak plainly in his presence."

Mitchell observed that the man looked near death in his hollow expression. At the same time, he could not discern any overt signs that the man had been tortured; the wound on his head remained the only visible injury. "Yumei, I can't say that I feel too comfortable about this, now that I think on it. How do we distinguish ourselves from Zhang Yong's ilk if we treat our enemies as such?"

Yumei smiled. "I'm not sure what you are imagining we've done to this man, but you are tenderhearted to allow yourself to be burdened with such concerns for your enemies. But you can also see that we were not barbarous with this one, even if he deserves such treatment a thousand times over." She sighed, turning to her hulking bodyguard. "My protector, Bo, has more cause than most to hate Zhang Yong's gang; his sister was lured in by them some years ago, and whatever happened to her we have yet to discover. They entice many young girls with expensive gifts. Some are trafficked far beyond the city, I fear, and even I avoid speculating on their sad fates."

"Feifei!" Bo suddenly rasped, tears forming in his eyes.

"It is not difficult to find households at the edge of his territory all damaged in some way by his activities," Yumei resumed, placing one delicate hand on the galoot's shoulder in comfort. "But for every angered soul, there are two intimidated ones who believe it's in their better interest to keep their heads down than to oppose him. This one here," she gestured back to the restrained man, who had shown no reaction to her words apart from the name of Zhang Yong, "has agreed to lead us to a place called Lin's Den—the headquarters of Yong's gang—in exchange for his freedom."

"Why should we need him to lead us there?" Roger asked. "Have you not lived in Chinatown your entire life?"

"I have not," Yumei answered coolly, "but even if I had, the northeastern corner controlled by Yong's gang is unknown to even longstanding residents—"

"—But say Zhang Yong dwells on his missing man here? He was very high-strung at the auction house. I'd imagine he'd take extra precautions, suspecting such information to be leaked," Mitchell suggested. "How many can you bring along, in case he is expecting trouble?"

"Bo here will be leading half a dozen brave men to the eastern edge of his territory and demand that Zhang Yong show himself while we head to Lin's Den," Yumei explained. "Occasionally, Yong must contend with such challenges to his authority, and the spectacle often draws onlookers, who watch the balance of power in our unhappy corner of the city. Yong suspects, correctly, that we will avoid an outright fight, but Bo will stall for as long as he can and retreat here when he must. The withdrawal will be another apparent victory for Yong's gang, as usual, but by then we will have concluded our important business at Lin's Den."

"So is Bei Yun the only one we hope to find there? You're sure he will be at this place?" Mitchell asked, regretting that they would not have the formidable Bo with them on their excursion.

"Bei Yun is, of course, our first priority, especially if there's any hope to solving the mystery of your statue. But this is too good of a chance to waste; it is troublesome detaining this one any longer." She jerked her head back in distaste. "And with a little luck, we could undermine Zhang Yong's whole operation."

The plan was fairly straightforward, and truthfully, Mitchell had expected the night to extend to some other mission or locale as a result of the rendezvous, though he dreaded it. Bo marshalled half a dozen men from the club, inspiring the more drunken ones to follow after him. The man's size always impressed, and minutes later, he set out to draw Yong's attention. Without delay, Mitchell, Roger, and Yumei set out into the streets of Chinatown just after nine o'clock. Their guide went forth uncomplaining with his wrists bound. Mitchell closely watched him for any furtive movements, but he could read nothing suspicious in his bearing. He did not doubt that Old Han, Yumei, had whispered some dark threat or curse to disincentivize any betrayal. Yumei had proven a formidable woman from their initial interaction; her attractiveness was outmatched perhaps only by her keen wit. Mitchell hoped that she had more concealed prowess when they at last came to the dark corner of Chinatown: the territory of Zhang Yong.

4

At the end of an alley, the party came to an unassuming one-story structure, surrounded by similarly cramped buildings, that was identified by the tramp as Lin's Den. The guide was released and scurried away after a strong warning from Yumei. "Is it not too soon?" Roger asked, shaking his head. "He will surely fetch Zhang Yong as quickly as he can." His face remained grim as the group watched the guide disappear from sight.

"No doubt of that," Yumei responded. "But it should take some time for him to reach his master, and that's if he finds him straight away. Mitchell," she began, turning to him, "you expressed your worries about my methods earlier, but know that I refuse to escalate my quarrel with Yong to killing, if it can be avoided. It has not come to that yet, and I would not have dismissed our prisoner if I weren't confident that we could conclude our business here before they return."

As they moved deeper into the narrow Chinatown alley, it assumed the air of one of those isolated backstreets that seems a separate world unto itself; everything was so closed in that if one spent enough time staring up at those uneven brick walls and overhanging slate rooftops, they might forget that there was a city, a world outside of this narrow dimension. Many of the buildings were clearly damaged by either quake or fire and had not yet been repaired. Shuttered windows, exposed interiors from collapsed roofs, and vine-infested cracks in the walls all testified to the silent ruin. Never had Mitchell observed the sounds and murmur of the city so utterly dampened. San Francisco had certainly been quieted in comparison to a couple years ago, but there was a remarkably stale near-silence that prevailed in Chinatown.

"The spirits of the dead jealously snatch away any escaping noises here. They won't suffer a disturbance to their peace," Yumei remarked with sadness. "The ripples of the earthquake are manifested in more ways than ruined buildings and insurance claims." The trio slowed their pace, warily approaching the structure. The architecture of Lin's Den had a noticeable slouch in its stonework; while the sturdy building material had kept the stout one-story building from collapsing in the earthquake, it was unclear whether the sloping stones and low, bowing roof were already present before the disaster. A very small sign to the left of the door identified the location in Chinese characters, and Yumei led the way as they stepped inside.

The restaurant's interior reminded Mitchell of the tomb from his dreams. The overall lighting was minimal; only a few candles illuminated the dining area, which was larger than he had expected from the outside. Only one table contained patrons, although Mitchell hadn't expected a large crowd this late in the evening. However, the overall size of Lin's Den made it obvious that it functioned as a staging area for larger gatherings. At capacity, Mitchell estimated at least forty men could be seated at the various tables, and that number could swell to double if more crammed themselves into the standing areas. *If Zhang Yong has that many in Chinatown under his sway, coming here was a mistake*, Mitchell thought, his heart racing. The floor, while tiled, was uneven and showed cracks and loose dirt in a patchwork of small fissures. There was an unpleasant smell that permeated the air, like meat just beginning to go bad, and wafts of fresh cooking from the kitchen in the back made an unpleasant mixture of odors that caused Mitchell to gag. From the first moment he stepped in, he wanted to leave the place.

Conversely, Yumei stepped forward with enthusiasm as Zhang Yong and his gang had seemingly been lured away by Bo's diversion and hopefully would be occupied until the group was long gone. The seated party of three glared at the newcomers and muttered amongst themselves but did not rise from their table. A miserable waif of a serving girl began approaching them with timid steps, but then was called back by the cook, a bearded Chinaman with graying black hair and prominent liver spots. He leaned forward at the counter and asked in Chinese, then in wary, broken English, what the newcomers wanted.

"We are looking for Bei Yun," Mitchell said, then repeated in his unrefined Chinese which he had slowly developed over the years from scattered interactions with patrons from Chinatown. Roger gave a start as one of the men at the table nearly bolted out of his chair at the name, but the cook put his arm out to assuage the startled patron, likely himself a gang member, who lowered back into his seat. Despite the show of diplomacy, the cook was plainly nervous, and upon returning his attention to Mitchell, he made a shooing motion with his free hand, repeating, "Never heard of him. Wrong place! Wrong place!" in his efforts to dismiss the inquirers.

Yumei then spoke in a harsh, clear tone, and Mitchell perceived the word *jǐngchá* as she gestured back to him and Roger. At this mention, the table of guests bolted up and fled out the front door, and after a whispered word from the cook, the serving girl followed suit. The cook then smiled and bowed profusely, saying, "Gentlemen of the law, please have your way, have your way," as he gestured to the kitchen area behind the counter. Mitchell realized that Yumei had conveyed that he and Roger represented a police-mandated search of buildings in the area. The lack of uniforms for the "officers" and late visiting hour had not hampered the believability of the ruse, it seemed, and Roger looked to Mitchell with a shrug as the two decided to quickly search the space to ensure that Bei Yun or other secrets were not hidden in the restaurant. Mitchell thought it certain that the chef of the hole-in-the-wall was a member of Zhang Yong's gang. *Hopefully he's been instructed to be cautious if he truly believes we are the police,* he thought.

Their search reached the kitchen area, which was

expectedly foul; mold was growing in a patchwork of areas, and meat and vegetables were stacked on dirty surface tops. There was one electrical lamp to afford enough light for the cook, revealing the true squalidness of the floors and countertops. There were three doors in the restaurant's rear: one obviously to a back alley, a bamboo curtain to a pantry, and another sturdy door to an unknown area. As Mitchell tried the knob, he saw that it was securely locked. "Basement . . . flooded, no can go in there!" the cook said alarmingly, shaking his hand at them.

"We need to get in," Roger replied. "You have a key?" He turned his hand in charade to assist his communication.

The cook hesitated, but then nodded his head and stepped off, presumably to retrieve the key. Yumei had stepped into the pantry, and Roger continued to examine the locked door. Mitchell pretended to do this as well, but in truth, he was watching the cook through the smeared reflection of some hanging cookware. The chef gave a sideward glance to make sure he wasn't being watched, then suddenly stooped down to grab a boiling pot of rice and came rushing forward with it in his hands. He used no protection for the blazing hot sides of the pot, and Mitchell could hear his flesh sizzling as he gripped it and cried out as he ran, "Abhoth! Shen! Abhoth Qīngchú!"

Mitchell was ready for him, and with a pivot, he sidestepped the charging cook and threw his weight into the man's side, leading with a jabbing elbow. "Gahhhh!" the man howled in equal measure of anger and pain as he lost his balance and his pot of boiling water flew against a low counter in the galley kitchen, splashing the contents against the cabinets just feet away from Yumei and Roger. The cook managed to keep his feet, and in an instant leaped headlong toward Mitchell, tackling him to the floor and pressing down with his weight. Mitchell seized hold of the man at his damp armpits. The act took great exertion; Mitchell's hold on the cook was just enough to prevent the man from biting into his face. The Chinaman's yellow teeth chomped inches from Mitchell's cheek while spittle and foul breath projected from the cook's rabid maw.

Then Mitchell's attacker sensed a new opportunity and instead wrenched his neck closer to Mitchell's bicep, biting into his flesh through the layer of his jacket. As Mitchell gasped in pain, Roger was soon on top of the man, locking his arm around his neck and constraining him tightly so that he could not threaten the hold with his teeth. The cook's face turned beet-red and his jerking intensified, but Roger maintained the hold as the man eventually slipped out of consciousness.

Yumei had Mitchell remove his upper clothing and found a small pan to quickly heat some new boiling water. Mitchell sat on a counter with Roger's help steadying him as Yumei carefully poured a pinch over the bite impression on Mitchell's arm. That pain was worse than the bite itself, and the whole patch of skin around his arm turned pink from the scalding water. After this, Yumei found a bandage and placed it in the icebox for a moment before carefully wrapping it around the bite wound. When she finished, to Mitchell's surprise, she gave him a quick kiss on the forehead, and for a moment he forgot about the pain as he put his shirt and jacket back on. His arm immediately felt both hot and numb under his sleeve. Roger, who had been searching the cook's body, gave a wry grin as he despoiled a key.

Recovering from the sudden attack, the three reexamined the door to the basement level. The cook's key worked on the lock, and Roger proceeded to undo the deadbolt above it, commenting how odd it was to find the bolt on the outside in addition to the standard lock. In dismay, Mitchell abruptly turned to his companions. "I'm sorry I've cost us precious minutes." He gestured to his bandaged sleeve. "I suppose we are out of time. Surely, we can't risk staying longer. Zhang Yong must be on his way," he emphasized after his first statement produced no reaction.

"Mitchell—" Roger began.

"Zhang Yong is dung, *shit*—that's the better word," Yumei interrupted. "You may be done, Mitchell Bernheim, and if you are . . . that's your business. This is not your neighborhood. These are not your people," she said icily, but without spite. "But I cannot be *done*. Not until I discover what else transpires here. The police came seldom enough to help Chinatown and its inhabitants before the earthquake and nowadays only come if a crime has spread to another neighborhood. The city's law reaches more slowly here; that is the way of things. That is why I cannot be *done*. I need to uncover the extent of Zhang Yong's evil and end it, if possible."

"Come, Mitchell!" Roger said encouragingly, planting his hand on the man's uninjured shoulder. "You'll regret parting from us now, however terrible things seem at the moment. But you have just as much reason—perhaps more than any of us, you must find the answers to that damnable tomb guardian."

Mitchell closed his eyes, unsure, full of dread, wanting nothing more than to be drinking a glass of wine in his den upstairs—perhaps with Wanda, but presently his fantasy began drifting towards Yumei. Yet life wasn't that way; rather, Mitchell was no longer sure of what his life was as it unraveled more each day. For the moment, he trusted his companions, and his faith in them would have to suffice. His hand reached out and turned the unlocked knob, and the door opened silently.

The darkness at the bottom of the stairs was absolute. While the rays of warm light from the main level helped reveal uneven wooden steps, it failed to shed light to the bottom. Roger had brought a kerosene lamp with him, and he reminded Mitchell how the incredible incendiary nature of a well-tossed lantern could get one out of unexpected scrapes. After fiddling with the knob, he kindled a bright flame to guide the party down the stairs. At first, the basement appeared mercifully small, only a cramped area of additional storage space for some extra pieces of furniture and general supplies. The walls possessed a sheen of moisture, suggesting last year's earthquake had caused some water damage or admitted some new seeping conduit to the Bay. Upon closer inspection, Mitchell and the others noticed and smelled a peculiarity: there were copious amounts of Palmolive cleaner in buckets in one corner. It was a strange sight to Mitchell given the uncleanliness of the ground floor. Opposite these supplies, the sublevel extended for eight more feet towards what would be the building's rear at the back of the alley. "Hold on, Mitchell," Roger said as he planted one foot on the lowest step. "There's a door behind these stacked chairs and some . . . unusual writing on it. Help me."

The three cleared the chairs out of the way. This door had a simple padlock, which was unlocked by the same key that opened the basement door. On the door was a bizarre drawing, what was known to Mitchell as a scrying circle. In a way, it resembled the *sefirot*, the intricate patterning that laid out the tenants of the Jewish Kabbalah, but instead of inscribed words interjoined in the organization of a column, it instead contained words in Chinese characters set within the circle. Yumei provided a translation of the words. Most prevalent was the name "Abhoth," which had been spouted by the gibbering cook, and other words reading as *birth*, *flesh, seal,* and *house.*

"Abhoth," Roger said the name vaguely. "I recall it now. The vilest man I know referenced it, and it was an adversarial entity to even him and his dark god. We must be ready for anything."

"It appears I was mistaken," Yumei said, downcast. "Yong's gang is not of the Anshi Cult. Abhoth is their god, not An Lushan's accursed deity."

"Abhoth," Mitchell whispered the name for the first time and found it nauseating, leaving a sulfurous taste on his tongue. "I can't allow the worship of such a being ignored in my city," he mustered with new courage.

Roger nodded, his face taking on a grim resolve that Mitchell had not before observed in the journalist, even when he recalled his story from 1903. With this, Roger was the first to step beyond the threshold. The others followed, and as the three stepped with *kerplunks* into a sudden pool, Roger raised the lamp higher to illuminate the new space. Their adjusting eyes provided insight as to where some of Chinatown's most desperate residents had interred their dead during the bubonic plague outbreak. The dark room functioned as an open grave. Cadavers in states of varying decay lined the walls to the left and right, stretching towards the opposite end of the room. Somehow, the bodies were propped up or affixed to the walls of the room so that they stood as silent sentries. The water damage was worse in here and muddled standing water came up just above the party's ankles. The pool of water did not spill out through the door to the other half of the basement they had come from; the floor itself was lower and uneven on this side—likely earthen. Some of the grim figures had empty, puckered eye sockets, while others still had putrefied globes leering out. Most of the corpses still had proud heads of hair, as well as beards, and tattered and moss-grown robes still clung to and covered much of their leathery, thin flesh.

The odor of this wet rot had a delayed onset, but when

it assailed Mitchell's nostrils, he recalled the faint preview he had sniffed on the main floor, and the oppressive smell caused his eyes to water and stomach to churn. The discovery represented the most horrifying affront to Mitchell's senses that he had ever experienced. The instinct to gag, cover his face, turn and flee the room, and cry out in terror all tugged at him without compromise. The net result was that he collapsed to one knee, sending up a splash of the foul water as he gave a seizing cough while his whole body tremored. Even with his eyes closed, the hollow stares of the corpse watchers had hauntingly impressed themselves in his mind.

"Steady, steady, Mitchell!" Roger said quietly, catching him under the shoulder and preventing him from falling headlong onto the flooded floor. "It's horrid . . . I know," he added quietly, helping the man to his feet. Roger brought Mitchell to a half-embrace that allowed him to whisper into his shaken companion's ear, "But it's our task to remain strong, especially as there's a lady present!"

That evoked a small laugh from Mitchell as his friend smiled back at him. Mitchell looked over to Yumei and suddenly felt a small pang of embarrassment at his swooning. The woman remarkably did show distress at the discovery, but Mitchell perceived that Yumei's frown was principally concerned with sullying her ankles and lower shins in the water, as she had already removed her delicate red shoes, which had been placed back on the raised floor on the other side of the doorway. *What horrors has she already faced to have such a bearing?* Mitchell wondered. She pointed to the far side of the room with a squint. Mitchell looked to the opposite wall, about thirty-five feet away. On a raised platform were three more corpses, their heads just inches beneath the room's low ceiling. These bodies were among the fresher specimens in the tomb, sporting robust, rotting frames. On the platform's foreground, flanking the left and right sides, were statuettes that looked of identical craftmanship to Mitchell's tomb guardian. They were stout depictions of the squid-like, winged humanoid, and Mitchell immediately believed that they were kindred constructions honoring the brief Yan emperor, An Lushan.

Spurred on by the sight of these, Mitchell wordlessly waded forward, ahead of Roger and Yumei, momentarily undeterred by the rotting columns of vigilant dead at his sides. An empty indentation was in the raised floor in front of the central corpse leaning against the back wall. *No doubt for a statue like mine*, Mitchell thought as he kept himself from looking at the horrors that surrounded him. Near the empty indentation on the platform was an open book, its pages showing the onset of moisture damage from the damp environment. Mitchell perceived Chinese characters upon the pages, and a surge of relief shot through him that the book would contain all of the answers he sought, the solutions to his nights of troubled dreams. *This book will lay the statue's magic to rest. All will be revealed!* he thought with manic anticipation. His companions followed after him more slowly.

"So what's to be done here?" Roger asked, covering his

mouth at the stench. The journalist had gently set his lantern into a small alcove near the entrance of the room, keeping a careful eye on the nearest corpse. "Yumei, can you identify if any of these bodies is your Bei Yun? I do see that this Zhang Yong has two sibling tomb guardians to match Mitchell's; no wonder he was so determined to retrieve another. What could he achieve, I wonder, were he to complete this set?"

"Few things are certain at this point, but remember, these statues are not of Abhoth, but of another. I'm sure Yong sought to corrupt their latent powers. It seems he is not completely without wit," she replied through strained breathing and speech, pointing to the book, "Whatever practices his cult fancies should be on those pages, and perhaps some understanding from whatever superior mind inspired this present madness." She looked over to Mitchell, who had crossed the room and pulled himself onto the platform. A small, approving smile formed on Yumei's lips, as much as she could manage in the setting. "It is best that we deprive him of his toys—"

"—Mitchell, look out! The bodies are moving!" a frantic Roger called out.

Mitchell had stooped over to first recover the book, and then the statuettes. Before Roger had even shouted his warning, Mitchell spotted a spine-tingling shambling in his peripheral vision that had frozen him. A breathless but unmistakable hollow moan emitted from the animated bodies that flanked him on the raised platform. The cadavers moved from their initial spot on the walls, and as they slowly lurched toward him, they pawed at his face, their long, curled fingernails catching a lock of his hair or brushing his cheek. Mitchell found himself unable to move in fearful paralysis, and the two undead began to coil their hands around his head, drawing their maws closer to his cheek. Mitchell observed that their mouths still retained enough remaining teeth to sink into his flesh or puncture his eyes, and at last he shot his arm out, shoving one of them back as he lowered himself away at the last moment. In this way, he was able to get himself down from the room's raised section, still clutching the book.

Mitchell's attention was wrenched from the undead guardians to a loud commotion of angry voices at the opposite end of the room. Zhang Yong and two of his henchmen had stepped through the doorway, returning to Lin's Den far more quickly than Mitchell and the others had anticipated. *Did a message reach them? Did Bo fail? Has he betrayed us?* Mitchell's mind whirled. Yong spat out furious words in Chinese and pointed at the intruders with one hand while his other raised aloft a great cleaver—the inscribed one that Mitchell had seen raked across his throat in his dream. The men at Yong's side brandished similar weapons, although for a moment they did not advance as they regarded their opponents.

Mitchell, Roger, and Yumei were at a supreme disadvantage, caught between the pair of animated corpses on the platform and the recently arrived Chinatown gang at the room's only exit. As far as Mitchell knew, neither Yumei or Roger had brought any sort of conventional weapons with them, and the situation had turned desperate. Yet the danger helped snap Mitchell further out of his terrified stupor, and he opened by tossing the heavy book straight at Zhang Yong. Such a throw would normally have been easy, but the tome not only had to clear the low ceiling but also sail past his own companions. Roger ducked instead of attempting to grab at it, perhaps understanding Mitchell's intention, and Zhang Yong cursed as he dropped his cleaver in order to catch the unwieldy book with both of his hands. Roger kicked up and created a splash of the foul water in the wake of this, which momentarily checked the other two men. He then reached into one of his jacket pockets and produced a jar that possessed a clumped shard of some tan-colored metal. In an instant, he removed the lid and lobbed the jar toward the feet of his closest enemy—perhaps eight feet away.

Upon contact with the water, the jar cracked and exploded, shooting out glass shards and a bright spark that added stark illumination to the room. For a moment, every detail of rotting corpses and furious visages were horrifically traced and bright with ghastly light from the curious explosion. In addition to the blinding display, the sound of the explosion reverberated deafeningly, and a sharp hissing sound and streams of steaming vapor emitted from the contact site. While Mitchell and his companions were just clear of the immediate aftermath, he perceived that the jar's shards had pierced the clothing of the Chinamen like shrapnel in areas of their shredded clothing. They also had been burnt from the flashfire, but Zhang Yong's formidable constitution not only kept him on his feet with such injuries, but also enabled him to proclaim words uninterrupted while he read from the book.

His ears ringing, Mitchell could not identify if Yong was vehemently shouting or whispering an incantation. Either way, he surged ahead, desperate now to wrench away the book from the cultist. His hearing was rapidly returning, and he could discern the rising volume of the insane utterings from Yong in addition to Roger and Yumei shouting something about the statues. Mitchell reached Yong, who seemed oblivious to his enemy's advance. But as Mitchell moved to wrest the book from Yong's hands, the entire assembly of watching undead now became animate like the pair on the platform; the nearest corpse slammed into Mitchell with a lifeless shriek. Mitchell grabbed the corpse by its head, his palms pressing hard against its forehead to keep the monster's horrible maw away from his neck.

In this deadly grapple, Mitchell risked a brief glance towards the back of the room and saw that Roger was contending with the undead near the statues while trying to grab the figurines away from the indentations where they rested. Yumei appeared at Mitchell's side and shot up her arm defensively, holding a swaying charm in her hand. The trinket kept all of the corpses at bay and instantly halted the grapple of the closest ghoul, who attempted to retreat back from Mitchell. As its body lunged away, its head tore off from its decaying neck, as Mitchell had still been clutching it in his attempt to prevent its bite. Yumei's ward, an effective bane against the ghouls, did not dismay Zhang Yong, who had thrown the book back to one of his minions. The accomplice was now limping out of the room with the book, careful to evade the lingering fires steaming in the water. Yong struck Yumei with a fist across her cheek, and she fell back. Another goon charged towards Mitchell with his cleaver, and Mitchell instinctively raised his arms with his improvised shield: the severed head. The cleaver buried itself into the crown of the supple skull, surprising the thug. Not squandering the opportunity, Mitchell wrenched the head towards the closest wall, slamming his enemy's hand between the hard stone and rotting cranium. The man dropped his weapon, and Mitchell swung his foot into the man's knee, sending him backwards in yelping pain.

While Mitchell had succeeded in disarming one foe, he remained exposed to Zhang Yong. Mitchell dropped the rotting head, and both men quickly groped in the foul water for the fallen cleavers. Mitchell found one first and aggressively slashed at Yong's exposed forearm. The cleaver sunk through both sleeve and flesh, but the off-balance strike did not penetrate deeply. Yong stoically ignored the wound while blood pooled under his sleeve, and as he recovered his inscribed cleaver, he counter-attacked. Mitchell clumsily raised the edge of his weapon to parry, but he was unaccustomed to using such an implement. Yong cut Mitchell's hand where his fingertips held the weapon, instantly disarming Mitchell and severing his ring and small fingers from his right hand.

Fighting through the pain and shock, Mitchell knew that if he didn't close the distance, he could be killed from Yong's next strike. He lowered his head and rushed forward to grapple with Yong, grabbing his arm and pressing him against the wall. With a wicked grin, Yong leveraged his weight and managed to push the antiquarian down to his knees. Yong drove his elbow into Mitchell's spine, and Mitchell felt Yong's other free hand clasp the back of his head—it pushed down hard and sent his head into the turbid pool of water. Initially, Mitchell was able to keep his mouth closed, but as the bottom of his chin scraped the hard ground beneath the water, he cried out in pain, intaking the foul liquid in which the feet and shins of rotting corpses bathed. Visions of a subterranean graveyard instantly manifested in Mitchell's mind: an infinite cavern extending impossibly in all directions, with endless craters of unclean spawning pools populated by worms and bloated half-alive humanoids. He tasted the vile water as it entered his lungs and grew faint, his body no longer possessing the strength to vomit or expel the pestilent liquid. Mitchell anticipated his death as time slowed, knowing that all Yong had to do was plunge his cleaver down. But then he felt an intense burst of heat above him, a slackening in the grip that pressed him down, but he had lost any strength to pull himself back up. All grew dark as he despaired of dying in the forsaken charnel house of living nightmare.

5

Mitchell awoke in the bed of a small room, his head slightly propped up by pillows. A soft light filtered through the blinds of a window, and the blinds swayed and gently clattered from a sea breeze that admitted through a small opening. As his vision slowly cleared, he could see a tapestry of Chinese woodblock art on the wall. His other senses subsequently returned, and he became aware of a bandage on his chin, his arm, and around the throbbing stumps of his severed fingers. A soreness in his throat and shortness of breath followed, along with an unpleasant imbalance of feeling too hot under his covers but chilled by the frigid air outside of them. "Hello?" he rasped, disliking the harsh croak of his voice, and he reached to the nightstand, finding a glass of water. "Is anyone there?" he asked more clearly after several gulps. He heard light footsteps and formed a weak smile as Yumei entered the room.

She sat down on the bedside and insisted that Mitchell not speak as she explained that she had treated Mitchell as best she could, sterilizing and bandaging his wounds. Mitchell considered going to the hospital, but reflected that little could be done to treat him that Yumei had not already provided, apart from pain medication. He had heard enough tales of opium addiction that he would allow himself to be consoled by alcohol instead, once he would have the stomach for it. When Yumei determined that Mitchell had regained enough strength, she finished the narrative of the dreadful encounter at Lin's Den. "Just as you fainted from the deathly water, Roger had freed the statues from the hollows, suspending the dark magic that animated the corpses. Together, your friend Roger and I were able to get the upper hand on Yong and the scum who was with him."

"What? How?" Mitchell asked, incredulous. "Yong was deadly with that cleaver, not to mention insane!"

Yumei hesitated, clearly troubled at the question. "Well, you saw that my Theravada talisman had some effect in repelling the unnatural life that possessed those corpses—don't assume that we are without tricks." She smiled, but it quickly dissipated as she observed that the response would not be enough to dismiss the question. "As for Zhang Yong's demise . . . your friend Roger . . . that would be a better question for him."

"Is Roger well?" Mitchell probed, the mention of his friend enough to momentarily derail him from the manner of victory at Lin's Den. "Unharmed?"

"Yes, he is safe too . . . he's been keeping your shop open on your behalf," she added, anticipating Mitchell's following question. "He would like to see you, I'm sure, so I will let him know that you are awake again when we have finished speaking. But to finish my account, we were able to get you out of the room but needed help bearing you up the stairs. I found Bo's group, and only with the assurance that Yong was dead and that he would not need to enter the accursed room would they come to the basement. With their help, we bore you up the steps and brought you here to my apartment. We then alerted the police that they would face a public health crisis if they did not dispatch a unit to the place, and at last they could no longer ignore the summons. I have been told that the whole building has been demolished."

"Already? How long have I slept?"

"It is Sunday, just past four in the afternoon, so not long . . . thirteen hours, perhaps. The police acted very quickly, for a Chinatown matter, and no news has been printed in the papers yet. It will tomorrow, I'm sure," she added. "We now possess the two statues from Lin's Den in addition to yours, and that is no small victory. However, the book that was in the chamber disappeared with Yong's man. It is my hope that his gang will slowly disintegrate without his leadership, and I hope the text we spied surfaces in the black market. You will let me know if it ends up in your shop?" she asked, smiling.

"Of course," Mitchell said, always heartened by any rare signs of tenderness from Yumei. A breeze kicked up again from the west, and for a moment, neither spoke. "So, Bei Yun never existed," Mitchell eventually added quietly, scrunching his forehead in thought.

"No, he didn't," Yumei responded in quiet apology,

gently planting her hand on Mitchell's wrist. "I am sorry for the deception. As I explained earlier, while Zhang Yong lived, none of my fellow Chinese would dare venture into the heart of his territory, fearing his retribution. The rumors of his command of curses proved true, and even my giant Bo would not withstand that sunken room of living corpses. I thought that by inventing this expert who would possess all the answers to your questions, it would be enough to convince you to accompany me. I am sorry for the pain it has caused you . . . but, because of our efforts, Chinatown is now free of Zhang Yong's shadow, and hopefully, Abhoth's."

Mitchell nodded at this, not feeling particularly angry now that he understood the evil and danger that Zhang Yong's cult represented to the Chinatown community. He doubted he could rouse himself to anger even if he wanted to in his weakened state. Without the added pretense of the all-knowing Bei Yun, Mitchell acknowledged that he would probably not have braved the trip in the first place. Yet he could not help but feel bitter about his now-crippled right hand, deprived of two fingers, and maintained a gloomy outlook of his life going forward. All of his woes had been wrapped in meeting the ill fate of the tomb guardian. "You have the statues here?" he asked, and Yumei nodded. "I don't suppose you'll keep them?" This time, she shook her head. "So then there is no knowing for certain of any of the statues' properties? Of the Anshi Cult? Perhaps with all of them in our possession, no further trouble will come of them?"

Yumei hesitated, then sighed. "You consulted with Nelson

Hastings, and I would give the same recommendation that he did."

"To go to China . . . to the remnant glory of the Tang. Was it Chang'an where An Lushan died?" Mitchell asked hazily.

"He had a palace in Luoyang, so I believe that is more likely the location that ties the power of the guardians together."

The replies brought Mitchell no relief, but heaped more dread upon the recovering man. Instead of asking Yumei further impossible questions on whether he would be able to obtain peace and answers from this journey, Mitchell instead dwelled on his options and decided that he would agree upon nothing until he had spoken with Roger. Yumei then left to summon him while informing Mitchell that fresh tea was ready in the kitchen, should he desire any.

Despite being light-headed, Mitchell had the strength to get to his feet and navigate Yumei's apartment. From the bedroom, he stepped into a narrow hallway, which adjoined an eat-in kitchen and another smaller bedroom that Yumei used as her study. Amidst well-stocked shelves and a full saturation of tropical houseplants, Mitchell saw one large book next to an open notebook on a writing desk. He eventually deciphered from notes in the margins that the large book being studied was *Great Tang Records on the Western Regions*, a historic work from seventh-century China by the celebrated monk Xuanzang. The notebook functioned as Yumei's research log and general commentary, and Mitchell perused a large paragraph on the open page.

Even among the religious, there are those who see death as a terrifying oblivion, a total separation from our current existence. Of course, the Pure Land Buddhists chant 'Amitabha,' anticipating paradise, much like the Christians who look to their heaven on the heels of the Day of Judgment. Yet they both have it wrong. I do not understand why the passage from life to death is imbued with such impermeable and fantastic properties by so many faiths. Death is not accurately described by either, although the dark road is much closer to oblivion than paradise. It is better understood as passing through a tall iron gate where one only has the strength to open it from the side of life owing to its design. While one is prohibited from passing back to the other side upon the way being closed, it is possible to gaze through in either direction. Those who are more motivated or desperate may press up against the cold bars and lunge through the openings to extend their reach, even slightly. It is imperative to understand that the further one tries to reach through this gate, the more dangerous the blind groping becomes. Imagine how vulnerable one's arm is when it is straining forward with every muscle, a person's head turning to the side to increase their reach by precious inches, but so that they cannot see where their hand extends. A sentry standing at the other side with a blade could chop off the appendage with one true swing. The nature of transgressing the gate of death is the same: the risk increases the further you stretch your grasp. It is my understanding that the scholar Xuanzang documented one such technique, perhaps secretly utilized it to assist his prodigious output of sutra translations. The secrets of this technique are surely inscribed in coded language on a stele or on a rotting palm-leaf manuscript in either Nanjing or near Xi'an . . .

The metaphysical discourse spoke with such authority that Mitchell had no doubt Yumei was able to hold her ground in correspondence with Nelson Hastings; Mitchell was quite impressed. *Transgressing the gate of death?* he wondered, remembering her words at Lucky Li's Club in reference to the invented Bei Yun. Yumei had suggested, even enticed Mitchell to venture to China, and now he had discovered some of her added motivations for going herself. *Whom among the dead does she wish to contact? A family member? Xuanzang? An Lushan?*

Mitchell waited at the kitchen table with his tea until Yumei and Roger returned. Roger appeared to be suffering under some new terrible burden, Mitchell decided, seeing a pained vacantness in his expression to match a paler complexion. Even when he smiled, seeing Mitchell conscious again, it was fleeting and unnatural. "Yumei told me that she debriefed you, so to speak," Roger said as he sat down along with Yumei. "But of course, some things could not be discussed until you awoke. I see you are made of very stern stuff, my friend." Roger's hands shook slightly, and he folded them together to steady them. "My old wound from the Haunchyville grotto has addled my nerves today," he dismissed. "Please begin, Yumei."

"As we established, it turns out that Zhang Yong and his gang were not members of the Anshi Cult, who call upon another dread god, a name I will not trouble you with here, but instead served Abhoth the Unclean, who warped the energies of the tomb guardians to reanimate the dead." Yumei's explanation was handled in her usual matter-of-fact delivery, but it was impossible even for the well-versed occultist to speak the names of the ancient ones without a momentary, shuddering concentration. "We have saved Chinatown, San Francisco, the whole of the Bay Area from the *gifts* of Abhoth in further plagues and madness, but the mystery of the original purpose of the tomb guardians remains. All we know is that they have cast great ripples in the dreams of dear Mitchell here."

"Could they not just be idols of worship?" Roger offered. "I would think that followers of these blasphemous gods are behooved to sabotage rival cults in promulgating their own practices." He sighed, then muttered something that Mitchell could not hear. "It is of some help to the sane and waking world that these crazed heralds are often at odds with each other. Otherwise I think some apocalypse would have consumed our frail world long ago."

"I would say that I agree with you," Yumei said to Roger, "but I would go further. I believe we remain at the brink of apocalypse, and calamities such as the earthquake may represent but a taste of what is to come if we turn a blind eye to those who would welcome it. I believe that the statue's true potency and other answers could be found—"

"—In China," Mitchell and Roger both interjected in unison.

"I am glad that I have been clear on this matter," Yumei

said with satisfaction, not minding the interruption. "I have resolved myself to go, before the spring's end. As with our venture to Lin's Den, I do not compel either of you to go with me but would be glad of your company."

"Yumei, would you excuse Roger and I to discuss this prospect in private?" Mitchell asked. "If you require us to step out—"

Yumei waved a hand dismissively as she was already out of her chair, and the woman strode into her study, closing the door behind her. "My first question: what was in that jar that you used?" Mitchell asked Roger. "I think the Chinamen regarded you as a sorcerer after you wielded that. It certainly bought us the time we needed."

"As much as I'd like to claim it as djinn's powder or angel dust, it was just a few ounces of caesium . . . element 133," Roger replied, not concealing his amusement at Mitchell's curious tone. "I've had enough contact with certain faculty of the University of Wisconsin's chemistry department to learn that a pinch can cause quite an explosive reaction with water. It's a rare metal and requires difficult conditions to produce as a solid in a lab, but it's about as unassuming as a piece of flattened copper to travel with. Why did I bring it?" he posed, reading Mitchell's expression. "I don't prefer the trouble of travelling with firearms and estimated there would be plenty of water this close to the ocean, should I have need of it. I expected to use it once I picked up on the distress inherent in your telegram."

"Yumei suggested that you also were responsible for

ending the fight against Zhang Yong. Come to think of it, I felt something like a surge of heat tremble above the foul waters that I had fallen into. Another chemical concoction?"

Roger's expression darkened on a dime. "I won't lie to you, Mitchell, it is true, but I should not speak to you of details, for your sake. I lost a piece of me when I called on . . . that power to overcome the Chinaman. If I were to heed Christ's command, I ought to cut off my right hand to prevent me from sinning." As Roger said these words, he looked down at the mentioned hand with its patch of darker skin from his burn wound. "There are old forces that can be called on, exacting great price on one's sanity and spirit to leverage their power. This was the first time I had done so, having studied certain abstruse and instructive texts, and I feel now more a husk of a man than I ever have before."

"Nonsense," Mitchell said, but in truth, he was alarmed at his friend's words, realizing that this dark incantation was the true source of Roger's sickly appearance. "I will ask you nothing more of how you saved Yumei and I, and I do mean that. God bless you, Roger." Roger did not look up at this praise, so Mitchell continued. "You'll have all the time in the world to bounce back from it, friend." Something about observing his friend's anguish inspired a new heroism in Mitchell. The fears and doubts of the voyage to China felt like a trifle in comparison. "You've done more than your share of investigation, and I have decided that I must go while you should seek the comforts that only family and friends can bring, back in Chicago."

"I would like to . . . I *should* go with you," Roger said with some difficulty. "Knowing what you will encounter, you will need my help again. Lord knows I came out alive from my little episode four years ago on the sacrifices of those who stuck with me."

Mitchell wanted nothing more than to encourage this line of thinking. Instead, he sighed and offered the hard truth. "Roger . . . I do not doubt that you would be the best companion I could ask for when leaping headlong into such madness. You've already helped me more and have been a greater friend then I had any hope of finding. But I cannot know, even with your aid, when we would be able to return to America. You must return to your home, to your wife, to your vocation. Should both of us become lost in this venture, I would worry for those we'd leave behind, that they would not have suitable watchmen to keep an eye on the dark things that we know surround us. You're a lucky man, you know, to have your Lucy, and you do not need to take on more darkness before returning to face her. Furthermore, a woman like that doesn't deserve a widow's mantle before reaching middle age, should something happen to us. You may not have Solomon's wealth, but you'd display his wisdom going back to her on the next train to Chicago."

Instead of an impassioned rebuttal, Roger listened to Mitchell's argument carefully, assenting with many grim nods. Something washed over Roger's expression, and for a moment, Mitchell perceived that some of the burden of the incantation may have lifted. "And they call Philadelphia the city of brotherly love, but the title may have been misplaced," Roger said as he embraced Mitchell carefully. "Mitchell, San Francisco will find itself bereft of one of its finest when you set out across the Pacific. Speaking of which, the Pacific Mail will allow you to send back what messages that you can— you have my address. I'll be checking my mail fretfully for the next several months. So long as you have the chance, I would like to be appraised of your progress."

"Of course," Mitchell responded. "I look forward to meeting Lucy upon my return!"

"We will all hold you to that," Roger said, a smile forming. "I am glad that Yumei is going with you. I can recognize that her company may be no small consolation for such a long journey," he added with an encouraging wink. "With a little luck, the two of you will pull through and come back enriched with some more Tang treasures. The non-cursed variety."

With a knock on the study door, Mitchell summoned Yumei back to the kitchen. "Roger is returning to his life in Chicago tomorrow morning," he explained. "But I will accompany you to China, Yumei, to settle the matter of the statues, An Lushan, Deep Ones, Abhoth." He sputtered the last word and found a bitter taste in his mouth. "And anything else that I'm missing! I'm quite sure I must go with you, once I've set my affairs in order."

"You are a true gentleman, Mitchell, and a handsome escort," Yumei said, causing a slight blush in Mitchell. "Today is Sunday, February 24th. Perhaps by the spring equinox, the

20th of March, you will be ready? I would prefer not to leave a day later."

"That should be manageable," Mitchell said, completely unsure of the truth of that statement. "I will update you on my situation when I can, though I expect we will be seeing much more of each other."

"Hah!" she laughed at the layered statement, offering Mitchell a sly look. "You are quite right. Perhaps I shall become a nuisance at your shop if you need further encouragement."

"Well, I should say that would be a nuisance most pleas—"

Roger had gotten up from his chair, wearing a wan smile. "I've witnessed this game before, when I was one of the players," he said through a laugh that nearly broke his weary aura. "But with things more-or-less decided, perhaps I should go back to your shop with you, Mitchell?"

Mitchell agreed, and with Roger's support, the two traversed from Yumei's unit in one of the sturdier Chinatown apartment buildings back to Bernheim & Hughes Antiques. For the moment, Mitchell's tomb guardian was housed at Yumei's apartment along with the other two; with Zhang Yong out of the picture, she was now willing to be their custodian until the voyage to China. Big Bo was one of several wardens who pledged their service to guard Yumei's home, along with the various prayers and charms she invoked to dampen the statue's potency.

Mitchell and Roger both drank that evening before going

to sleep, exchanging a final series of revelries and questions of their previous evening before the Chicago journalist would take his leave. Even at the prospect of parting and with their lingering injuries, they spoke lightly, praising each other like warlords around the feasting fire of a Norse mead hall. The main difference from this analogy, apart from the choice of beverage, was that their commendations focused not on sword jabs in the shield wall but rather on the split-second decision-making in the sunken basement of Lin's Den. The deft toss of the blasphemous book, the utilization of the explosive jar, Mitchell's cleaver duel with Zhang Yong—the narrative flowed until the action arrived back at Roger's technique that vanquished Zhang Yong. "I . . . I will not press you further on it, friend," Mitchell slurred. "Oh confound it, can you at least tell me what happened to the man? I'm not asking for any instruction, but I should think that I will always wonder about it should you leave without a description!"

Roger remained silent for so long that Mitchell was startled when he at last spoke. "Imagine the fist of a star of blackness lunging forward and striking the frail, mortal coil of your opponent. It is mostly an unseen spectacle, but Zhang Yong's body was crushed like papier-mâché," he said, avoiding eye contact with Mitchell. "It will suffice to say that Zhang Yong is dead as a consequence of my actions. He was a vile menace, but I am still troubled by it and have likely removed myself from the grace of God—for I know that the means that I called upon were not from Him." It was difficult for Mitchell to believe Roger, even from what he had witnessed, and Roger must have perceived his friend's skepticism. "Yes, it is *impossible*, in one sense," he continued. "But when you become so driven out of delusion, fantasy, or desperation to see how far you can bend reality, you'd be surprised. Reality can indeed be bent, most often these days through science, but also by other means at a price always greater than what is bought."

"We . . . we both acknowledge Yahweh. Are not all things ultimately from Him, or orchestrated by His will?" Mitchell offered in response, now feeling compelled to take his faith more seriously in the face of such dark wonders.

"Perhaps," Roger replied tiredly, looking down at his empty glass and placing it aside. "Let us entrust our dreams to His keeping this night, at the very least."

Mitchell had none of his usual nightmares as he slept, but his terrors originated from a different source that night. He had not returned to the usual locus of his dreams, but to the cavern of rotting death that he had seen when going under the foul water at Lin's Den. *Abhoth's Den* he thought the more appropriate title for that place as he remembered the name of the foul, great, old one mentioned by the gang members and Yumei. In his dream, his instincts were to move quickly and thrash with every muscle to escape the horrid place. This was made impossible by observation of his own body and appendages; his extremities had transformed into worm-like tendrils. Every synapse and nerve suffered from an intensifying pain. In his faltering movements, he saw further abominations, smaller versions of himself, worms with starfish shapes and humanlike heads who gnawed at his corpus. Mitchell had become akin to beached prey, and his eyes were the last thing to be consumed as he saw the monsters multiplying from their recent nourishment of his flesh.

Roger had awoken him, his hands shaking Mitchell's shoulders as he stooped over him. Roger suffered for the intervention as Mitchell sprung up and attempted to throttle him, perceiving his friend as one of the abominations. His effort was pathetically weak with his delirious state and maimed hand, and just as quick as this outburst began, Mitchell regained his senses and ceased, apologizing profusely to Roger as the morning sun came through the windows. "It's alright," Roger replied, coughing. "Had I gentler means of waking you, I would have done so, but you were sweating and muttering horrible sounds in your sleep—I don't think you would be able to replicate them in the waking world."

After further apologies, closing the shop for the whole day, and a long breakfast on Mitchell's treat, he at last saw Roger off at the Oakland wharf. As the journalist's train began its trip back to Chicago, Mitchell wasted no time in returning to the store. The day was gray with waves of rainfall followed by shrill, damp breezes, and Mitchell found himself miserably exhausted from the night terrors. His broken sleep must have still amounted to at least six hours, but he had found no refreshment from the insufferable dream vision and he sweat constantly, even without exertion. *I won't be able to keep things up if I have another night like that*, he acknowledged.

Thinking of no other recourse, Mitchell visited Yumei at her apartment that afternoon, requesting to take back custody of his tomb guardian. "I'd accept the influence of that smothering and drowned city over the horror of last night, which I cannot put to words should the description of that misery rekindle the memory," Mitchell explained to Yumei, leaning sideways against the doorframe as he found himself suddenly faint.

"This is my handsome Mitchell?" Yumei asked, putting her hand on his cheek. "You are much worse for the wear than yesterday. I . . . I do not wish to alarm you, but I fear you may have caught some blight from those tainted waters, though I administered herbal medicines."

"Oh Lord," Mitchell muttered, terrified as he immediately thought of his intake of the foul water which had birthed the abhorrent visions. "Perhaps I should go to a hospital and you should keep your distance. I'm likely contagious!"

"Nonsense," Yumei replied. "What do those doctors know that I do not? This isn't any natural affliction that's befallen you. I saddled you with this problem when you chose to help me, so now you are under my care, Mitchell Bernheim." Yumei helped Mitchell into her apartment's sole bedroom. "You need proper rest, hot beverages, and a little luck before you can resume things," she said with a matter-of-fact resolution.

Mitchell took heart at her words and certainly did not object, until he anticipated an issue. "But where will you sleep? I cannot exile you from your only bed!"

"I have nodded off many times in that little chair of mine in my study, and maybe with the acquisition of a proper ottoman, that will serve me just fine," Yumei replied along with several interruptions to override Mitchell's refusals. "If you truly wish to satisfy your chivalric urgings, then recuperate quickly so that you may return to your own bed!" she said sternly but not unkindly, and they shared a smile at the compromise.

The following week was not pleasant for Mitchell. On one account, his dreams were now more conflicted; residing in the same house as the tomb guardian effected that his dreams had become a battleground for the two dark gods dragging at his consciousness. At times he would be back in the claustrophobic earthen tomb or walking amidst the overwhelming majesty of the teal-auraed monoliths. These locales had now developed such a degree of familiarity that he no longer feared them; indeed, Mitchell no longer experienced overtly terrifying or painful sensations with either location, apart from the lingering sense of a great presence. It was not so within the realm of Abhoth, and with each passing day, those dreams began to dominate his sleep. He asked for Yumei to bring up his tomb guardian to his room, and despite her discomfort, she honored the bizarre request. The protocol had some success initially, but the power of Abhoth's realm continued to ascend in the house of Mitchell's spirit. When he would awake with his heart racing, he could feel his throbbing pulse painfully in the stumps of his lost fingers.

The sole consolation for the increasingly delirious antiquarian were his conversations with Yumei. The two had ample time to discuss their pasts in the quiet, long hours of the late winter days. Mitchell only wanted to hear about Yumei, but she snapped at him, saying that he could at least provide stories for the care that she provided. The rebuked man shared what little life details he found worthy of Yumei's consideration. His aging father Elazar the Rabbi was likely anticipating retired life within the next few years. Mitchell's mother Miriam consistently reminded Mitchell at infrequent gatherings and through correspondence of the possibility that his parents would take their retirement in San Francisco. "They desire the Bernheim family name to carry on," Mitchell explained. "And they understand correctly how magnified the pressure will be for me with them in close proximity," he added with a strained chuckle. "Isaac is my younger brother, but at the age of thirty, is not young as far as marrying-age is concerned. He works for a shipping company in Duluth, Minnesota, and I hear even less from him than from my beloved parents."

"You failed to mention your previous marriage," Yumei probed gently.

"Ah yes, Magdalena Kaplan. A match made in heaven as far as my parents thought, and hers, for that matter. The closest thing to an arranged marriage in America, a perfect Jewish union," he commented, his voice now tinged with melancholy. "The most painful thing about it was that the both of us thought so too, at the beginning." Yumei was an excellent listener, and through all of Mitchell's long pauses, she never asked unnecessary or leading questions, as Mitchell would always arrive at them in his own time. "It's possible that we simply didn't complement each other, but I can't tell you when exactly things began to deteriorate. Everything was good for a couple years, although Mag's only pregnancy ended with miscarriage. I don't want to say that changed things, if anything it brought us closer for a time." Weak tears were spilling from Mitchell's eyelids. "Do you think it's possible that sometimes when things don't work out, it's not the fault of either party? I feel that we both became islands, shouldering troubles, inconvenient dreams, and eventually daily thoughts on our own as never to trouble the other. We both lived our lives, but they never became as one, as it's always said should happen in marriage. My mother said it was because we had no children, and my father insisted it was our lack of piety. Had he known of the troubles while we were still married, I'm sure he would have stepped in as a counselor. I don't feel that he's ever forgiven me for that, but after eight years . . . Magdalena and I both became aware that for us to continue on in our world of immaculately polite coldness, we would be adding an indelible layer of quiet pain to our time on this earth."

"You must allow yourself to heal from this taint, as you did from your time with Magdalena," Yumei said gently.

"Have I healed from that?" Mitchell asked, his eyes widening. "I wonder."

Yumei informed Mitchell that his response merited the

sharing of her life story. She had been born in the early 1880s to Franz Bonhoeffer, a Lutheran missionary of the German Empire, and Han Mei Lin, a daughter of an affluent family in Beijing. Her mother's parents saw the relationship as an opportunity; conversion was a small price for their daughter to marry one of the influential foreigners. "It was a good childhood, if a hard one," Yumei said distantly, recalling the memories. "My father came to spread the Gospel of Christ, but even if my mother had never understood a word of the Bible, I believe they still would have married. Theirs was a very powerful attraction, and my mother was baptized the day before she married my father. She did her part in the Beijing Church, and I was raised to love Jesus, but aside from my religion, my parents could not agree on my future. My mother wanted me to find a Chinese husband and continue to promote the church within China, while my father intended for me to return with him to Europe and marry a high-status German or an Englishman, reflecting his own parentage. 'The wonder of Europe you shall be! My sweet May-flower, my marvelous May,' he would say to me. He always called me *May*, for short."

"What did *you* want to do?" Mitchell asked.

"Back then, only to please them—a feat that was much more difficult with my father. He insisted that I be raised learning three languages: my mother spoke to me in Chinese, my father in German, and many of the books that I learned to read were in English, the language of the 'Great Empire,' my father would remark." Yumei sighed and rubbed her shoulders from a sudden draft of chill air that filled the room. "It was a very valuable curriculum, I can say that now. But in a way, it felt like my soul was divided up into three, and I spent far too few hours away from my little flower-painted study desk at home. I was Yumei to my mother, May to my father, and Han Yumei or May Bonhoeffer as I traced in my writing. There is one thing about books—it made the walls of my small home seem much larger, the ceiling much higher, when I discovered how to transport myself into the stories and histories that entered into existence with each line that I read."

"No wonder you became such a bookworm," Mitchell said, risking a comment that could evoke either a scowl or a smile. Perhaps on account of his condition, Yumei went easy on him as they exchanged a grin. "My history is a little fuzzy," Mitchell confessed, "but I remember the news of that horrible violence in China against the Christians approaching the turn of the century. The Boxers?" he asked. "I don't know why they called it that, but I know that the U.S. and some of the other Great Powers tried to clear things up. Were you there for such terrible times?"

"I'm not surprised it was described as such in the West, but it was not nearly so simple. Those Great Powers you mentioned had caused much hardship for many communities. The *gweilo* defeated and humiliated China in several wars, forced the right to promote their faith, and imposed oppressive treaties. Even among some of the Chinese Christians, there were rumors that soon all of China would likely become partitioned colonies of England, France, and

Germany. One had to only look at how they strutted down the street, thinking themselves above Chinese law, and in many cases they *were*. Some of my father's own countrymen organized into a roving band, taking what they wanted—goods or women—and would end their sprees by promptly returning to the legation and escaping punishment. Not all were like this, and my father set out to confront the group that was causing the most trouble in the early summer of 1900. His body was found heavily mutilated, and the official story was that he was murdered by one of the early Boxers, so called for their embrace of traditional Chinese martial arts. But my mother and I both believed that Father was killed by the German men he confronted. Those were in the early stages . . . as the siege later reached its climax, we took refuge in the Legation Quarter as rumors of massacre were heard everywhere. Anyone who was known to be Christian was a target of the Boxers. Eventually the Europeans brought enough soldiers and found enough support among the Chinese, but before then, my mother was killed by a Boxer mob who had momentarily breached the quarter and found our home, and I only survived by hiding in a stable's haystack while I heard her screams."

Mitchell muttered what apologies he could for her hardships and listened as Yumei described her escape from Beijing aboard a vessel operated by the United States Navy, the name of which she had forgotten. Its port of call was San Francisco, arriving in October of 1901, one year before the Chinese Exclusion Act was made permanent law. "Although

I think, given the circumstances, a refugee of mixed ancestry arriving on a naval vessel would be spared from the prohibition of the law, even if you had arrived later," Mitchell suggested.

Yumei nodded indifferently. "Years later, I came to understand that the Boxers were fighting for causes both low and noble, and I learned to detach my hatred for them. It was only hurting me, I realized, and those of the Boxers who had not found their own graves from the rebellion were quite unaffected by whatever grudge I held. I tried instead to reinvent myself here, as many who come to this country wish to do. I lived comfortably in China, but in America, I had nothing save for my education and youth." There was a long pause, suggesting to Mitchell that Yumei still faced her most difficult memories to recount. "I told myself I would retain only what traits were helpful and discard all the rest to survive. I embraced the family name of my mother, the education of my father, and the identity of my new sanctuary in America. Chinatown became a home to me, and I have gotten by through a . . . variety of my talents, mostly as an intermediary for the residents of the neighborhood who speak almost no English."

"Does working as an interpreter pay all that well?" Mitchell asked, risking insensitivity.

"You wish to know if I have ever plied another trade? Yes, Mitchell, you are not the only one charmed by my body," she added acidly. "You think I could have avoided starving to death? How pristine and wonderful your reality must be!"

"Yumei . . . I did not mean," Mitchell stammered, then coughed. He doubted he would have the strength to pull himself up in the same way that she had managed, but was hopelessly unsure of what to say to her.

"And now I am the villain for working up a fit in you," she replied, more sad than angry. "The past few years have been better. I do have my endeavors in scholarship, as you are aware, and occasionally even that leads to small payment. It was only possible with the libraries in the area, although I find I never have enough time to get into anything proper."

"Nelson Hastings would disagree, as would I," Mitchell offered with a vanishing smile as he rested one hand on his throbbing forehead. "Have you ever sought them out? Those among the German legation you believe to be responsible for your father's murder?"

"As if I could touch them . . . I can scarcely remember the names of the men I had become suspicious of. They are beginning to blend together," she sighed.

"Surely, you can remember something!" Mitchell felt a new energy in thinking about the issue. "One name may be all it would take."

Yumei seemed to notice the improvement in Mitchell on the topic. "You can be very persistent at times. There was an Adolphus, or an Alphonse, Adolf . . . no, I cannot remember the name of their leader, though my father mentioned his name along with some of the others to my mother and I more than once. They did not practice Christianity; instead, they were part of some order . . . *The Brotherhood*," she said resolutely. "That was the name, although likely not the full name . . ."

"Then I would bet if you were to see a roster or list of some kind, you would remember the names, and we would have our next great mission ahead of us," Mitchell added with as much energy as his voice would allow as it continued to dry up.

"I don't expect I shall ever obtain justice for my parents. I don't let this distract me from what I can do . . . what justice we may yet obtain. But if looking even further to the future is what revives your strength, then plan many more expeditions, dear Mitchell."

Despite long and revealing talks such as these and Yumei's comforting care, Mitchell eventually knew beyond a doubt that he was dying. He developed a fever alongside splitting headaches that assailed him during the daylight hours, and soon even the melodious narrations of his caretaker became abrasive to his throbbing synapses. Any thought of preparing for the voyage to China vanished, and Mitchell made further demands of Yumei, asking that all three guardians be brought up to the room. As his teeth began chattering at night, Yumei began sharing his bed to help keep him warm. As comforting as this had been and as joyful Mitchell would have found this under his right mind, in his desperation, he eventually scorned this in favor of clutching the guardians under his arms in his bedridden misery. The fresh meals of soup or broiled meat and vegetables that Yumei prepared for him he could no longer retain; by the eighth day after he had entered her care, the slightest morsel was likely to cause an episode. His lymph nodes at his neck grew swollen and painful, and he suspected that whether he had the plague that had ravaged Chinatown years earlier or suffered from Abhoth's curse, he would not survive much longer.

On Monday, March 4th, Mitchell asked Yumei to send a telegram to his mother and father in Los Angeles, advising them of his condition. He also thought to call for a lawyer, perhaps J.R. Longstreet, but in his dizzying illness, all things were feeling pointless. "I . . . I don't expect they shall make it in time. I waited too long to message them, damn fool that I am," Mitchell said weakly. "Now that it comes to it, I have yielded far too much ground to my own shame and fear before my father, and now I shall not see his face again while I live."

"Nonsense," Yumei replied with her signature rebuttal, although Mitchell could at last perceive that her tone had been battered down and bereft of its natural resilience, gnawed by the week of sleepless vigils and observing the undeniable truth of Mitchell's decline. "You are a fool, Mitchell Bernheim, but only in that you count so little of your own constitution! You want to prove something to your father, then stay alive, recover to your full health, you imbecile!" For the first time, Mitchell noticed a quaver in her voice.

Mitchell had gone far beyond the point of feeling sorry for himself, and any energies for his own tears were long spent. Yet as he looked upon Yumei's face, he thought that he noticed a sallow flush in her cheeks, a swollenness near her neck that she had thus far concealed with the height of her collars or delicately-wrapped scarfs. "My God, Yumei!" he croaked, his eyes red and deprived. "Don't condemn yourself to this same slow death on my account! I did not ask for you to put yourself in such danger! Please . . ." he began, his words the chords of a broken soul, knowing that any warnings he could offer were already too late. "Don't doom yourself too! You have too much still before you!" Even as Mitchell said this, his breath became utterly short, and he felt consciousness slipping away as his pain began fading into a great numbness creeping up from his chest.

"No, Mitchell!" Yumei shrieked, her eyes full of tears. She leaned over him, and he could feel the warmth of her chest against his as she cradled his head, one hand stroking his hair. In doing so, the scarf around her neck slackened, exposing a large *bubo* on her delicate skin: the emblematic blisters of the fatal bubonic condition. The sight was too much for the shriveled and overworked heart of Mitchell. He now understood that Yumei, who represented the continuation of purpose and his own redemption, was now doomed alongside him. As he became aware that his chest no longer heaved in labored breaths, his final thought was not on his own extinguished spirit but on his own condemnation of a woman he might have loved.

Part Two:

Ocean's Grave

6

Utter darkness surrounded Mitchell, and he perceived himself to be as nothing, though his cognition remained. *The void of death? My consciousness lingers?* Mitchell's mind raced with questions and musings on the afterlife, drawn from his memories of the prophets of all faiths of the earth, when he perceived a crack in the night that enclosed him. He was amazed to be able to see anything at all—to have any perception or semblance of the senses. The sliver of light grew into a rectangle: a warm and softly brilliant portal. Inside the portal, he saw the unmistakable outline of humanoid forms. There were three of them. *The Father, Son, and Holy Ghost?* Instead of reexamining his religious outlook, Mitchell paid more attention to the growing light, which was slowly illuminating the space around him. He was not occupying an endless void, and to his great shock, the space was not large at all. Distant sounds, voices, like those heard underwater from across a pool, began to register. Now details began revealing themselves all around him and he recognized, *recognized* the place! His conscious mind beheld the basement of Lin's Den, and he had been looking towards the sole door and only entrance to the room of corpses. He saw the flanking rows of the dead at his sides and their gruesome visages, and at last, the faces of the approaching party.

Mitchell already knew who to expect, and he beheld himself, Roger, and Yumei scanning the room with caution and fright. As anticipated, he witnessed himself nearly keel over at the sight of it all, and Roger steadied him, helping him up. If lightning could course through every cell of his body and petrify his spirit like a pillar of granite, Mitchell could begin to relate the crushing emotions he experienced as revelations surged through him. *I look through the eyes of a tomb guardian once again! It's not just a vision . . . my very spirit has fled my body and resides within this ancient figurine! And such power resides not just within the piece I acquired at auction . . . they all must have this function, this soul transference! What triggers it? Why am I so fortunate and so cursed!? Are they not bound by time's linearity? Before, I beheld my death in my own home before it happened, and now am I to witness the cause of my death after it already transpired? Did both deaths happen? Did neither death happen? When shall I awaken? Would that I could spring from this clay prison and seize hold of my flesh and blood once more, I would warn them! I would prevent that dark death from seizing Yumei, from seizing myself!*

Everything was playing out just as it had done, and Mitchell feared that he would either be brought back to his own body too late, or not at all. *Perhaps this time I shall remain this way*, he dreaded. Zhang Yong and his subordinates had already stumbled onto the party, and every action transpired precisely as Mitchell remembered in burning clarity. Mitchell narrowly avoided the bites of the ghouls, he tossed the book at Zhang Yong, Roger unleashed his improvised explosive on the gang. With blasphemous commands in the name of Abhoth, Zhang Yong roused the other corpses in the room to assault his enemies. Mitchell watched himself fend off the attack of the gang member with the shield of the severed head while Yumei rushed to his side with her raised charm to ward away the other undead. But now, Mitchell had a much better view of how Roger had fared in the frantic seconds of that encounter, and he saw him duck under a groping lunge of one corpse as he reached out straight towards Mitchell's perspective and grabbed the base of the statue that the antique salesman inhabited.

The sensation of rushing wind that followed was so engulfing that Mitchell could think of nothing other than being uplifted and at the mercy of a raging tornado in the Great Plains. When he landed from this feeling, he found that he was back in his body, holding the rotting head and seeing Zhang Yong before him. Mitchell had a fraction of a moment to act. Fortunately, he had not burdened his mind only with helpless questions in his second out-of-body experience, but also prepared a course of action. Zhang Yong deftly scooped down to recover his inscribed cleaver from the water, and as he did so, Mitchell stepped forward, not searching for his open weapon, but holding the rotting head aloft. He bellowed out, sustained by the branded memory of the bitter reality he had come from and hoped to escape. The shout caused a moment's hesitation in Zhang Yong, who looked upward, and at that moment, Mitchell brought down the putrid head. He struck Zhang Yong's crown with all the intensity of Samson when he collapsed the pillars of the Philistine temple. The decomposing matter within the skull and loosely-hanging flesh cascaded down Zhang Yong's head, entering into his eyes and mouth.

Zhang Yong screamed with tortured hysteria, the whites of his eyes the only discernable features under the new mold of rotting innards that covered his face. Mitchell only held a fraction of the shattered skull of his improvised weapon, which still had the other assailant's cleaver protruding from it. No sooner had Mitchell removed the cleaver from it than he saw Zhang Yong recover and charge at him in a frenzy, cleaver again in hand, the only name on his lips being "Abhoth! Abhoth! Abhoth!" Yet the man faltered as all around him, bodies of his animated thralls hit the floor, returning to lifelessness as Roger surged ahead from the far side of the room, creating small splashes with long strides, cradling one statue in each hand. Yong stumbled as a body fell directly in his path, yet even as he began falling, he used the momentum to swing down the cleaver with deadly force at Mitchell. Roger had come up beside his friend and used the broad side of the statuette to deflect Yong's cleaver. Yong fell in the water, and Roger nearly dropped the tomb guardian he cradled in his left hand, but Mitchell took it from him and helped Roger keep his balance. Yong sprung up, spitting and coughing the foul water, and as he wrenched his body upward, Roger drove the base of the tomb guardian downwards, landing such a blow to the man's head that the thud echoed in the flooded chamber. "You're right, they make the most uncanny little weapons," Roger remarked to Mitchell.

"Let's get these out of here. Perhaps we can track down that fellow that ran off with the book," Mitchell replied, stepping over the incapacitated Yong, who floated facedown in the foul water. Mitchell knew well the debilitating power of the water and found it fitting for Yong to be admitted to the realm of his lord Abhoth in such a grave. He expected Yumei to wish to confirm the death, but instead, Mitchell labored to keep up with her lithe movements as he carried one of the guardians along with Roger out of the flooded room. Yumei had grabbed her shoes, but she bolted up the stairs barefooted. *Is her motivation to obtain the book that strong?* Mitchell wondered as the three made their way out of Lin's Den. As his adrenaline subsided, he felt in a trance, the dreamlike wonder of a new reality released from the taste of the slow death of the plague. It was such a sudden and profound reversal of fate that he wanted to cry out in joy as he found his footfalls marvelously light as they ran through moonlit Chinatown alleyways. In that moment, he welcomed and celebrated all aspects of life, both troubling and pleasant.

Disturbing dreams, unpleasant encounters with insurance agents or criminal patrons, dark investigations alongside new friends, he would embrace them all, a new opportunity purchased by the strange magic of the tomb guardians.

Even with the assistance of Big Bo and Yumei's other allies, who attempted to close the escape routes from the vicinity, once again the trail went cold for the gang member who had fled with the grimoire. Nonetheless, the three rallied the whole district for one night of celebration, even as they watched from afar while the summoned city authorities concluded their brief survey of Lin's Den and swiftly prepared its utter annihilation as a disease vector. "You will have quite a responsibility," Roger remarked to Mitchell, "in opposing whatever voices that call for the destruction of Chinatown as a whole after this discovery. I fear that the city may opt for broad and clumsy strokes again instead of a restoration in response to the fears of another outbreak."

"I shall do whatever it takes—I am not without some resources myself," Mitchell agreed, prompting a smile from Yumei.

Roger and Mitchell did not talk much as they returned to Bernheim & Hughes Antiques exhausted and footsore. Mitchell slept dreamlessly that night, the first instance since obtaining the statue. Thus he awoke more refreshed than he had felt in a month's time, rising before Roger and examining himself in his bathroom mirror. Like the phantom scar along his neck, he found a curious new pair of scars that ran parallel across his ring and small fingers on his right hand—the two fingers he had lost in the erased encounter with Yong. He then proceeded downstairs, the wooden steps creaking underfoot, to his secured storage drawer and unlocked it.

Here Mitchell reexamined the tomb guardians. Previously, he had regarded them of identical make in terms of their craftsmanship, displaying the sculpted bat-like wings, octopus head, and hybridized humanoid appearance, and had observed gentle hues of tan, red, and green in their complexion. But now two of the statues, the same ones that Mitchell had momentarily inhabited, were defined by a monolithic, blue-gray layer that dominated the new coloration. The persistent dampness remained, as observed earlier by Professor Hastings, but a distinct change had come over the two that had temporarily housed his spirit. Mitchell further noticed cracks running along their design; it was as if they were living organisms that had aged a thousand years and had "died" in his stead. He regarded the third statue that remained fully intact and in original color, hoping that he would not require yet another revival before all of this was over.

The rest of that day was one of the most curious Mitchell had ever known because he had recently experienced it, or something very near to it, in his previous life. At Yumei's apartment, over rice, chicken, egg drop soup, and hot tea, Mitchell surprised both Yumei and Roger with his resolve to set out as soon as possible to China and settle the matter of the tomb guardians, the Anshi Cult, and any other connections to Abhoth. But this revelation was only the beginning; his greatest task was sharing with them his new understanding of his limited immortality. Previously, Mitchell had described to Roger his throat-slashing by Yong in his own apartment as a dream vision, but he now would attempt to explain to his friends the statues' miraculous property to transfer consciousness and life itself, which he had now experienced twice.

"In the first instance, I alone had been killed in the presence of the statue in my apartment. The next time was our first visit to Lin's Den, the erased past, which transpired differently to yesterday. We were all worse off, but I succumbed to bubonic plague in just over a week's time after intaking the blighted water. That is why I think I was brought back again. The Mitchell Bernheim before you now is one that continues on only because of strange magic." It remained difficult for Mitchell to theorize while recounting such horrors, and Yumei and Roger listened patiently.

After considerable silence, Roger spoke through steepled fingers. "So the reviving effect is triggered by touch?"

"I'm fairly sure that's how they function; upon my death, my spirit transferred back to my body the moment another person . . . when you, Roger, touched one of the tomb guardians."

"Meaning anyone could tap into this power," Yumei suggested. "But shouldn't Yong have been brought back then in the most recent encounter?"

Roger nearly got up out of his chair as if to rush back to the sunken basement. He stopped himself, sighing. "It is true we only left him for dead, but the entire structure was destroyed . . ."

"I'm unsure if the statues have formed a special bond to me," Mitchell offered, "or if the only requirement is for someone to die or acquire a fatal condition in the close presence of one of the guardians. But one thing I'm quite sure about is that both experiences, both deaths . . . *happened.* The pain . . . the clarity . . . the length of my sufferings are all too great to have been dreams."

As their astonishment sublimated to tenuous belief, Roger and Yumei asked more detailed questions of what precisely had happened, feeling poorly represented in Mitchell's account, which possessed the implication that they had been unable to offer the dying man any remedy or comfort. Finally, they asked for proof, knowledge that Mitchell could have only obtained from this other existence. "Roger, I have little to say on your account, although as Yong nearly drowned me in the water . . . you called on some unseen power to overcome him. You would speak almost nothing of it to me afterwards, although you briefly described it as the fist of a black star."

"There is only one such technique you could be describing that would have been of any use there, and I do not doubt the truth of your words that I would use it to preserve us," Roger said distantly. "You have my great thanks, as do the tomb guardians, I suppose, for keeping me from such desperation."

"Oh, also you had identified the contents of your jar as caesium," Mitchell added.

As Roger nodded at this, Yumei in turn was easy to convince, as Mitchell began retelling her life story—and she interrupted him as he began the sad tale of the Boxer Rebellion and the demise of Franz and Mei Lin. "If only you had the presence of mind, the understanding that you would be brought back . . . you could have uncovered something far more useful in your purchased time. What would you have had to fear knowing your life would be restored anyway?" Yumei asked with unmasked disappointment.

"It's not that I understood all this at the time!" Mitchell protested. "You seem quite unimpressed for someone who converses with one who has lived an alternate future! And you were so sweet as you cared for me," he retorted playfully, although he found that he was altogether glad to see Yumei's usual and uncompromising curtness. "There could be an issue . . . while I would never be able to verify it, I feel that each statue becomes . . . *expended* after transferring this effect. Both my statue acquired from the auction and the one that I looked out from in the flooded basement no longer have the same tricolor patterning as they once did. Instead, only a trace of color can be seen through the blue-gray rot that seems to have set in."

"That explains your peace that Yong has not been brought back. One of the three statues remains fresh," Yumei replied, prompting a slow nod from Mitchell. "Nonetheless, we shall still take all three with us and hope that your recklessness has not cost us too much." She sighed. "Don't look so wounded. We are of course glad to have you back."

"Speak for yourself," Roger interjected, causing the three of them to share in a laugh.

For the second time, Mitchell wished Roger goodbye after again persuading him to return home. "The parting is not any easier this time, even with all of my fingers and good health!"

"You have only to send me a wire, and I shall dismiss everything to come to your aid again," Roger assured him, clasping his shoulders. "Confound what Yumei says," he whispered to Mitchell in the doorway of her apartment. "If you need the statue to save yourself or Yumei, you do it! Nothing compares to saving a human soul . . . whether it's unveiling some mystery or obtaining secrets from the dead . . . promise me, Mitchell!"

"I . . . I promise you," Mitchell replied, and with an embrace, Roger stepped out into the street to make his way to the train station. Silence was Mitchell's only companion on the walk back to Yumei's apartment. Over tea, she declared the spring equinox as the latest desirable time for leaving, though Mitchell cautiously posited that they could depart sooner. "I will keep my agenda simple: get the business's affairs in order, try to locate that book in the black market, and . . . visit with my parents during the Passover Feast."

"The first day of Passover is March 17th?" Yumei asked to confirm.

"Yes, and I suppose that's St. Patrick's Day this year as well. But in lieu of attending the parade, the evening will consist of the Seder meal and some catching up, that's all," Mitchell said. Yumei nodded and resumed reading one of her books. "There's one other thing, Yumei. You should know that at the end of my memory, when I had succumbed to the plague . . . you had also contracted it by that point. There was no mistaking it."

"I do not doubt that," she replied casually, but marked her place in the book to look up into Mitchell's eyes. "I do not feel any illness," she began, "but if I am the one to die this time, then perhaps I will be wrenched back to the final statue in the basement of Lin's Den."

"I pray you do not," Mitchell said. "We grew very close, you understand. You were far kinder to me than I deserved of you."

An amused smile formed on her lips. "I cannot imagine what came over me. Perhaps it was a consequence of this wasting plague that you described?" She held up an arm to mute Mitchell's reply. "Maybe it's not so surprising, but now is not the time for any dalliances. We both have much to attend to. If you dream of sharing a cabin with me across the Pacific, perhaps that will be motivation enough to keep your focus in these upcoming days."

Mitchell showed himself out, frustrated, now understanding that Yumei intended to use his attraction toward her to her own ends. Deciding that there were worse fates, he returned to his shop alone on the evening of Sunday the 24th of February. The following weeks ushered a return to Mitchell's routine, lending new energy and focus after the man's two brushes with death. Nonetheless, he undertook a project unknown to Yumei; he would attempt to determine if a roster or census of the German legation existed at the time of the Boxer Rebellion and obtain it if possible. While Yumei had declared that any mental wound of her father's murder had healed, Mitchell now understood that she would show no exterior weakness regardless of whatever pain the injustice still caused.

As for Yumei, she committed her remaining time in the city to further researching two principal matters: the location of Xuanzang's lost texts and the possible locations of An Lushan's tomb in the vicinity of Luoyang, China. She had become convinced that both were necessary to end the statue's adverse effects on Mitchell's dreams as well as understand the wider role of the tomb guardians. They would need to be returned to their original home, but this alone would not be enough to put their energies to rest or avert the dark portents of the age. Some recitation or ritual would be required, knowledge long forgotten save for where it may be inscribed.

The efficiency of their route would be critical upon reaching China; they both wished to avoid fruitless wanderings in the expansive territory. As a result, while Yumei feverishly searched for clues among piled books of history and myth, Mitchell understood that the logistics of the trip would be his responsibility. He inquired at the docks for outbound vessels to China and discovered that room was available on the S.S. *Asia*, a British liner in the prestigious White Star line. The *Asia* was now operated by the Pacific Mail Steamship Company, who recently acquired the vessel from the floundering Occidental and Oriental Steamship Company. Mitchell's view of the older ship in the harbor suggested its long service, and while its primary function now was running mail and parcels, as an ocean liner it could accommodate a fair number of passengers beyond the crew and cargo. Its typical passage normally ran from San Francisco to Hong Kong, but starting in March, the ship's scheduled journey was to arrive in Shanghai first and then proceed to Hong Kong for supply running. Since they understood An Lushan's tomb to be somewhere in north central China, Mitchell and Yumei would be best served to get off in Shanghai and continue inland from there. Its next scheduled departure day of the evening of Tuesday, March 19th represented their best time of departure.

The dock agent informed Mitchell that the duration of the voyage was estimated at twelve days, averaging a speed of about twenty knots on the open ocean, but was subject to delays or even slight improvements based on weather conditions. Mitchell returned the next day with Yumei, and he purchased two one-way, first-class tickets for forty dollars each after they had provided their passenger information. The fare included standard meals aboard, but not bar tabs. She promised to repay him, but he shook his head, saying that it was *his* repayment for the care she provided to him in his final days.

"You understand how odd it is to hear that as an explanation?" she asked Mitchell, who laughed. "But I'm more than happy to take credit for it, you pleasant fool."

"Is it better to be a pleasant fool or a brilliant humbug? Truly, I wouldn't know which you'd prefer."

"You're concerning yourself too much with my preferences," she said, smiling. "I like Mitchell best when he's . . . his own man, the immortal investigator who will persevere."

Yumei accepted Mitchell's arm as he walked her home from the wharf. *Immortal* . . . he reflected on the meaning of the word. He had no illusions regarding himself in such arrogant terms. Indeed, he was unsure of what mindset would serve him best in the upcoming weeks. Dwelling on the pain and oblivion of the slow death he had suffered was always enough to direct his thoughts toward future trials.

7

The next day, Mitchell went to the offices of J.R. Longstreet. In preparation for his trip, he wanted to set a will, and since Mitchell had no personal lawyer, he would approach the man who had once represented his business partner Roland Hughes. From a brief exchange of mail, Longstreet indicated that he was more than happy to accommodate Mitchell as a new client. The lawyer's office had recovered considerably from the last time Mitchell had called upon him. At last, the bevy of inquiries and claims appeared to be winding down for Longstreet's firm, and Mitchell immediately found that the square-headed man was much more in his element in this encounter. "New chairs for the office. Sears leather," he remarked, rubbing his hands up and down the leather arms. It was clear that his firm, like Mitchell's antique business, was one of the number that were prospering as the city rebuilt.

Roger Merrick, Mitchell's parents, and Wanda Silverman were designated to receive various selected items from Mitchell's antiques inventory while nearly everything else would go to his brother Isaac. Mitchell had already carried out a soft breakup with Wanda at a dinner date earlier in the week, indicating that he may have found someone else. "How nice for you," she had replied dryly before ordering more than her customary number of glasses of wine.

Mitchell was unsure that this was the best course of action, but even should nothing develop between him and Yumei, he increasingly felt that he may never return from China, or he'd come back with some new dangerous mystery hanging over him. He still had feelings for Wanda, and, by the end of the dinner, felt better about insulating her from whatever dark portents his future offered. Even if he could not convey that to her now, he intended to do so in his will. "I'll also be leaving the country for a time, should you need anything," he added to her as they made a final promenade in the street after dinner.

Wanda shook her head. "Whatever has gotten into you? You're not my same Mitchell," she added, stroking a finger across his cheek. Wanda had never allowed herself to be wounded in Mitchell's presence as per the nature of the dalliances, but she now appeared genuinely distraught, which made the exchange all the more difficult. "Where are you going anyway?"

Mitchell hesitated. "China."

Wanda clearly expected no such answer and laughed a bitter laugh as she parted from him. "China!" Mitchell heard her repeat to herself as she rounded the corner, passing out of sight.

Longstreet, in his perfunctory manner of speech, asked

if there was some upcoming journey or perhaps doctor's results that had prompted the initiative. "Not that any such impetus is required. It is always a sensible thing to do," he clarified. "I just wish to be best suited to serve your interests, Mitchell, as you now have entrusted me with a duty that I take most seriously."

"I actually have been feeling in good health lately. But I will be taking a trip to China, and you know . . . it seemed appropriate, given all of the unlikely but possible calamities international travel can pose."

"China! Oh indeed, very prudent of you. The Pacific Mail line . . . the *Asia*, perhaps?"

"Yes . . . you are rather astute about that. Done much sailing yourself?"

"Well, I first knew it as the *Doric*," Longstreet began, clearly delighted to show off his knowledge. "At least, I was acquainted with the news about it in the early years of its operation. It ran between London and Wellington—yes, all the way down to New Zealand! A very fine, very *tested* ship . . . she's starting to show her age a bit, you might say, but I would wager that any difficulty you might have on this trip will not be on her account."

"Thank you very much for the assurance, Mr. Longstreet."

"It's nothing, and good voyage to you! I hope you are able to bring some lovely new items back from across the Pacific!" The two ran over final details of the will's specifics. When they were concluded, the men both rose from their seats and exchanged a firm handshake.

"You never did receive any update on the fate of Roland Hughes by any chance?" Mitchell asked.

"No, not a whisper, and from what I understand, his relations—which are distant—are content with the matter as it stands. Can you believe that? They are not requesting an investigation or anything of the like . . . the requisite time has elapsed for him to be declared legally dead."

"You did meet him in person at least once, right?" Mitchell asked, his curiosity drawn in by Longstreet. "I suppose I've never really asked you before, silly question—"

"No, no, I quite understand! You need to satisfy your curiosity. He is a man of some mystery after all. Yes, I suppose now that he has passed on, it is not insensitive to tell you that I did meet with him twice, however briefly. I remember both occasions. He was a clean-shaven young man, about your age or slightly younger. That surprised me the first time, having such business acumen so quickly. He had accounts on both coasts, mostly in specialized merchandise and antique businesses, such as yours. Exceptionally well-dressed, his suit was much more expensive than mine . . . *that day*," Longstreet emphasized, brushing the expensive fabric of his suit. "He had a face you don't soon forget—one of those fellows whose bone structure comes through a little too tightly through the skin in the face, but he was polite enough!"

Mitchell still had Roland Hughes's old mailing address on hand from the considerable forwarding of revenues and correspondence before the earthquake. He had never personally visited it, but it was convenient for him to stop there on his walk home from Longstreet's office, as he had taken the rest of the day off from the shop.

The afternoon was overcast, but the canopy of clouds trapped a comfortable warmth. Mitchell checked the address and confirmed that the location had indeed become a ruin. The freestanding house had lost most of its outer supporting walls, but its remaining foundations suggested the Queen Anne style. The polygonal tower at its southwestern corner still precariously stood, reaching its full height of three stories, and a pang of regret touched Mitchell that he had never become properly acquainted with his departed business partner. An impulse guided Mitchell to step further into the rubble, and the antique seller risked the crumbling structure around him to head to a remaining corner he deemed intact enough. The frame of a fireplace still stood, and before the earthquake, Mitchell would have wagered that he would have been standing in a small parlor or study. The room was bereft save for the cracked, vine-infested floor. Mitchell, amused by following his whims this far, decided to check for a secret cache, reminded of an old tale of a Huguenot family hiding a Bible from the old country.

Looking back out into the avenue, Mitchell saw that he was quite alone. He got down on his knees and stuck his arm through the fireplace and up the chimney shaft. He parted cobwebs as he swept his hand along the interior chimney wall closest to him, and to his great surprise, he felt a cool metal surface distinct from the soot-lined brick. A steel lockbox rested in a crevice of the stonework, perfectly hollowed to house the hidden container. Eventually, Mitchell was able to grip the box with enough leverage to slide it out, and he lowered it down with ashy sleeves and hands. The box was unlocked, and he opened it to see a piece of paper as well as a Remington 95 derringer pistol set in a felt-lined impression. Mitchell took the weapon and the note and quickly set the empty box back in its place, then briskly walked from the site.

He was not followed. Once home, Mitchell noted that the small pistol had both barrels loaded and seemed in brand-new condition. He unwound the note and vaguely recognized the handwriting from his correspondence with Roland Hughes.

Matthew,

If you have found this message, do not look for me, for I will be beyond contact. The compact gun can be useful for concealment in case you ever get in a scrap—there may be some unpleasant fellows asking around. Don't let them intimidate you or follow you, and don't listen to anything they have to say. It's not true.

Roland

The cryptic note provided Mitchell a number of clues. It would be simple enough to look up to see if a Matthew Hughes existed, or to confer with Longstreet if he knew of any of Roland's acquaintances by that name. It wasn't unheard of for people to store such open-ended messages in the event of disaster. There was a preparedness in the letter,

Mitchell decided in his own lens of psychology. He was convinced the note displayed that Roland's concerns were more concentrated on whoever this group was rather than a generalized greeting in the case of unexpected death. For now, Mitchell would hang onto the derringer for "Matthew," and truth be told, he was glad to have the easily concealable weapon with his trip fast approaching. He was unsure whether to introduce this evidence to Longstreet or Yumei, but he had time to decide on that.

It had proven difficult searching for the Beijing legation census from the years corresponding to the siege of 1900, or any year for that matter. But by March 13th, Mitchell at last had success in arranging a meeting with a Mr. Herschel Graf, an investor with Oriental connections. Graf was a member of the prominent German-Jewish community in the city, which had elevated itself to something of aristocratic caliber. Graf had involved himself in the motion for a permanent German consulate in the city, though the initiative had been set back by the earthquake. In sending a telegram, Mitchell had endeared himself to the man on account of being Elazar Bernheim's son; Herschel Graf promptly replied that he esteemed the rabbi greatly and would accept an appointment with his son.

They met in the Union Square plaza that afternoon, where Mitchell found Herschel sitting on a park bench that looked east to the Dewey Monument, the grand column atop which stood the Goddess of Victory. "I wonder how she compares to Nelson's Column in Trafalgar Square?" Herschel asked lightly, gesturing for Mitchell to take his seat alongside him. The man had a finely trimmed beard and rather thick eyebrows just beneath the brim of his gray bowler hat. A tan folder rested in his lap, and he handed it over to Mitchell. "This information represents a rather poorly kept public record, but I believe it is trustworthy. I maintained such a list for business matters, though for a time it was regarded as a bit sensitive in light of the Boxer Rebellion," he explained. Mitchell had prepared an elaborate explanation of his need for the roster, but Herschel broached no questions for him. "All told, there were less than three thousand European civilians in the quarter at the time of the siege's onset, so the total number of Germans are very manageable—provided they were documented. From what I understand, hardly any were slain in that dreadful siege."

"Much appreciated. There's a close friend of mine who's trying to confirm the whereabouts of certain parties who lived in the legation, and I had given up hope any such list existed," Mitchell replied.

"Ah, well it is a pleasure to be able to assist. I have a copy for my own records, so no need to return it. Hopefully you may find who you are looking for in there."

"Thank God for men such as yourself," Mitchell thanked him again.

"It is nothing," Herschel replied unctuously. "A hello and a wish of good health to your father from me will more than suffice."

With the dossier acquired for Yumei, the remaining

matter, apart from Mitchell informing his customers of a temporary closing of B&H Antiques, was to track down the grimoire from Lin's Den—if it still remained in the city. Several of the usual channels for rare merchandise were instantly checked and ruled out. This type of item would not surface at an auction, and Mitchell doubted that the text would be pawned off to one of his competitors or fortuitously grace the selling table of his own establishment. The man who had retreated from Lin's Den had presumably done so under the orders of Zhang Yong and likely knew something of its worth. Mitchell understood Zhang Yong's gang to be limited to the city, but if the man with the book had been instructed to take it to some hidden cache spot, it would never be recovered. Even with the city's cult of Abhoth crumbling without Yong's leadership, Mitchell still hesitated to leap headlong into the black market.

Yumei had been assisting with the search; her friends and contacts kept their ears to the ground throughout Chinatown for any word of it or of larger transactions. The same evening that Mitchell had met with Herschel Graf, Yumei heard news of an unconfirmed, large transaction within the community. "It's vague to the point of uselessness," she explained tiredly to Mitchell. "We know that a Western businessman had passed through the other night and that there was fresh cash moving through one of the neighborhood's brothels later that evening. By the time I learned of it, both the buyer and seller had vacated."

"We can only hope it was some other dark transaction,"

Mitchell replied, observing the lines of concern in Yumei's face. He was also looking closely for any signs of the plague, but to his great relief, he discerned nothing and trusted that the two of them had been spared the horror of the deadly condition. He thought to present her the dossier of the legation, but the time seemed inopportune to introduce yet more projects and concerns. "I don't suppose anyone in the neighborhood knows the gang member?"

"Most of Zhang Yong's gang were assimilated by one of the Tongs; the Hip Sing has been adding the most . . . my Cantonese is too poor to keep me fully appraised. But some have also turned up to work at the dockside, trying their hand at either more honest or criminal labor—both can always be found in abundance there. But as for our man, our best opportunity may be if he has the same instinct to flee to China, perhaps with the cash earned from selling the book."

The next morning of Thursday the 14th, Mitchell manned the shop like any other day, but with the somber knowledge that it could be one of his last routine schedules. There were a number of patrons and acquaintances stopping by to wish him well or inquire of his journey, and he handled these with a polite endurance. What he really wanted was to scrounge up as much cash as possible before the journey, but most who had actual business at the shop that day were coming in with offers to sell instead of purchase. By three in the afternoon, he had made thirty-one dollars from the sale of a set of vases, a rocking chair, and a set of commemorative half-dollars from 1892, celebrating the 400th anniversary of

Columbus's discovery. Despite his intentions not to purchase anything, he made one on a whim: one of those Russian matryoshka dolls that were popping up all over the place since they became the toast of Paris's *Exposition Universelle* in 1900.

In truth, such items could scarcely be called antiques, but Mitchell was not strict with the age of most items. This particular doll showed impressive craftsmanship for the sampling Mitchell had seen and cost him twelve dollars. The item was particularly large for its kind, portraying a rosy-cheeked, blond-haired woman bundled up in colorful winter clothes, and contained miniature versions, which Mitchell imagined as the woman's daughters, inside of each respective statue. As the afternoon waned, it took an unpleasant turn when Louis Malcom came through his door. "Just so you know, everything is marked double the listed price, just for you," Mitchell greeted him.

"Then, my dear Mitchell, I must resign myself to purchase half as much as I planned to," Louis replied woundedly without making eye contact. He removed his hat and took care to scrape the dirt from his shoes onto the floor.

"In that case, Mr. Malcom, maybe if you try to divide nothing in half in your head, it will explode," Mitchell replied, not caring to hide his hostility while in his own shop.

Louis seemed amused by that, as his moustache curled even more as he grinned. The agent was in a brown lounge suit today, wearing a checkered bow tie of mustard and white. "My friend, I live not only to disappoint, but also to torment you. Didn't you know that?" With satisfaction, he approached the counter and rapped his fingers on the fine wooden surface while his other arm cradled a large case. "But since my cranium is still perfectly intact, perhaps we can do business instead." Louis lifted the attaché onto the counter, stifling Mitchell's rebuke. "I am *not* here to advertise any policy of Malcom Insurance," he clarified.

"I suppose there's a first time for everything." Mitchell was genuinely surprised, and a touch curious.

"I propose a truce. A cessation of hostilities. An alliance—"

"I'd rather jump into a bed of snakes," Mitchell interrupted drolly.

"Then you ought to have *your* head examined, because I am not without gifts to make the peace." Louis fidgeted with the side locks, spun the case around, and opened it just enough to show a decrepit book inside, secured by the straps. It took all of a second for Mitchell to recognize that tattered binding, even in the amplified lighting of his store as opposed to the sunken squalor of the accursed basement. Mitchell did his best not to react, but it was impossible for his eyes not to widen, his mouth not to open slightly at the object of his bitter search. "I understand you've been looking for this," Louis added knowingly. A small smile saturated with deep satisfaction formed on his lips, proclaiming his victory.

Mitchell decided there was no use in feigning disinterest. He could not possibly ignore the dangerous fact that his enemy had not only discovered, but acquired the book of incantations from Lin's Den, though Mitchell doubted that Louis had any inkling of the book's terrible precepts. Mitchell considered trying to talk sense to the man that he was in way over his head with such an insidious tome, but such a course ran the risk that Louis would be more encouraged to bleed a higher price. "Alright, Mr. Malcom, for the sake of this peace offering, I am willing to forget our troubled history and, as a bonus, dismiss the peculiar fact that you knew I was looking for such a thing."

"Now that's more like it!" Louis said, his fingers resting on the case's side, still poised to reopen or relock the attaché. "After that incident at Butterfield's, I naturally had to introduce myself and my services to that belligerent Chinaman Yong, which was not easy, mind you. But after we established lines of communication, it happened that one of his associates remembered me—once his superior met his mysterious demise," he explained. "The fellow who had the book wanted an exorbitant price for it, but lucky for me, one Chinaman is not all that intimidating when you meet them on your own terms."

"You must be very proud of your initiative to share the details with me," Mitchell replied tiredly, again surprised that Louis bothered to inform him in the first place. "Yong found me so quickly after the auction . . . you must have alerted him to my shop!"

"What a strange accusation," Louis replied, his voice touched with nervousness for the first time. "One that you could never prove, unless Zhang Yong were to confess it himself. That will prove very difficult for him given the fact that he's dead. I wonder if you had anything to do with that?"

"I can see this will get us nowhere," Mitchell replied, subduing his anger. He was convinced that Louis had aided Yong, but such knowledge would get him no further to the book. "About the peace offering then?"

"My gift to you," Louis said unctuously. "Of course, *this* gift will not be granted freely, as you already suspected." He swept his chin down to denote the case. "However, I will be representing Malcom Insurance in Hong Kong at the behest of my father. A tremendous business opportunity has presented itself, one so large, perhaps, that I shall no longer need to pursue more modest outfits such as yours for our clientele. So there's a double benefit in it for you, potentially. I may just leave you alone for good should this prospect turn out."

"I am aware of your penchant for obtaining private information," Mitchell replied, deducing that Louis had also learned of his trip, which was very troubling. "But I'm surprised that you would want anything from me, unless you really just want to make up that badly."

"I care very little for your friendship," Louis rebuked, tugging his briefcase slightly back towards himself. "However, I understand that you have somehow endeared yourself to the sorceress of Chinatown, and her protection and linguistics I *do* value."

Mitchell snorted. "Sorceress? Do you hear yourself, Mr. Malcom?"

"Do you have a more suitable title to offer?" he asked

161

sincerely, displaying unmasked desire to understand the enigma of Han Yumei. "I've heard you are on good terms, but I've also heard that Old Han was a living fossil and Confucian scholar from Confucius's own time—the stories have been morphing rapidly."

"If sorceress translates to scholar, interpreter . . . occultist perhaps, then yes, I suppose that's fair," Mitchell said, realizing he was giving too much away in his haste to match his adversary. "In fact, Louis, you best not anger her, or me, her implacable ally, or you will surely be transformed to a gnat or ghost."

"Snide comments are not a convincing stamp of our expired animosity, friend," Louis warned. "You called me Louis!" he suddenly observed, grinning. "Yes, perhaps this is indeed the beginning of a new era!"

Mitchell cursed under his breath. "One sign that this conversation has been going on too long. You've flaunted quite a bit but still have not actually tendered anything either," Mitchell responded, his eyes resting on the satchel.

"You'll get your book after I've met with Miss Han and certainly not a moment before. Sufficient room remained on the *Asia* for myself as well as my . . . auxiliaries, so we will have plenty of time to negotiate on the way to China." The agent resecured his case and stepped away from the counter.

"Sure I can't interest you in buying anything?" Mitchell asked.

Louis scanned the room with theatrical disdain. "I try to avoid filling my home with junk."

"Then you are remiss to cross your own threshold at night," Mitchell countered.

The two men glared at each other. The exchange of barbs had nearly run its course. "I don't suppose you've turned a profit on that little statue of yours?"

"I somehow feel you already know the answer to that, Mr. Malcolm."

"And those are always the best questions to ask," Louis replied snidely, stepping out to Van Ness Street, admitting a gust of wind that ruffled some of the tapestries on the shop's walls. *Everything is nearly in order*, Mitchell recognized. The Passover celebration with his parents loomed alongside the dark dreams ushered by the tomb guardians, but a crucial piece was now revealed. Mitchell had survived both the Great Earthquake and the confrontation with Zhang Yong's gang, but he braced himself at the creeping idea that these were only the opening acts in a darker saga which would threaten all the earth.

8

It was the Ides of March, Friday the 15th, two days from Passover. Mitchell's parents had become his houseguests, having arrived that morning to avoid travelling on the Sabbath. The forty-eight hours of their visit prior to the Seder proceeded at a crawl, and the upper apartment had been rearranged by Mitchell to accommodate the approaching meal. He busied himself by being a consummate host, but avoided mentioning the specifics of his "business trip" which demanded his departure on Tuesday. Each occurrence where Mitchell concocted a way to explain his dark situation, he instead chose inaction. He would be obligated to explain everything following the recitation of the Exodus at the Seder meal.

Mitchell also had an introduction to make; he had invited Yumei for that evening. There were general prohibitions to inviting a non-Jewish person for the meal itself and to partake in the food and drink, so Yumei would arrive after the ceremonial recitations had been made. It was still somewhat tenuous to share company with such guests on major festivals, but Miriam in particular implored Mitchell to invite whosoever he wished. He suspected that his parents would see such courtship and exposure to Jewish custom and tradition as an excellent opportunity for conversion, and for their son to, at last, remarry.

The antiquarian had come back from the dead, engaged in a deadly melee with living corpses, and had peeled back the veil of the mundane world to expose a cavernous oblivion of spirits and unseen powers. Despite this, there were few individuals who could wither Mitchell's resolve like his own father. He loved his father and tried to do right by him, but for a very long time, Elazar was never *only* his father, but also the rabbi. And however tender his father could be, the rabbi would come to pass judgment. Yet ever since he arrived, Elazar had been content to talk diluted politics, graze on appetizers, or read the newspaper or the Torah as the day turned over to the Sabbath. "The greatest struggle of keeping the Sabbath holy . . . 'two letters shall not be written, nor erased,'" Elazar reminded Mitchell the previous afternoon. "Almighty God tends to bless me with all of the best insights on Saturdays, and it's my burden to remember them for commentaries or sermons for the following day!"

Mitchell's mother had a more ambitious agenda that first day and had successfully isolated him to discuss his relationships just after their light supper. "I have heard that you've been seeing Wanda Silverman," she said to her son, planting a hand on his wrist. "That wouldn't be a bad match. I've heard good things about her. Leave your father to me, I will make sure he's amiable. Miss Silverman will be your guest tomorrow?" Mitchell did not answer right away, so she continued speaking. "You shouldn't consider the door closed on yourself, Mitchell, but you shouldn't *let* it be closed on you either! Your father would love nothing more than for *grandchildren* to learn the faith while he is still alive to lead the Seders!" Mitchell nodded, his mouth an awkward shape of muted indecision. "My precious boy! Is this how you act when seeing your mother for the first time in over a year? Come now!"

Mitchell hugged his mother, remaining in the embrace for a long time. He could feel the fragility and thinness of her aging frame as she rested against his chest, and tears formed in his eyes. "Mother, I don't want you to be distressed on my account, but Wanda Silverman and I are no longer . . . in courtship."

"Oh Michel," Miriam spoke his birth name gently. "Is that all that has troubled you? That separation is no bad thing, we had not exactly invested our hopes in that relationship." Her words surprised him, indicating that gossip had reached them of the nature of that romance. "You know your father and I are very traditional about divorce—"

"My trip has nothing to do with business, but an investigation of a mystery older than a millennium," Mitchell began spurting out, his mother's arm on his shoulder all the while. "My companion on the trip is our guest tomorrow, a Chinese-German woman who immigrated in the wake of the Boxer Rebellion. She speaks perfect English, Chinese, and German, and is—"

"Most welcome," Miriam finished for her son, reassuringly. "I look forward to meeting this lady. Chinese-German, what's the story behind that?" Mitchell gave his mother the long account, and the night grew late by the time he had finished. Miriam assured her son that everything would turn out well as she wished him goodnight. Mitchell remained restless, but eventually his mind burnt itself out in its overtired exercise.

As the table was set on Sunday evening, Mitchell decided to inform his parents of his acquisition of his antique business, making him the sole owner in the wake of Roland Hughes's disappearance and prearranged buyout agreement. This news was well received, perhaps the *only* tidings Mitchell knew his parents would be pleased by in the upcoming hours.

"My son! My son! That is splendid," Elazar beamed. "Perhaps the next step will be opening another branch? That is no small feat. So your partner Mr. Hughes perished in the earthquake then?"

"They do not know for certain, but he has been missing for so long that it is the most likely explanation. But look, Father, I did not forget your birthday this year, and your gift is on that table over there," Mitchell added, redirecting Elazar's attention.

"Birthday gift? When's the last time you . . ." But then Elazar's speech was checked as he saw the formidable hardbound books set before him. "This is . . . the wonderful Mr. Singer's work, the brand-new *Encyclopedia*? All volumes? I did not know it was available already!"

"It arrived by parcel from New York City, where it was published."

"Oh my son! A better gift was never given," he said, clasping his arm around Mitchell's shoulder. "I needn't leave my study now when writing! What other references would I need?" Elazar then put both of his hands on Mitchell's shoulders, looking at him squarely. The gesture was reassuring, and for a moment, Mitchell thought he was about to receive a sort of blessing. "Your mother tells me you are nervous about this Seder; you must never be nervous on my account. I may not always express it, but you and Isaac are forever my pride. You have done very well for yourself, and everything is in God's hands. We must always be ready for His call, wherever it will take us."

Mitchell embraced his father, realizing that Elazar could not know how true his words were in the moment. For Mitchell had heard a burdensome and dark call, and it was about to take him somewhere his father would not dream. Regardless of how the rest of the evening would go, the momentary expression of his father's love would have to sustain him. They settled in at the table, and Mitchell's father sat at the head, wearing his *kittel*, and began with his recital of the *Kiddush* blessing and drinking of the first cup of wine. The meal commenced, and Mitchell breathed relief, knowing that his father would allow nothing to disturb or addle him during its official components. Every phase of the meal, from the washing of hands, the blessings, food, wine, recitations, all the way until the declaration of the

Nirtzah, was recalled by Mitchell, who had not forgotten the numerous times he had sat next to his brother Isaac while their father proceeded or asked them questions about the Exodus or a section of the Torah. The ritual of the Seder ended with the toast "Next year in Jerusalem!"

Mitchell found that the whole affair went by in a blink. A knock at the door signaled Yumei's arrival for the later refreshments. Mitchell thought it difficult for anyone to turn away such a guest in that moment as he led her in to exchange handshakes. Yumei displayed a delicate grace and warmth, wearing a black dress and her hair up to reveal the lovely contours of her intelligent face. A waft of subtle fragrance filled the air as Mitchell offered her a seat. He and his parents all had drank three glasses of wine by that point, which would hopefully moderate the rabbi's examination. Elazar poured more wine for all of them.

"So, Miss Han, what precisely is your relationship to my son, and what is this trip that you two are going on?" he asked directly, but with a deliberately casual air as he reclined in his chair.

"I am a consulting scholar for St. Ignatius, and your son and I are looking to bring back some rare sutras from the Chinese mainland," she replied pleasantly. "You've noticed that he has the beginnings of some finer pieces from the Orient, but we have recently made new findings that demand further investigation."

Elazar raised his eyebrows at that, but eventually begrudged a nod, affirming a kind of respect at the claim.

He then made a joke about the oriental decorations down in the storefront, and the situation defused. Yumei had bent the truth expertly; Nelson Hastings, and perhaps numerous historians, owed wide-ranging insights to Yumei that would never be properly acknowledged, but of course she held no such status officially.

"So your acquaintance is professional?" Miriam asked, and Yumei nodded. "I hear that more and more women are earning degrees and being recognized in medicine . . . even broad academia these days. Do you think that someday we may achieve a parity in university departments?"

"Perhaps more than parity," Yumei suggested warmly, gently swirling her drink as the two shared a smile.

"Sutras," Elazar spoke dismissively. "But I suppose for academic interests, it is meet to have a comprehensive understanding of the Eastern faith traditions. But travelling in the midst of the Passover holiday is inadvisable, even when the trip is more-or-less sensible."

"The ships to China unfortunately do not operate in accordance with our faith, Father," Mitchell said firmly.

"Then wait for the next one! Why is it so critical to depart now?" Elazar asked, becoming agitated. "Who will look after your business? You're the sole owner now after all!"

"The availability of the texts is a time-sensitive manner," Mitchell replied, attempting to prop up the words with importance. "Certain knowledge could be lost forever."

"Well, I see where your priorities are and how much value you place on the faith—and my counsel, as always,"

Elazar sighed, pouring more wine for himself. "Are such trips dangerous?" he asked. "I don't think I could ever be persuaded to make such a journey. When are you slated to return?"

"You did once," Mitchell reminded him.

"That was to come to America! To remove ourselves from danger, for *family*," he emphasized.

"Ours should be no more dangerous than the Atlantic crossing," Yumei interjected diplomatically. "And as far as your son's Chinese is concerned, I will make sure it is conversant by the time of our arrival. As for our return date . . ." She looked over to Mitchell, hesitating. "It will depend on how quickly we find the artifacts."

"Surely by autumn," Mitchell said with much more confidence than he felt.

"You have worked closely together in the past?" Miriam asked.

"Yes, I have learned to tolerate him," Yumei responded through a small laugh, her cheeks now touched with more color. She and Mitchell shared a smile that added a new freshness to the room.

At this, the atmosphere threatened to regress into a completely pleasant and cordial affair. Elazar took a drink, his eyes resting on Yumei's hand that cupped her own glass. "You are unwed, Miss Han," he remarked abruptly.

"That is true," she replied.

Elazar took a long minute to assess things, ushering a terrible silence that suddenly filled the room. It looked as if he was preparing to excuse himself, but instead he sat up straighter in his chair. "God above," Elazar rasped, turning to Mitchell. "You are going to leave everything behind and take to the sea with a Chinese whore . . ."

"Damn your ignorance, Father!" Mitchell protested, bolting out of his seat, while Miriam looked mortified but resigned to the outburst.

"It seems that the Page Act arrived a shred too late!" Elazar added, also rising, which brought his son to stare him down just inches apart. "I am no fool, Mitchell." Both of his hands were raised up, indicating he would speak his piece before any response would be accepted. "Nor was my remark fair to Miss Han here. She is certainly too well spoken to . . . well, the simple matter is I cannot go on pretending I abide this whole situation." The rabbi's tone had become exhausted. He looked to Miriam, then to his pocket watch. "I will pray that you have a safe journey, but now I must also travel during the Passover. Your mother and I may yet find a train to Los Angeles this evening, but if not, we shall find somewhere to rest overnight. Thank you for the books."

Miriam made some conciliatory remarks to Mitchell and Yumei when Elazar left to ready the luggage. An impulse sprung up in Mitchell to show Elazar the tomb guardians, perhaps even track down Louis Malcom and present the grimoire as well to add sinew to the dark world he concealed from his parents, but the urge quickly dissipated. Introducing his mother and father to the true ugliness of his business was not worth the small chance of mending the breach that had formed, he decided. Within half an hour, they were ready to leave, and Yumei waited upstairs while Mitchell bid goodbye to his parents. A stoic Elazar offered an embrace and a final word of blessing, although Miriam lingered longer. "You must understand, your father has spent a long time fretting about you and Isaac," she explained. "I do not defend his outburst, but he has been keeping a lot in, and things never quite seem to work out in the manner that he prays for."

"Something all of us can learn from," Mitchell replied.

"I believe that when you return, he will be begging for a chance to catch up again," Miriam whispered as she embraced her son and kissed his cheek. "Oh how I would love to see your name in the newspapers with some historic find!" Her small confession of excitement brought a smile to Mitchell. "But I have to know, I'm rather embarrassed but . . . I cannot recall, what was the Page Act?"

"It predated the Chinese Exclusion Act," Mitchell explained dryly. "It was made specifically to prevent immoral Chinese women and harlots from immigrating."

Miriam's expression turned hollow with unmasked shock. Elazar beckoned for her, and she gave Mitchell a final glance as he watched them disappear down the avenue. He returned upstairs to his apartment where Yumei waited for him, sitting on his bed. He sat down next to her, and for a while neither spoke. "I believe it was Jesus who said that a prophet is not welcomed in his own town," Yumei broke the silence, her head resting on Mitchell's chest. "I can see the truth of that now, even if I'm stretching the application."

Mitchell knew that Yumei was not evangelizing, but

sharing one of her many pockets of knowledge. *She doesn't turn her nose up at any insight*, he thought with a smile. "How woefully inappropriate for a Jewish man," he remarked, and the two laughed. "But you already called me immortal a couple of weeks ago. This mantle is growing heavy if I must become a prophet now as well."

"We both must be many things to defy the Anshi Cult and the followers of Abhoth and still live, or remain sane."

"I can be whatever you need of me as long as you stay right where you are," Mitchell whispered, and Yumei did not return to her Chinatown flat that evening.

Monday morning afforded Mitchell a final chance to check his luggage and tally his store inventory. J.R. Longstreet agreed to check up on the store on a weekly basis and forwarded the updated legal information of Mitchell's estate and B&H Antiques to the INA offices. Over lunch, Mitchell at last brought Yumei up to speed on the situation with Louis Malcom and his acquisition of the *Book of Abhoth*, as he referred to it. He avoided galling her with excess affection in light of the previous evening, yet Yumei's disposition had certainly brightened, and he could not help but smile constantly when looking at her.

"Need I be worried about this Louis Malcom?" she asked Mitchell. "You say he's one of the worst men in the city, but he wants my friendship? I don't think I understand . . ."

"I believe that, despite his posturing, the man is terribly uncertain about an upcoming business negotiation. He wants you as an advisor and translator, nothing more. He seeks the insight of someone who has mastery over both languages, the culture, and who has been to China before. Preferably Hong Kong . . ."

"I don't suppose you informed him that my Cantonese is poor or that we do not intend to go all the way to Hong Kong?" she asked with a growing smile.

"Of course not! The plan is to leave him high and dry while we take the book! I know it was that bastard who helped Yong find me so quickly the night they broke in. Louis has never truly needed my help for anything, but now that he believes he does, I finally have some leverage on the bastard. Of course, we'll need to persuade him to part with the book first, so please be cordial, at least from the onset."

"Then I shall enjoy myself. Has he any idea of the importance . . . the potency of the book that he has acquired?"

"If he did, then he's as mad as Zhang Yong for seeking it out, and madder for holding onto it."

"You didn't attempt to dissuade him with such an argument?"

"No, and it has nothing to do with my dislike of the man," Mitchell insisted. "I have no desire to see him consumed by the book's foul energies. But for one, I doubt he'd believe me, and second, it might somehow convince him that he can wrangle more for it. I feel that it is for the best that we simply say nothing to him of its contents for the time being."

The day of the journey dawned, Tuesday, March 19th. It was required that all passengers be aboard the *Asia* by 8:10 in the morning, and in the predawn hours, Mitchell confirmed his belongings. He packed five complete outfits, two jackets, the tomb guardians, one hundred and twenty dollars in cash, a roll of his antique silver rounds, and a medley of personal items, including his new Russian doll. "It looks . . . cheap," Yumei commented amusedly after a yawn as Mitchell loaded the item and closed his suitcase.

"You never know, it may come in handy for a bartering—a bargaining chip, that's the expression. It's also outstanding for smuggling contraband," Mitchell added. He had discovered that if the miniatures were removed from inside the largest matryoshka doll, there was substantial space for hiding contraband for anyone unfamiliar with the design of the figurine. He had therefore removed all but the second largest doll, which he considered using as a separate hidden container entirely. He had composed a small note addressed to Roger Merrick and placed it inside the secondary matryoshka doll inside of the largest one should any of his effects be recovered in case of disaster. Deciding it prudent, Mitchell included the derringer pistol and some of his silver coins in the luggage, concealing the small firearm on a strap beneath his arm sleeve. The statues he placed in their own suitcase, which required a four-number combination on a dial lock to open. Ironically, Mitchell anticipated that the statues would pose no trouble with Chinese customs; most ports in Shanghai were run by European dock authorities, and the statues were unlikely to be scrutinized as cultural theft or contraband—especially since they were entering, not departing, China.

Mitchell and Yumei settled into their first-class cabin,

Room #5, which had a full-sized bed, the largest either of them had seen aboard a ship before, two small wardrobes, a writing desk, a standing mirror with a gilded frame, and plush carpeting that only smelled faintly of dampness. There was no *en suite* lavatory, although a steward assured them that private, heated baths could be arranged and that they would only be sharing theirs with a handful of other cabins. "It's much more comfortable than my crammed space when I last crossed the Pacific," Yumei remarked, tracing the frame of the mirror with her hand. "This is a palace in comparison."

"It is no *Lusitania*," Mitchell quipped, remembering the lavish specifications he had read about the new British ocean liner. "And she's showing her age a bit, but we could have done worse."

"I'll be more concerned with what we can manage for the return journey," Yumei replied. "Dear, you haven't convinced me you'd do too well in a fishing trawler."

Mitchell acknowledged the truth in that statement, figuring that Yumei made a far sturdier seafarer. But as the ship began moving, he found that his stomach was not troubled by the large vessel's movement, and the couple explored the sections of the ship's interior that were open to the passengers. Between the division for first- and second-class cabins, there was a dining hall as well as a bar lounge and music room with a piano. The ship seemed nearly full as far as passengers were concerned, but Mitchell could only speculate what other cargo lay aboard. Yumei only had a few scraps at dinner, as she was exhausted, burnt out from allowing herself almost no sleep in her research in the preceding week. As she returned to their cabin from the dining hall, Mitchell decided to linger in the lounge that evening, sitting at the bar while the piano man did his best to play Joplin's blitzing "Maple Leaf Rag" as requested by a man who ostentatiously shoved a dollar into the player's jar. When the ill-performed song mercifully ended, the player, a balding fellow with a large nose named Micky, resumed with a more relaxing and manageable assortment of pieces.

Perhaps most of the passengers were just finding their sea legs that night; Mitchell counted only a dozen patrons lingering at the lounge, who kept their own company for the most part. There was a friendly Irishman sitting next to Mitchell at the bar named Shane McSweeney who offered some conversation. Shane introduced himself as one of the economy passengers who had been drifting westward from Ireland for half a decade, working for various fishing operations. He had just finished his run of drinking at every tavern along San Francisco's "Barbary Coast," and the brusque Irishman also had done stretches in New England and Seattle and now was hoping to find employment by one of the European outfits in Shanghai or Hong Kong. "I wouldn't guess life as a fisherman would involve moving around so much," Mitchell offered as politely as possible.

"I'm a bit of a strange case, but in truth, I enjoy that sort of wandering," Shane responded as he drank from his dark brew. His hands suffered from the condition of slight webbing between the fingers, but Mitchell reminded himself not to stare. "It's not that I'm bad luck. Quite the opposite, they turn plenty o' fish where I cast my nets. So maybe I just want to be a blessing to as many I can?" Shane posed the quip with a wide smile, although a certain twitch the man seemed to suffer from hamstrung the effect. "They never factor that into my wages, though."

As they continued talking, they learned that it would be a first journey to China for both. They also commanded about the same range of stuttering Chinese, and as drinks flowed, they laughed as their exchanges grew sloppier and more rambling. "I'm quite the opposite. I've been in San Francisco most of my life," Mitchell stammered. "I don't think that I could do it, Shane . . . the few sailors I've met just boast all the time! Doesn't matter how old or drunk they are, they all claim legendary conquests. Women in every port of call . . . although some of them slur the stories so badly, I hear names and words I've never heard before! Were they fish or women that they bedded? Maybe they were too drunk to remember the difference?"

Shane laughed at that. "Oh Lord, I don't know how many bastards I must have by now," he similarly boasted, but Mitchell didn't believe him for a moment. "It's a perk I guess you could say. Although I still don't have a proper idea of why *you're* making the trip?"

Mitchell caught himself before blurting out the secret purpose of his journey and instead reached again for his drink. Shane seemed to notice Mitchell's strife and frowned. "Not to offend you," Mitchell stammered, then stifled a belch. "It's just a sightseeing tour. My lady and I both have some interest in some of the historic sites. But what do you suppose we are hauling below deck, Shane?" he asked, finding some other tangent to keep the conversation. "Apart from mail, of course."

"I don't have the faintest," Shane replied before polishing off the remnant of his glass. "I can tell you what the old *Doric* would be bringing if we were going the other way though! Opium! They'd weigh the poor girl down to the ocean floor with that balm. They'd pile it to the ceiling! The stacks of money you'd get in return for a haul like that . . . it'd only end up a head shorter than the product!"

"I've avoided keeping my nose in the stuff," Mitchell replied cautiously. "Although my brother was given some for treatment when he broke his leg . . . when was that, eleven years ago?"

"They favor morphine now," Shane acknowledged as he distractedly looked across the room. "But as far as what we're hauling now . . . if I were to wager on it, I'd say maybe leather? The Chinese enjoy California gold too, there's no questioning it."

"Tomorrow, Mitchell, dinner at seven o'clock," Louis Malcom's voice said, and Mitchell then realized that Shane had been distracted by the approaching insurance man. He wheeled about in his stool to regard Louis, who looked pale in his evening jacket, and Mitchell could discern a layer of sweat on his brow. "We shall discuss the terms of Miss Han's assistance and my conditions for handing over the book. She must be present too, of course," he managed before placing a tissue to his mouth. Without another word, he turned his back and exited for the first-class cabins.

"Heading for the lavatory, no mistaking that," Shane said with clear amusement. "There a lot of people that you know aboard the *Asia?*"

"Just that odious fellow, my travelling companion, and now you, Shane."

"Oh, Miss Han?" he quoted with Louis's inflection. "I would be much gladder to meet her than that other fellow!"

"With your reputation, perhaps that's unwise."

"But mate, that's only if you believe all that I'm tellin' you!" he replied innocently. "You *can* believe I'm a right gentleman to my mates' gals!"

Mitchell saw a standing clock display the time as past midnight and rose from his stool. "In that case, just don't be too much of a gentleman." He padded the man's shoulder as he stumbled back to his cabin to retire for the night. Yumei was sound asleep inside, just a few feet away from their cargo of the tomb guardians. It was then that Mitchell realized just how long this oceanic journey would feel. He had no reason to suspect any difficulties, with the exception of Louis Malcom. Yet the near silence of the *Asia*, the perfect innocuousness of the whispering waves, caused him to distrust any notions of security. He prayed for the first time in years as he tried to sleep that night. Yet the dreamlands held their own hazards, and once again, Mitchell returned to visions of the teal-veiled city and the suffocating tomb.

9

The next night, Mitchell and Yumei sat down at Louis Malcom's table in the dining cabin across from him and one of his "assistants," who appeared to be nothing more than a bodyguard and enforcer wearing an untidy tan shirt that surely did not pass dining room protocol. Yet any polite requests for the man to change his wardrobe or simply leave were curiously never initiated by the serving staff. In fact, the man was so muscled that he looked miserably scrunched in the chair beside his superior as he took care not to crowd Louis Malcom, who in turn reclined with a sprawling relish. Despite this, Louis did not look comfortable and seemed unable to shake a sickly hue. "Mitchell, Miss Han, so good of you to join us," he said courteously, summoning the waiter to receive their wine order. "I'm sure your charming escort has horribly misrepresented me up till now, Miss Han, but I hope you'll give me the opportunity for a better impression."

"It is an opportunity I would never forfeit, and even if he had misled me, those words would be dispelled on meeting you in the flesh," she replied, her eyes glowing as she regarded Louis. Mitchell immediately recognized her signature persuasion, but managed to keep a stoic face from his side of the table. "Whatever you need, Louis," she emphasized his name, "I will be happy to assist."

"Slow down," he rebuffed, tossing a quick glare over to Mitchell before regarding her again. "You haven't heard my terms yet, but they are simple and generous, I would argue. Upon our arrival in Hong Kong, you will serve as my second at a meeting with a group of investors and interpret and speak when I ask. I can already see that it's true of your reputation—you have a formidable aura about you, Miss Han. Regardless of the outcome for my company, I will provide you the book the moment after the meeting has finished. If the meeting is successful, I will also cover your expenses back to San Francisco. If Mitchell is still hanging about, he will have to scrounge up his own fare."

Yumei hesitated. Clearly the two had no intention of heading all the way to Hong Kong, but an outright refusal might have made recovering the book nearly impossible. "I only have Mitchell's word that the book is, in fact, what we seek, and he only got the briefest glance at it," she redirected.

"Allow me to guess your request, and it is a reasonable one. *You* may view the book in my cabin to confirm it," Louis replied, immediately looking over to Mitchell.

Mitchell understood that Louis intended to goad a reaction out of him, perhaps out of protective jealousy or chivalry, but Mitchell displayed no flinch of emotion. Louis likely wouldn't try anything against Yumei, and if he dared, Mitchell believed the man would likely stagger out of his cabin begging for mercy. "Perfectly reasonable indeed," he said.

"Let us not delay then," Yumei offered.

"Come now, my dear! Dinner first, and we have a long way till Shanghai," Louis insisted. "I'd love to hear about how this book became so prized by such . . . interesting people."

After the remainder of a series of halting conversations interspersed with a rather wholesome dinner, Louis at last agreed for Yumei to inspect the book at the conclusion of their meal, allowing for half an hour in between. Now that it had come to Yumei visiting Louis's cabin, Mitchell found himself less sure of the proposition, his mind restless with the prospect of something happening to her. "I will be fine," she assured him. "After all I've seen, this Louis is not even remotely intimidating . . ."

"Just take this with you," Mitchell insisted before she could continue. He placed the Remington derringer in her palm. "It's loaded, of course."

Yumei regarded the small gun, then placed it in her handbag. "A thoughtful gift," she remarked. She kissed him, then left the cabin to head down the hall to meet Louis and inspect the book. They had not set any secret plan for the rendezvous; Mitchell trusted in Yumei's discretion as far as any opportunities to take the book from Louis, either now or later in the journey.

The next hour or so passed slowly while Mitchell waited. Yumei returned some ninety minutes later, noted by Mitchell on his pocket watch. "He constantly pestered me and leaned in close while I looked it over. His breath was quite foul from the seafood," she explained, taking a seat on the bed while Mitchell sat at the desk chair.

"I'm sure he remained his loquacious self," Mitchell commented with sympathy.

"Why are you looking at this page so long?" she quoted mockingly. "Oh, something must have caught your eye here! Can you explain the meaning of this diagram to me?" She continued Louis's inflection, tiredly. "But . . . I believe by the end that I avoided agitating him and indulged him just enough to be polite."

"I pray you don't catch whatever illness is hanging over him either."

"As for that, I think that is more attributed to the book itself. The binding, the pages, all of it has an odor of decay . . . rotting flesh. It was unmistakable in that tight space whereas the effect was masked at Lin's Den. I feel I would look much the same as Mr. Malcom if I were the custodian of that dark book in close quarters all day . . . its aura is too strong."

"I wonder what strength Zhang Yong had to master it, or at least to not seem so afflicted by it." Mitchell thought back to the grim Chinatown gang leader, who seemed inversely affected by the tainted magic.

"We did discover the book unattended at Yong's shrine, which suggests that even he deigned not to be in its presence all through the day," Yumei countered.

"I don't know how I'd ever rest if I had a mind as sharp as

yours," Mitchell replied, earning a smile from her. "Anything else that you noticed? Other items of contraband?"

Yumei squinted. "The room's layout was unusual—there was a service ladder in a corner of the room, leading down."

"To below deck? That's very odd indeed." As Mitchell pondered the detail, he rose out of his seat and crossed the room. He embraced her, then sat down next to her on the bed, resting his arm across her shoulders, massaging her lower neck. "You have endured a great deal," he added quietly. "But what of the book's contents? Could you discern anything?"

"It reads much like the Middle Chinese poetry of Li Bai or Du Fu, but foul and dangerous. I discovered its proper name is *Xīn ròu de yīnyuè huì*, roughly, *Concert of New Flesh*. It would take months perhaps to properly digest its inane style, but it can be crudely surmised as a book of necromancy and chants and prayers to Abhoth the Unclean."

"Of what value could that be to us?" Mitchell asked, trying to dissuade her.

"In truth, very little," she replied, surprising him. "It would take me months to be able to channel it in the same way as Zhang Yong. I did take some notes on a small section, but I am doubting that a careful readthrough would be worth the spiritual taint from wading through such madness. I once considered such mediums for a chance to communicate directly with Xuanzang, but I will accept what written traces remain of his lesser-known studies, if any."

"It would be easy enough now to simply accept the idea

of Louis retaining the book," Mitchell ventured. "I imagine he would have a miserable time selling it. But should he sell it to a dangerous party . . . perhaps we'd be better off destroying it."

Yumei agreed on that, although they did not yet agree how to go about doing it. They introduced and discussed options, and very quickly Mitchell's preferred idea was to steal the book from Louis before reaching Shanghai. "If I could manage to sneak into his cabin, I could grab the book and toss it into the ocean. Ideally, it should be on the day of arrival, as late as possible in the journey . . ."

"Discarding such a book in the ocean is not good enough," Yumei insisted. "I would see it burned instead. But I also feel we are ignoring one very straightforward path. We could be open with him, convey to him of the greater good in destroying it."

"I would not expect you to have such a rosy outlook on human decency," Mitchell replied glumly. "If I had any such faith in the man . . ."

"Perhaps I will speak with him once more before we disembark," Yumei interjected, and the matter was laid to rest to allow more time for thought.

*　　*　　*　　*

"I will make no attempt to persuade him," Yumei said the next morning. "The risk is too great if I cannot convince him, and we can't afford him being more paranoid than he is already." She paused, forming a thin smile. "Since it was your idea to steal it, I will trust you to carry it out. I am many things, but an ill-practiced thief."

Mitchell was also inexperienced in skullduggery but, to his relief, believed he knew of someone who may be of assistance aboard the ship. He made his way over to the ship's lounge the evening of the seventh day of their oceanic journey. Mitchell waited, looking out the port window to the south, knowing the islands of Hawaii were somewhere out there beyond the horizon. Eventually, Shane entered the room and took a seat at the bar, and Mitchell joined him, ordering a gin and tonic and toasting Shane's health amidst the usual greetings. "Would you like to make some money?" Mitchell eventually asked Shane, nonchalantly.

"Always," he swiftly replied, shifting his glance from his mug to Mitchell.

"I seek the master key for the passenger cabins," Mitchell replied just as bluntly. "I need to extract an item from a certain room number, unless you can break in through other means."

Shane shook his head while finishing his gulp, but it was not from the criminal bluntness of Mitchell's proposition. "Locks on these liners are usually of higher quality. They are of English make, after all. It'd be easier to obtain a key, I'm sure."

"So what do you suppose . . . the captain's cabin, or perhaps they keep extras in the bridge?" Mitchell asked leadingly.

"Hah! Suddenly I see why you're consulting me!" Shane posited. "No need to do two break-ins when some simple pickpocketing will suffice." He leaned forward and whispered, "Most of the lower officers I'd figure would be so embarrassed that they may not even report the loss of their key to the captain. And even if they do, I can always return it—by that I mean drop it under a stool or near enough to where I grabbed it in the first place. No harm done at the end of the day. Could even *borrow* the key from the cabin's occupant instead, if you'd care to point them out to me, though I may be able to guess the target."

"That would be perfect!" Mitchell exclaimed, drawing a glance from the bartender. Much more quietly, he added, "I was hoping you could take care of it all solo. My plan was to distract Mr. Malcom in conversation in the lounge." He included his target's name, abandoning any remaining discretion. "Otherwise he's sure to suspect me for the deed."

Shane frowned at that. "I can get you the key, but I'd rather not go further, not unless the payment is more generous than what I'm imagining. I've come to learn that you're at the mercy of the captain, or whatever he tells the authorities at the dockside, when breaking the law on the high seas, and I imagine you'd be better suited for backing your way out of that. You've got that high society feel about you." Mitchell and Shane discussed the prospect further, and upon the man's payment expectations, Mitchell would have to finish the job once the key had been acquired. "What are you after anyway?" Shane asked casually. "Must be something very special for an upstanding gentleman like yourself to resort to such means. Wasn't there something about a book?"

"I'll keep that private for now, Shane, if you don't mind. Now perhaps if *you* were the one retrieving the item, then of course I'd be obliged to tell you . . ."

"I see your game," he laughed. "Well, maybe I'll change my mind, but I wouldn't gamble on me growing so curious. Stop looking so glum though. I'll share this little item with you as a courtesy." He glided a document of card stock towards Mitchell, who stopped it as it slid across the table.

"The passenger manifest," Mitchell remarked with amazement, successfully keeping the volume of his voice in check. "A fine testament to your abilities," he added, fully confident Shane would be able to do the job when the time came. He scanned the passenger list, hopelessly curious while not concerning himself with what Shane wanted with the document. Indeed, it occurred to Mitchell that the Irishman perhaps needed no reason, but occasionally pilfered such things to stay in good practice. He prepared to return the paper back to Shane, but then stopped, noticing a familiar acquaintance. "This can't be correct . . ." Mitchell stammered, his eyes locked on the name. He should have revealed nothing but nearly counted the Irishman as a full co-conspirator at this point. "Roland Hughes has been missing since the earthquake, for nearly a full year!"

"I'm afraid I don't follow. How could it be a mistake?" Shane asked. "Look, there's me, you and Yumei, that Louis Malcom fellow, it all looks correct. Who is this Roland to you anyway? Maybe it's just another gentleman with the same name?"

"He's my business partner. I've . . . never met him. Room 13. Room 13," Mitchell repeated vacantly, confirming what his eyes were seeing.

Shane and Mitchell negotiated the payment for the theft of Louis's room key and confirmed the job for the last anticipated day of the *Asia's* journey. After handing over an advance payment in cash, the two agreed to see as little as possible of each other in the interim days before the theft. Since they had confirmed all the necessary details of the plan, further meetings would only add suspicion. Mitchell returned to his cabin, explaining the strange discovery to Yumei of the passenger manifest. She suggested confronting the cabin's occupant at once. Mitchell was less certain, but Yumei pressed him. "I had to sit close to that insurance peddler as he brushed up against me for the better part of two hours while I examined the book. Yet I did the job all the same. Now we have the opportunity to meet someone considerably more interesting, save for your trepidation."

"Very well, but let's continue our policy of you bringing the derringer."

"You'd be hard-pressed to separate me from it. One of the most practical gifts I've received," she replied pleasantly.

The two found that Room #13 was not far from their own cabin, on the same side of the hallway, in fact. Mitchell hesitated, then gave a tremulous knock. There was a pause, but definite movement was audible from inside the room. The door opened a crack, still secured by the chain, as a keen, blue eye regarded them for a moment. The door shut again and grating and unlocking noises followed. "Come in, Mitchell," a man's voice called through the door. "It's unlocked now."

Mitchell stepped into the cabin and nodded for Yumei to remain waiting just outside. The presumed Roland Hughes was already sitting back at the room's desk, holding up a book, as if he had been interrupted in the midst of a reading session. *Does he mean to convey that this meeting is of little consequence as an interruption? Or is there a theatric streak in him?* Mitchell wondered, then suddenly recognized him, although it took him a moment to place his face. *The auction house,* he realized. The man sitting before him had been the leading bidder wearing the top hat—who had hastily fled upon spotting Zhang Yong as his competing bidder. "The man who couldn't stop fidgeting," Mitchell remarked, keeping his eyes locked on the young man who remained calmly seated.

J.R. Longstreet's description of Roland Hughes came to mind, and the resident of Room #13 matched them. He was thin, and his cheeks were prominently high-boned. The top hat had obscured most of his features at Butterfield & Butterfield, but Mitchell could see that the man's overall facial structure gave him a certain grimness and resting frown. Mitchell was not the best judge for spotting expensive wear, but his evening jacket had a luxurious look to it, and there was a certain delicacy in his posture that suggested wealth. "You're Roland Hughes," Mitchell said, his delivery more certain than his assertion.

"Very good," he replied and rose up to shake Mitchell's

hand. "A firm handshake for a firm business partner," he said solemnly. Roland leaned to the side, gesturing to the door. "Your friend Miss Han should enter as well. I'd prefer to not draw attention in the hall." Yumei let herself in, and Roland gave a respectful nod to her. "I apologize for the long deception, but my 'death' became necessary after I made myself a target of some very unpleasant connections, and the earthquake was perfectly suited for this ruse. I suspect the trick shall only work once, if it has at all. Miss Han, it is an honor," he added, cupping her wrist and slightly bowing. Roland had an detached coolness and smug confidence to his bearing, giving the completely opposite impression of the nervous bidder at Butterfield's.

"You were already such a recluse," Mitchell remarked, "so I'm not sure which of the two Rolands I've witnessed so far is more genuine. It's true that I managed to track you down aboard the *Asia*," he said, carefully avoiding references to his Irish conspirator, "but I'm having trouble squaring the reason for your appearance at the auction. Oh, I should also mention, I found your pistol at your old address, along with the note—"

"You may keep it," Roland dismissed the object with startling disinterest. "As for my appearance at the auction . . . I am not a trained actor. But I achieved what I wanted out of that embarrassing farce at Butterfield's. That is, that Zhang Yong is dead, you are *en route* to China with all three tomb guardians, and the legendary Old Han is your guide, all this with less than two months elapsing since the auction.

I realize this has caused both pain and stress, but surely you agree—a great success, all things considered."

Astonished, Mitchell wondered if such events could possibly be components of an engineered plan. Feelings of anger stirred within. Roland's words presented him as the engineer of Mitchell's recent miseries, his deaths! Yumei seemed to sense the strife within him, and her hand on his shoulder was a greater comfort than any internal wrestling Mitchell could rationalize. He sighed. There was nothing he could do at present about the past. For his own sanity, he had been constantly repeating to himself that he had met his destiny, and if the aloof Roland Hughes was the vehicle of that, he would try not to resent his part in it. Mitchell needed to remain analytical. *So he's the sort who prefers others doing the work for him?* Very quickly, Roland's story seemed to click, with a few difficulties. "The first statue, the one at Butterfield's—"

"Donated by me, through proxy," Roland quipped. "I acquired the statue through some trouble and ultimately decided that the Butterfield's auction would be the best stage for it. Suspecting the two sibling statues were already somewhere in the Bay Area, I decided to risk one to gain the others. I did not know where the other two were, nor who exactly would become my agent, but I hedged for it to be you, Mitchell. I'm *glad* it was you."

"How would you have knowledge of the other statues? What use do you have for them? What are you . . . playing at with such things?" Mitchell clumsily asked.

Roland paced his cabin, hovering mere inches away from a wall that was shared with an adjacent cabin. Mitchell decided he must have been listening. When Roland was apparently satisfied, he sighed heavily. "For the last nine years, I have been a member of a certain cult, one that you can't leave willingly, not to mention it being a bit of a family tradition . . . but now I am trying to make amends for my household's role in the proliferation of his worship. Of Great Cthulhu," he concluded with exertion.

It was the first time that Mitchell had heard the name, and he was reminded of the lengths Yumei had gone to in avoiding uttering the awful name as she frowned in acknowledgement. The pronunciation was replete with a wet saturation as Roland brought his tongue to his teeth to give the word a subaqueous fullness that rendered the word unpleasant. He tried to imagine the terrible god, wondering of its age, of its rank alongside the gods and idols of Canaan and elsewhere described in the Scriptures. The very exercise left him strangely faint, and he contented himself with the depiction of the tomb guardians.

"The Hughes' fortune in part derives from such a history, such partnership, but the wealth was always bought at too high a price," Roland continued. "I was tired of seeing what a heavy toll it took on those I loved. Since you eliminated Zhang Yong so deftly, I could remain in the shadows for precious additional months. As for the statues, I do not doubt they have been burdensome, but I am convinced they are instrumental in maintaining . . . *his* slumber. Do not misunderstand me, nothing made of mortal man, regardless of skill or arcana, could contain or affect beings such as him. Rather, were they to be mistreated, they could produce a great stimulation, great enough perhaps to bring waking ruin. As such, we must make for Luoyang in the Henan Province of China as quickly as possible."

"An Lushan's tomb," Mitchell responded knowingly.

"Exactly!" Roland smiled. "I see that you and Miss Yumei have not been idle."

"So because you were a good business partner and demonstrated that we fit into your grand plan, Yumei and I are just supposed to trust you? When were you planning to reveal yourself to us? Or was it your intention to surveil our progress from the shadows all this time?"

"So many questions!" Roland replied, for the first time with agitation. "Are you supposed to trust me—of course you are! Do you think if I had any inclination to harm you, we would be having this conversation? With everything I have orchestrated?! You would have been destroyed!"

Yumei laughed at the display, as if daring the man to try on the spot. Her lukewarm reaction to the proud declarations seemed to turn off Roland from granting the answers to Mitchell's questions. "That's just the kind of thing I'm talking about," Mitchell answered, folding his arms. "I do not doubt you've been . . . *helpful*, but we still know almost nothing of your aims."

"I am sorry," Roland apologized, stroking back his hair across his forehead. "It has been a long process, putting things in place. They are always searching for me." He crossed back to his desk and took a long drink of a clear liquid. "From what I understand, at An Lushan's tomb . . . we need only to deposit the tomb guardians alongside the others in some fashion. Lushan's tomb functions as a major shrine for the cult, and provided all of its guardians have not been pillaged, the earth will return to a state of relative stability and Cthulhu may yet sleep for millennia to come." Roland's voice had quieted, and he hung his head in anticipation. "I was still unsure of when I would reveal myself to you, but now that minor issue has been resolved. After the business with the statues is concluded, we all may go our separate ways. Return home, if we are not intercepted or otherwise waylaid."

"Have you been to the tomb before?" Yumei asked. "That is information I would actually be impressed by."

"No, in fact, this will be my first time going more than a few miles inland from the coast," Roland explained. "But I will . . . I *should* have people waiting for us in Shanghai. From there we can take much of the way by the Grand Canal. In the remaining days of our voyage, you should keep as low of a profile as possible. Hopefully no one else aboard is of the cult, but they operate across the globe and many are unknown to me. We still have a three days' travel until Shanghai, and I would advise staying in your cabins as much as possible. Especially avoid the deck at night."

"You have people in Shanghai, but no one else aboard the ship?" Yumei asked.

"Captain Neal is a friend, and I am fairly confident the crew are not to be feared. But my network has been shrinking, either by those who now shun me as paranoid or insane, or by those whom the cult has reached. But we would have no chance of success were our numbers too large either. I am concerned about your entanglements with that busybody Louis Malcom," he added, changing the subject. "Having him aboard the ship is very troublesome."

"Could he be in league with this . . . Cthulhu cult?" Mitchell asked.

"If so, he has kept that an exquisite secret. I, of course, monitored him and his business while in San Francisco. I cannot imagine that he is, but just make sure you don't have him following after us when we arrive in Shanghai. I don't believe *Concert of New Flesh* would possess any insights worth risking our mission over."

"We've made that same judgment, but mean to destroy it," Yumei explained.

"That would be best," Roland agreed. "But again, it would be troublesome to draw his attention merely because of it."

Before leaving Roland's cabin, Yumei pressed him as to exactly how much he knew of the tomb guardians. Roland procured a bottle of Scotch and refilled his glass. Rubbing his forehead, he began sharing what he knew of the statues' history from the oral traditions he was privy to within the cult. They were created by a "dark consecration" that took place in the aftermath of Lushan's assassination. An Lushan's favored son, An Qing'en, who had lost the throne to his half-brother Qinxu (the very son who murdered his father), initiated a ritual with the purpose of reviving his father Lushan. Qing'en summoned all of Lushan's closest eunuchs and servants, and a sacrifice was held of an unknown, exceedingly large number in the rites and honor of Cthulhu.

The dead emperor was not revived. Instead, it was said that the eight idols of Cthulhu which adorned the chamber of the ritual became enchanted with a timeless power, bearing the life force of those sacrificed. The chamber was a secret to all but the cult for nearly four hundred years, where they employed it for the rituals, culminating with the ascension to become higher lifeforms, Deep Ones. The Deep Ones then left the region, taking whatever path they could across the long miles to the sea, to the great timeless city of R'lyeh, the home of the slumbering Great Old One, Cthulhu. However, the adroit Emperor Gaozong of the Song dynasty discovered the place, put all of the cultists he found there to death, confiscated many, but not *all* of the tomb guardians for his own imperial treasury, and sealed the chamber in an unknown manner.

So ended the history, but Roland had obtained further insights from his own investigation. Emperor Gaozong's method was inadvertently opportune in preventing disaster. The removal of some of the tomb guardians and the sealing of the chamber ended the ritualistic power of the site. At the same time, leaving enough of the tomb guardians behind prevented any ensuing natural disasters or cataclysmic ripples from R'lyeh across the earth's ley lines. An Lushan's tomb became inaccessible and forgotten, until some calamity in the spring of last year displaced a further two statues or more.

"How this is possible, I have never determined," Roland said softly. "The location of An Lushan's tomb is secret, and it is sealed. I can only suspect it as the result of some strange magic, be it by the servants of Abhoth, some other god, or even members of the Anshi Cult themselves. It's possible the tomb guardians were transported out of the chamber with no one even setting foot there. The statues themselves may have been wrenched through thousands of miles of oceanic currents by the very will of Cthulhu."

Mitchell looked to Yumei, as he was more curious as to how she would receive the information. The cunning lady never objected, but nodded along slowly with Roland's narration. Yumei seemed to notice Mitchell's gaze and folded a hand over his. "Your business partner speculates often, but reasonably."

"Yet one thing I am certain is that they must have come from the tomb itself, as the world has been destabilized," Roland replied. "San Francisco was not the only place touched by the Pacific to suffer from a quake last year. In January, a quake struck Ecuador and Colombia, and in August, Chile was touched with death." He straightened in his chair, and a cloud must have passed in front of the moon, for the light from the port window lessened. "Yet I do believe these were the particular guardians that ended up in Zhang Yong's possession. But it is said that if all the tomb statues are removed from the tomb—"

"—Cthulhu will waken, and the earth will become no home for mankind," Yumei finished for Roland, clearly familiar with the portents of such an outcome.

"Indeed, meaning that the world may be perilously close to Cthulhu's realm and his terrible form bubbling over the sea level and ushering in a global, submerged necropolis," Roland added, now noting that his glass was empty. He did not refill it. "You have seen the city in your dreams, Mitchell? Know that I have as well."

"Roland, you should know that I've accessed the power of two of the statues," Mitchell said. "By all rights, I should be dead twice over . . . both times on account of Zhang Yong. Instead, two of the statues that were near me at the fatal hour have . . . lost their color."

"That will translate to some misfortune before all of this is over," Roland replied after a long silence, his face darkened. "I do not know if this will nullify them as wards, but we will have to press on all the same. At least we still *possess* all three, even if two are spent in some degree."

"Please help me understand something," Mitchell began. "In what way are we opposed to the cult then? Not that I want to be friends with them! What I mean is, if they desire the awakening of their master, how have these statues remained in the tomb for so long under their keeping? Could they not have accomplished that many centuries ago before the Emperor Gaozong raided their shrine?"

"Because then, as now, there exists little communication, and even less unity among the various orders save for madness," Roland replied. "The Anshi Cult, as the Chinese branch of Cthulhu worshippers is called, regards itself as the fit caretakers of this mortal plane until their lord awakens on his own time and in his own potency. They were less zealous to usher the oceanic apocalypse that the awakened Cthulhu might bring, favoring the power that the tomb guardians provided them in this mortal realm. I suspect their practices were largely secret, but now the knowledge of these idols has spread to the dark corners of the earth, and many will vie for the idol's power or attempt to empty the tomb regardless of understanding the statues' purpose." A man coughed somewhere in the cabin hallway, and Roland checked his watch. "You should leave," he instructed them. "Hopefully you have heard enough from me to understand that I am an ally, and there will be time enough to clarify our plans upon reaching the mainland."

The dark conference concluded, and Mitchell and Yumei returned to their cabin. Yumei asked Mitchell not only if he trusted the man, but if he believed that it was, in fact, Roland Hughes. "I . . . I do feel that I trust him, for now," Mitchell at last replied with some difficulty. "But I'm certainly not ready to make hard and fast judgments about his claims. He clearly knows too much that we can't afford to ignore."

"A very sensible perspective," Yumei replied approvingly. "From what I understand of that note you discovered, the little pistol I carry was intended for Roland's brother . . . Matthew, was it?

"Yes, and clearly he's made his peace with you retaining

it. It would seem his family lost their lives when Roland decided to leave the cult. I . . . *we* should probably not speak to him of it. I would think that the memory would be very painful. It is quite near, after all."

"Revenge is among the most powerful motivators," Yumei offered.

Mitchell nodded. "Let's hope we don't get caught in the crossfire, but I can imagine no better way for Roland to make peace with his past than to stave off this apocalypse."

The party would enjoy two more days of peace, but the final day spent aboard the *Asia* before reaching Shanghai was destined for theft, secrecy, and with a little luck, an escape from a very gradually growing claustrophobia and the waxing aura of whisper and suspicion. The vastness of the ocean surrounded and enclosed the *Asia*, the closed-off universe that Mitchell inhabited with the tomb guardians. *Who else aboard this vessel shares some link of fate to the cult or the statues?* Mitchell thought while sleep remained distant. His consciousness must return to the earthen chamber, or to the place he now knew as R'lyeh. The consolation that Roland shared his dreams did not dilute the arresting terror of the dead city.

10

The final day of the *Asia's* journey dawned, as per Captain Neal's announcement that the vessel was holding course for Shanghai and benefiting from favorable conditions. Roland had left a note under Mitchell and Yumei's door suggesting that they rendezvous at the Palace Hotel upon arriving in Shanghai the next morning. Just past noon, a warning was issued for passengers to remain in their rooms starting at five o'clock due to signs of an approaching storm. The tidings provided an excellent window of opportunity for the theft of the book—it was Mitchell's hope that Louis and his attendant bodyguard would be out stretching their legs before the episode of turbulent weather. Conversely, there would be virtually no chance of entering Louis's room unnoticed after five o'clock. Mitchell informed Yumei that he would now take his chance and look for his contracted pickpocket in the parlor.

Mitchell was still dependent on Shane producing the key in time, and to his relief, the Irishman nonchalantly approached him just past two thirty. "Beg pardon, chap, you must've dropped this," he said as he padded the key against

Mitchell's chest. "There's a press of folks against the taffrail catching some fresh air. All of them so interested in watching the storm clouds coming in . . . it's a shame, you never know what you might lose when bumping into people," he added more quietly and swept his hands in dismissal. It was obvious he was quite pleased with himself.

"Capital! Just try to keep him up on deck for a few minutes if you can!" Mitchell replied as he already began moving towards the passenger cabins. The way was deserted, as it seemed that many of the crew were also either observing the conditions from the bridge or monitoring the larger presence of passengers on the deck. Mitchell examined the fob of the key to read Room #2 and paused as he reached the door. There was no one coming, and he entered inside as quickly as he could manage in one fluid motion while quickly closing and locking the door behind him.

As Yumei had indicated, Malcom's room had an odd layout. It was spacious, but there was an access ladder in a corner of the room that led further below deck, suggesting that the space had a different original purpose when the vessel was the *Doric*. The room was dim, as thin blinds had been lowered over the two ports. Avoiding distractions, Mitchell rummaged through a pile of belongings on a table near the bed while his eyes adjusted, then proceeded to the dresser drawers. His heart raced as he spotted the leather satchel that Louis had used to present the tome to Mitchell in his store. Upon loosening the strands, he could clearly hear a commotion in the outer hallway, murmured voices and loudening footsteps. Mitchell hesitated. If he attempted to leave the room now, he risked being spotted while leaving. But lingering behind rested solely on the hope that the room would not be entered, and he would be trapped if Louis returned. He stole a glance inside the satchel—the ancient book was not inside, but instead there appeared to be a set of proposals for Louis's clients in Hong Kong.

Not knowing if Louis had been somehow alerted, or if he himself had been betrayed, Mitchell could spend no time in thought and left the satchel behind. The clicking sounds of the door unlocking spurred him to grab hold of the ladder and descend. He lowered himself just out of sight from the floor level when he heard the door open. "Look, Oleg, he's already been in here! My satchel's been gone through!" Louis explained hysterically. Mitchell reached the bottom of the ladder and found an iron door. It was locked, clearly to afford some privacy to the occupant of the unusual room. He tried the room key, and to his great relief, it worked on the sturdy door. It creaked loudly, prompting more urgent babble from Louis. Before being spotted through the ladder shaft, Mitchell closed the door behind him.

He was now in a maintenance hallway dimly lit by service lights. He needed to get clear of the landing from the ladder to avoid being discovered by Louis or 'Oleg' and find another way back to the passenger area. He moved down the passageway, noting signs to the boiler and engine rooms. Much further down the hallway, he saw crew members coming through a bulkhead door in his direction. Mitchell tried the nearest door, which was locked, and then another door further down the hallway. He stepped through into the cargo hold, a comparatively cavernous area, and took cover behind a large mail crate.

Moments later, the same door that Mitchell had taken opened, and a pair of crew members stepped through. Mitchell assumed that they were performing a routine walkthrough until one man took out a pipe and the other produced a pouch from within his jacket. The men sat down with their backs against the wall just to the left of the door, preventing Mitchell from leaving in that direction. An unusual odor permeated the room, which Mitchell guessed to be opium. He crept to the opposite end of the room, aided by dozens of rows of crates, turning carefully to block the line of sight from the two men. Mitchell had momentarily entertained the thought of identifying himself as a lost passenger and asking for help, but certainly not after they had produced the illicit drug while on duty. He waited for some time, but the smoking break was proving interminable. *Hopefully my time here has thrown off any search on the part of Louis Malcom.* Mitchell decided he could not delay long and weaved between more containers and crates, carefully noting when the men were conversing and not gazing further into the room. Eventually he had worked his way to the opposite side of the cargo hold, which presented more options for an exit. Apart from the large hatch to the deck, there was another door here that was cut off from the line of sight of the two crew members, which Mitchell took to escape.

Back out in the lower passageways, Mitchell spotted a stairwell leading up. He seized the chance, but as he reached the lower steps, a door opened at the top just in front of him. A deck officer stepped through, discernible by his coat and cap. He was not the captain, but perhaps a navigation or staff officer. "How the devil did you get down here?" he asked Mitchell, alarmed. "Trespassing in the lower compartments is strictly forbidden! Your ticket, sir, show it to me," he pressed Mitchell, who had not found an appropriate response through his stammering.

"Of course, I'm Mitchell Bernheim," he said, presenting the ticket. "I was on the terrace of the deck with the other passengers when I was seized by a bout of seasickness. I was looking for a lavatory . . ."

"It will have to be reported, Pacific Mail standards," the officer responded uncaringly. "Although I do hate to inconvenience the captain with this . . ."

Mitchell understood full well that the man was asking for a bribe of some kind. He cursed under his breath; nearly all of his cash was back in his room. Any sort of trouble aboard the ship could lead to a room inspection, which would be potentially disastrous if the statues were confiscated or if Louis's room key were discovered on Mitchell, still in his pocket. "Perhaps we can work something out," Mitchell replied.

"Not unless you're an electrician," the man replied, clearly disappointed that Mitchell made no reach for any wallet.

"I have done some work with electrical circuits," Mitchell

replied, perking up. "I work in antiques, and a number of items I've restored just need a little wire replacement or adjustments."

"I'll be damned," the officer said, rubbing his chin. "Right then, come with me."

The officer, who introduced himself as second officer Taylor Leighton, led Mitchell to an electrical panel not far from the generator room. The power was shorted out to the crew quarters and kitchen, leading to significant inconvenience. The ship's engineer had failed to report it in San Francisco in time for departure, but the captain would not risk delaying the journey as such problems were rarely encountered. The secondary technician aboard had extensive knowledge of the boiler and steam engine systems but was vexed when it came to most electrical difficulties. Upon being provided with an electrician's toolkit, Mitchell was able to repair the circuit in about forty minutes, managing to avoid dangerous shocks in the process. "Just some rotted-out wires," he explained as he double-checked the connection points and removed his gloves. "I've never worked on a unit this large, but there's a first time for everything."

"Why do you think it gave out?" Officer Leighton inquired with a note of admiration.

"At first I thought they were all running quite hot, just normal strain from high-power use, but I believe it's more from the proximity to this pipe," Mitchell added, wincing as he brushed his fingers against it. "It must be running from the boiler."

"There's been a good deal of retrofitting to update the ship," Officer Leighton explained, and the two suddenly braced against the wall as the ship took a large wave. "Storm's arrived, it would seem."

"Please excuse my wandering," Mitchell said. "An honest lapse—"

"Of course, not a word!" Officer Leighton replied as he escorted Mitchell back to the passenger cabins. It was implied that the officer would be taking credit for the repair to the circuit, which was fine by Mitchell. Now that he had finally escaped from the crew compartments, his fear of a formal investigation of his cabin turned to anger and confusion over the failed theft of *Concert of New Flesh*. *Had Shane tipped off Louis?* Mitchell wondered. *Louis's timing was disastrous, and why should he have the book on his person that afternoon if not anticipating a theft? Had Shane been working with Louis all along, or was it a betrayal of opportunity?* Mitchell looked out the ports in the hallway and saw that the sky had grown dark. Either the storm had come earlier than broadcasted, or he had been down in the crew compartments longer than he had thought. Indeed, it was difficult for him to estimate how long he had spent in the dark, steel passageways.

Mitchell at last returned to his cabin, finding the door unlocked. Yumei was nowhere to be found, and the room displayed an untidiness that suggested she left abruptly, or perhaps by force. Her perfume kit was open, and the derringer was not there. Mitchell hoped that somehow she had still concealed the weapon, but dreaded that it too had been found and seized by whoever had forced their way into the cabin. Panic began to grip him. When he recovered his senses, he abruptly realized that his backpack had been taken as well as the tomb guardians secured in his extra suitcase and some blankets off the bed. The scrapes along the brass metal of the suitcase frame indicated that a knife had been plied into the gap to force open the dial lock. Finding himself tremendously short of allies aboard a ship that now seemed entirely hostile, he moved down the hallway to Roland Hughes's room. The man, as if expecting Mitchell, quickly opened the door and ushered him in before he could knock.

"Yumei's gone. I think she's been taken," Mitchell began frantically. "And the statues are gone as well! Louis Malcom's work, it has to be . . . perhaps Shane is working for him too. You said you were friends with the captain?"

"I would not entrust our hopes to Captain Neal unless we must," Roland replied uneasily, and the two suddenly braced themselves as the ship lurched from a wave. "I must try to keep a low profile, and besides, in these conditions he will be sorely pressed as the ship comes into harbor—"

"Then we can't wait! Yumei can't!" Mitchell replied. "Let's check Louis's room. I still have his key!"

The two did this, finding Room #2 vacant. Without the whereabouts of Shane's room, they had few options to consider in continuing their search. "Perhaps I was overconfident, but it seems that Louis Malcom may indeed be a part of the cult," Roland intoned bitterly. "He made his move, and I was oblivious. I had hoped that the worshippers of Cthulhu did not have the resources to monitor all ocean crossings, but perhaps their number has grown large indeed. We are now close enough to China that they will act bolder," he continued with analytic dispassion. "If they have not already cast Yumei overboard, then they are—"

"Up on deck," Mitchell finished.

Roland retrieved a case that had been concealed under his bed and opened it. Inside was a German Luger pistol as well as additional magazines for the weapon. "I had hoped to not need this aboard the ship," he said as he loaded it. "And there's no guarantee that guns will be of help here."

"Not to mention the authorities," Mitchell replied as they moved quickly through the cabin hallway to the stair accessing the deck.

"Incarceration is meaningless if the statues are lost," Roland replied darkly. As they reached the hatch to the terrace, they found a crewman. The man was likely stationed to prevent passengers from heading out in the conditions, but instead, he was slumped over to the wall. Blood trickled down from his hair, and Mitchell guessed that he had been knocked out from significant blunt force. Roland wordlessly opened the hatch to the tempest.

The lights of Shanghai were visible in the west as the storm raged, but visibility was poor on the deck of the *Asia* as the spray of the ocean raked its way across deck while the ship bobbed and turned. The waves waxed to mighty whitecaps, and streaks of lightning flashed above the towering clouds of blackness. Water was beginning to lap onto the deck's surface, making it slick and treacherous as Mitchell moved closer to a congregation of dark figures he perceived at the aft of the ship. Roland followed him, keeping a low stance to help his balance while he concealed his pistol beneath his coat.

Shane had a knife to Yumei's throat and his back to the *Asia's* taffrail. Yumei had gone limp, her eyes wide, and Mitchell saw a trickle of blood from the contact point of the knife against her neck. Louis Malcom and Oleg were standing nearby. Mitchell recognized two satchels the insurance man held, one likely contained *Concert of New Flesh* and the other was Mitchell's own leather backpack that held one of the tomb guardians. Oleg held a bundle under his left arm, which Mitchell thought must be the second and third statues, and wielded a shotgun in his right.

"Louis!" Mitchell called out over the noise of the storm. "You've crossed the line! What the hell do you think you're doing?"

"You meant to cheat me for your damned book!" he retorted, raising the case with the tome inside. "Mr. McSweeney also told me of your little plan to dispose of me in Shanghai!"

"*Dispose* of you? What—by God, he's got a knife to her throat, Louis!" Mitchell shouted angrily. "It's obvious that he's playing both of us!" Mitchell turned to Shane. "If you hurt her, I'll send your body to the ocean floor!"

"That's square with me. I've got plenty o' friends down there after all!" the Irishman replied through a frenzied smile. "Friend, I don't need to kill anyone right this moment—

much as I'd like to, I just need to make a deposit." He gestured to the statues held by Louis and Oleg. Shane leaned over to look over the side of the ship, and Mitchell strained to see what he was searching for. It was then that Mitchell saw the shapes moving just under the surface of the water. "Looks like we're just about ready," Shane added.

The figures were man-shaped, or slightly larger, and coursed through the waves with a grotesque effortlessness. Fortunately, Mitchell's vision was too dimmed by the mist and darkness to discern them with detail, but as he began to turn away from them, another bolt brought sudden light. That fleeting glance, touched with the sky's white light, was forever seared into memory. The upper bodies of the creatures displayed gray sheens of slime thicker than water, and their faces were just barely humanlike, to implant the chilling idea of relation to their abominable species. Everything else in their contours and appearance were of an overgrown fish, blue veins and layered corruption in the folds of flesh. Shane called out, entreating them with some aqueous babble through his teeth as Mitchell discerned the name *Cthulhu* amidst the sounds. "Toss the statues overboard!" he commanded Louis and Oleg, returning to English.

"If you make any such movement, I will kill you both myself!" Roland shouted, his pistol drawn and leveled at Oleg.

Oleg bristled at that and aimed his shotgun back at Roland while he took a step closer to the railing. Louis hesitated, perhaps realizing that coming to the *Asia's* deck with McSweeney was a mistake. To Mitchell, it seemed that Roland was moments away from taking his chances with his pistol; the man had just made it clear that he would not risk losing the statues. There was no scenario Mitchell could conceive where Yumei emerged from this standoff alive, and his thoughts raced regarding the final statue that had not yet stored a soul. But he still retained one advantage. "How pleased will your monstrous friends be if you throw them my Russian doll as a gift?" Mitchell shouted over the storm. "You haven't got all three guardians; I've got the final one hidden away!"

Louis's face turned to ash for a small moment before he stiffened. "Of course I checked your bag, you idiot!"

Shane was not nearly so certain, and it appeared that even the fearsome Irishman would not lightly risk angering the horrors in the water by throwing random debris at them. Oleg removed one of the cabin bedsheets to reveal the two tomb guardians that he had been carrying. Again, Louis gave a ghost of a nervous look. Shane shifted, positioning Yumei directly in the line of Roland's shot, and glanced over to Louis. "Take it out first," he said to Louis. "Show me!"

There were two clasps that Louis needed to undo in order to open the backpack. He fumbled as he loosened them, constantly glancing over to Shane, who seemed to unsettle him far more than even Roland with his pistol steadily leveled. At last, Louis groped inside and produced a statuette, lifting it up carefully at its base. To his horror, instead of the tri-color tomb guardian, he held aloft the garish Russian doll, and Shane shrieked out in frenzied anguish, which caused a terrified Yumei to scream as the knife dangerously pricked at her. "No, that's impossible!" Louis yelped. "I know he kept it in this bag!"

"Mitchell, we'll make an exchange!" Shane proposed, speaking in his friendlier tone as he had so often on the voyage. "I have no quarrel with you. I'll just be needing that last statue! Your miss can go once I have it! A damned good trade on your end!"

"Let her go first! She'll be dead by the time your nervous hand stops twitching across her neck!" Mitchell shouted back.

"She's not leaving my arms until all three statues are overboard!"

It had not occurred to Mitchell in the drawn-out seconds of that stalemate how relatively calm conditions had been on deck with the storm continuing to rage all around. The false peace ended as the *Asia* was broadsided by a tremendous wave that sent a great spray of water across its prow as the entire vessel rolled to its port side. Mitchell nearly kept his feet, but a rush of seawater surged and lapped across the deck, sending him sliding into the opposite rail. His side ached with pain, but he scrambled up to his feet, avoided slipping again, and rushed forward as the ship regained a level bearing. Mitchell looked up to see that the lights of Shanghai had indeed grown bright through the gloom. Louis Malcom was scrambling back to his feet, trying to get behind his bodyguard. The case with the book was no longer in sight, but Mitchell spotted the Russian doll rolling about on the deck on its side. Yumei was free of Shane's restraint, although her hand was bleeding, presumably when she shielded her throat against the knife as the ship had suddenly been buffeted. Her other hand shot up to her ornate silver hair ornament, and a moment later, she had removed it. Her long silken hair cascaded down, and Mitchell perceived the derringer in her hand as well, having been concealed as part of her hair ornament.

"Oleg, shoot them! Shoot them now!" Louis screamed.

Mitchell at last spotted Oleg, who had dropped the statues and the shotgun from the ship's violent tossing and was scrambling to recover his weapon. Yumei trained the derringer on the man and shouted a warning. He briefly looked up and laughed at the shaking woman, then snatched the shotgun off the ground. A gunshot rang out with a flash of light. Two small red holes began pooling blood in the side of Oleg's bald head as he slumped to the deck of the ship.

Shane had wasted no time and alone had kept his footing. Unlike Oleg, he moved straight for the two statues, and before anyone could stop him, he casually lobbed the two overboard, and Mitchell could hear excited splashing on the side of the ship. "I shall be honored in R'lyeh! I bring the idols of great Cthulhu home!" he proclaimed and already was crossing over with proud and sure strides to regain his hostage. Roland had recovered his balance and his weapon and immediately fired two shots at the Irishman. Shane held up a webbed hand in defense and spat out loathsome babble that harmonized with the murmuring waves surrounding

217

them. The very air around the man seemed to fluctuate and waver, heavy with pressure and drawing the surrounding moisture that had been splashed on deck. The bullets from the Luger became visible as they dramatically slowed when entering that arcane field, and Mitchell saw their trajectories change; the first slung down and to the left, passing through Yumei's shoulder, and the other flew up harmlessly into the tumultuous sky. "Roland Hughes!" he called out knowingly as he regarded his assailant and, ignoring all else, began sprinting towards him.

The ship was listing slightly, but Shane kept his feet as he rushed at Roland. Mitchell would not be able to see how the charge ended as he was forced to turn his attention to Louis, who moved toward the fallen shotgun. Louis was surprised from behind by Mitchell, who kicked the gun away and grabbed Louis by his shoulders as he turned to face his attacker. Mitchell slammed him up against the taffrail as the list of the ship increased, creating a slight verticality and making it far easier for either one of them to go toppling over into the raging sea. Louis, finding his position more secure with his back firmly planted against the railing, suddenly jabbed at Mitchell's eyes. Mitchell was able to protect his right eye, but wailed in pain as Louis's fingers pressed against his left eyeball. The seeds of a longstanding rivalry and antagonism fully sprouted from this attack, and Mitchell struck back furiously, landing savage blows square in the insurance man's face. Mitchell's fist throbbed after the last hit broke Louis's nose, which at last caused his attacker to falter and break away. The Russian doll rolled back to clang against the rail next to them, and with his uninjured eye, Mitchell stole a glance to observe its movement. *Another lurch and the doll will surely go through a gap,* he acknowledged. Louis also regarded the doll with new clarity. "Of course," he proclaimed victoriously, clutching his nose. "It's inside!"

The insurance man twisted away, no longer regarding Mitchell, and recklessly lunged forward in a dive that put him on his stomach within reach of the doll. He seized it, and Mitchell tried to jump on top of him, but Louis anticipated his foe's pursuit, swiftly turning over and delivering a jolting kick to Mitchell's lower chest. The antique salesmen went stumbling backwards, coughing up a hunk of blood. Louis brought himself up, leaning heavily on the rail. He looked strangely calm; the man had clearly decided his victory had afforded him a moment to inspect the inside of the Russian doll and confirm that the tomb guardian was within as he began turning the figure to open it.

At this moment, the tide of the storm rose up once more, and Mitchell heard frantic shouts from across the deck; a lifeboat had been knocked loose and was sent slamming into the entangled Shane and Roland. But nearer to Mitchell, the rising wave ushered the return of the grotesque fishlike humanoids, the Deep Ones. Up with them came a horrible and burning air of rot and fish oil, and in his shock, Mitchell could only hope that no lightning strikes would reveal them in closer detail. Sensing easy quarry, or drawn by the call of the idol, their webbed, pallid hands seized hold of Louis's shoulders. Before the insurance man had even pried the statue out of the matryoshka doll, they wrenched his body with terrifying strength, and his neck snapped back so that his eyes beheld their horrifying faces just inches from his own. Whereas moments ago Mitchell felt nothing but hatred for the man, he was filled with pity and revulsion at the wail that issued from him. If one believed in the soul, they must also believe that Louis Malcom's left him at that very moment.

The Russian doll rolled across the deck, now freed from the grasp of Louis, and Mitchell was able to perceive it through his blurred vision. A barrage of gunfire sounded from Roland's pistol, and Mitchell noticed spurts of discolored blood spray up from the Deep Ones where the bullets found their marks. But the monsters did not withdraw below the water until they had twisted the body of their quarry through the bent steel of the railing, taking Louis below. Roland's marksmanship was all the more impressive since Mitchell saw that he was hanging at the railing just further down from where Louis had been taken. Fighting through shock and terror, Mitchell forgot the statue for the moment, instead returning to the dangerous territory where the monsters of the sea could reach out at him. He clasped Roland's free hand and pulled him up back up onto the deck, and they both wasted no time in moving away from the ship's outer edge. Roland quickly lagged behind, limping severely, having been struck by the lifeboat in one of his shins. "Bone might be broken," he grimaced. "But McSweeney's overboard. May he be crushed under the ship! Where is the last statue?"

"I have it!" Yumei called to them, herself wobbling forward with one hand clutching the Russian doll and the other between her bleeding neck and shoulder. As she handed the doll off to Mitchell, she slumped against the cabin's outer wall while he steadied her, relieved that her wounds appeared nonfatal.

Roland shook his head. "It's unacceptable! Even with two statues, the Deep Ones will be emboldened. Far greater miseries will come from this!" he shouted over the sound of the waves, wide-eyed, and pointed his gun to his own head. "But I know what will happen! My death will pass in the twinkling of an eye and give us a second chance at this whole encounter. Mitchell, this time you will not have to face death. I can share in the burden! We will push back time and lose nothing!" His hand was shaking, but his grim expression suggested his resolve, and Mitchell did not doubt his intention nor that the bizarre enchantment would act precisely as Roland anticipated it would.

"It's too late!" Yumei protested, moving toward Roland while clutching her wounded shoulder. Blood streaked down her dress from her hand, neck, and shoulder, and Mitchell knew she could not carry on much longer without the attention of a doctor. "This *is* our second chance, you fool," she said more hoarsely, each word touched with anguish. "If you shoot now, you will only succeed in blowing your brains out, and Mitchell and I will have to move on without you.

Although . . . if you are this great of a fool, perhaps it is an acceptable loss!"

"What? You mean you've . . ." Roland faltered, and Mitchell saw the gun barrel tilt away slightly. "What chance do we have, does the world have, without all of the statues? I would have sensed something, surely, if you were to have been revived." He lowered the gun back to his side.

"My life ended in a streak of pain across my neck minutes ago on this very deck," Yumei said hoarsely. "And if it hadn't happened, then one of our enemies would have been revived from your gunshot, if you understood the properties of the statue!" And at that, Roland looked truly stunned. Mitchell himself was confused, now thinking that the statue ought to have revived Oleg, who surely perished from the shot to his head. "But I don't ask your death for compensation," Yumei resumed, "only that you forsake such madness."

"Listen to her, Roland! It's true," Mitchell added as he picked up and opened the top half of the Russian doll, inspecting the coloration of the previously unharnessed statue while it rested in the base. It appeared grayer and more colorless in the limited light, but in truth, Mitchell could not be certain in the low visibility. He had already decided to support Yumei's claim in either case and affirmed this by closing the statue inside the doll once again. "We will have to manage as best we can without the other two. We need to get Yumei to the ship's doctor!"

Roland hesitated. Yumei collapsed, shivering and complaining of coldness as Mitchell caught her in his arms.

At this, Roland at last holstered his gun and, with Mitchell, helped Yumei back inside. All three of them were drenched with sea and rainwater, and Captain Neal and a security officer immediately intercepted them, leveling pistols at them.

"You will all be entering the custody of the Shanghai Municipal Police! No one move!" the officer commanded.

Mitchell knew that Yumei was in no condition to entertain thoughts of escape, so he looked over towards the indomitable Roland Hughes. The man looked exceedingly calm, carefully placing his gun down with the barrel pointed inwardly to his feet. Clutching at his leg, he stood as straight as he could manage and raised his hands up. He gave Mitchell a very slight nod, conveying that it would be no great setback to go along with the authorities. Thus, beleaguered, cold, and injured, the three reached the coast of China, injured, despoiled of all but one of the magic guardians, and under suspicion of murder.

Part Three:

Angels of the Promise

11

The guardsman, who spoke with a cockney English accent, wished Mitchell a happy Easter as he stopped by with his breakfast early the next morning. Mitchell peered up from his cot, sore, tired, and unable to see straight, his left eye throbbing. He unhappily noted that his great victories left little in the way of satisfaction or reward, apart from reinforcing his tenuous grip on his sanity. Mitchell's night in the cell had not been entirely without solace, however; he dreamt no dark dreams and the room was warm enough and dry, allowing him to shake the spray of sea-salt chill. Waking was much harsher; pain and memories of unspeakable sights returned and battered the man. The guard had set out a plate of ham steak, rice, chopped onions, celery, and peach preserves, along with a cup of coffee and some juice. "You picked a good time to get locked in the slammer. Warden's always extra generous the day of the Lord's resurrection."

"I'm in need of a resurrection myself," Mitchell rasped, evoking a not unkindly laugh from the guard. "I hope it also counts for something that I haven't been convicted of a crime yet."

"None of those in this ward are convicts, but they're awaiting due process. Believe me, you wouldn't be in such a comfortable suite 'gov!"

Mitchell hesitated to drudge up the point, then sighed, regarding his plate. "What would change on this charming plate if I mentioned that I'm Jewish?"

"Oh, blimey . . ." the guard replied, leaning forward to take a closer look at his prisoner's face, as if that would settle the claim of ancestry. "Well, uh, we don't get too many people of the Old Testament, you understand? Uh, I can take this away if it bothers you, but I'm afraid the alternative might be dog meat, but . . . I don't know if that's kosher either."

"I'll manage," Mitchell replied, raising the cup of coffee before picking for the kosher parts of the plate. His thoughts turned to his companions. He hoped that Yumei had been stabilized and on the path to recovery and that Roland's shin was indeed not broken as he had feared. The greater danger perhaps was in Roland overplaying his hand with whoever may have been questioning him, but Mitchell knew nothing but the small world of his cell framed by the gray light of morning through a cramped, high window. His vision was nothing but a blurry mess from his left eye, and his right eye strained to compensate. Mitchell therefore made an effort the rest of the day to keep it shut or cover it with his hand. *A mirror would be useful. I wonder if blood is welling up?* This was not his only material desire, but by the end of the day, he prioritized by asking the guard for materials with which to write. "I would like to send a letter," he told the guard, who he now knew as Paul. Despite their awkward introduction, Paul had taken a curious interest in checking on Mitchell more frequently than his patrols necessitated. Mitchell was amused to think that the man felt some pronounced guilt on account of the ham he had presented him. "And Paul, if it isn't so much trouble, something like a patch to cover my eye. I can pay you for it."

By the next morning, Paul had brought Mitchell both items, charging him only for the eye patch. Mitchell sorely needed the remedy; his current condition had grown miserable. In waking moments, the walls of his cell took on wavy motions, the lines of sooty brick blurring into folding waves. It was as if he was staring back at the dark and infinite sea from which the *Asia* had carried him. The guard idly turned the eyepatch over in his scarred hands, having some difficulty finding his choice words. "If you have a pound sterling, that would suffice, or the Chinese coins if you have a few pieces of silver . . ."

"Of course," Mitchell replied, finding his wallet fortunately intact as he handed Paul three silver dollars. The guard in turn passed him the eyepatch. Mitchell marveled at the condition of the leather, not to mention the strap, which still had a full and thick thread. "Is it new?"

"Somewhat . . . it belonged to a fellow guardsman. He passed away, as it were, while off duty, a nasty scrap after a bit o' drinking. Well, that is to say . . . we all thought he'd make a recovery from his injuries, and he had this ordered while at the hospital. It turned out he didn't recover after all, some bad infection from a knife wound. So we've just sort of had it sitting around, I bought it, so to speak, from the other mates, and I'm just asking for what I paid . . ."

"You're a right saint, Paul," Mitchell replied after Paul finished his account, and the two of them had a laugh at that.

Mitchell wrote a two-sided letter to his friend Roger Merrick, giving him a full appraisal of his current status as well as the challenges their mission now faced with the group only retaining one statue. There was only so much warning he could give, that he would dare to give, concerning the Cthulhu cult, yet he risked it in his letter all the same. He confirmed his intended destination of Luoyang in the attempt to find An Lushan's burial site and promised Roger that he would write him again if he and his companions were prevented from reaching there or were forced to divert. The only matter that Mitchell wavered on was how much he would try to explain of the enigma of Roland Hughes, worrying that he may provide more questions than answers in the space afforded on the parchment. Ultimately, Mitchell erred on the side of detail, and at the very least explained that his reclusive business partner, still universally acknowledged as dead in the United States, was very much alive and travelling with him. The letter was sealed, and Paul promised to get it over to the post office for him.

On the third day of Mitchell's detainment, a Detective Cecil Eddington interviewed him about the events on the final day of the *Asia's* voyage to Shanghai. The small room that Mitchell had been moved to was not much different in nature from his cell, apart from the brighter lighting of a large carbon-filament bulb that hung from the ceiling. Eddington removed his policeman's cap to reveal a flattened tuft of brown hair and sat down across from the antique salesman, opening a file and angling it so that its contents were shielded from Mitchell. "Let's just start with your story then, Mr. Bernheim," he said tiredly.

"I would like to have news of my friends, in particular the lady who was injured," Mitchell answered.

"Sir, it is not my intention to be rude, but I am here to obtain your account as it pertains to a criminal investigation. Until the Shanghai International Settlement determines whether to press charges, I am not to provide you any information of the status of other suspects," he recited stoically.

Mitchell sighed, then told the story nearly straight, that he and his travelling companions were robbed of certain artifacts and assaulted by Shane McSweeney, Louis Malcom, and his bodyguard on the deck of the *Asia* during the storm as it was coming into port. "Your forensic examination should have identified the defensive wounds from my friends' accounts," Mitchell explained, "and for your information, the man I've referenced several times, Louis Malcom, tried to puncture my eye with his fingertips before he was washed over the side of the ship by the storm." He removed the eyepatch to demonstrate his swollen eye.

"Your condition has been noted," the detective said uncaringly, though he jotted down a line in the report. "Vision returning?"

Mitchell had left the eyepatch on almost continually the past few days, but as he strained, he thought perhaps instead of the absolute fuzzy blankness there was a now a slightly more defined texture in his overall vision. "God willing."

"What reason brought you to the deck during such turbulent conditions?" Eddington asked.

"Miss Han was missing from our cabin. I alerted my friend Mr. Hughes, and we decided to search for her on deck. Thank God that we did, as she had been forcibly brought up there by our assailants."

"Would that not be a matter to report to the captain and crew?" Eddington asked abrasively.

"You must not forget the storm, detective, or the fact that the closest crew member we found was incapacitated, and I'd bet anything he was attacked by McSweeney or Oleg."

Eddington nodded, then turned to the next page of the report. "And please repeat for me who fired the derringer pistol shot that killed the bodyguard, the bald man we've identified as Oleg Mendeleev."

"It was Miss Han."

"And, in your opinion, lethal force was justified?"

"Tell me, Detective Eddington, that if you had been shot in the shoulder, scratched by a twitching knife at your throat, or threatened to be thrown overboard, would you take care to hold back in your own defense?"

Eddington hesitated, but then stiffened. "Since you mentioned Miss Han's shoulder wound, the round recovered from Miss Han's shoulder was matched to a gun possessed by your companion Mr. Roland Hughes, not this bodyguard, Oleg."

"They'll tell you the same thing, if they haven't already. It was an errant shot intended for McSweeney, who was restraining Yumei with the knife." Mitchell, of course, had no idea if his friends had been consistent in that detail, but he decided to be confident as it was near enough to the truth.

"And as for Louis Malcom and Shane McSweeney, they both fell overboard by sheer Providence? None of you had a hand in that?"

"Each of us had grappled with one or all of them at some point, but neither myself, nor Mr. Hughes or Miss Han were responsible for them going over. Call it Providence, if that's what you want to call a loosened lifeboat slamming into you."

"That's enough for now," Eddington said, scratching underneath his chin. "Your cooperation is appreciated."

"What of our possessions that were thrown overboard?" Mitchell asked as Eddington prepared to escort them from the room. "There were two little statues and a briefcase with an old book."

Eddington hesitated, then shrugged. "No further evidence has been recovered from Hangzhou Bay, although it's shallow enough that you might have some luck if you wanted to search it yourself, should you have the opportunity. Though I can't expect a book, even inside a case, would have any chance in the water that long."

Five more days passed without Mitchell being spoken to by another investigator, legal counsel, or any other authority apart from Paul the guardsman. It was such a numbing vigil that Mitchell thought his mind might break, but he kept himself going with thoughts of home and Yumei. On the eighth day of being detained by the Shanghai Municipal Police, Paul arrived slightly earlier than his usual patrol time, smiling proudly. "I've got your luggage here, Mitchell. You're free to go! Investigation's closed, case has been managed!"

"That's outstanding, my friend. Managed?"

"That's right . . . your mate Roland got a lawyer, fast as lightning, and from the ways I understand it, he's paid some sort of uncontested misdemeanor fees, mostly concernin' undeclared possession of a firearm and customs violations. That lawyer fellow though, he expedited things like a marvel! Otherwise they can drag on a bit . . ."

"And just when I was starting to like the place," Mitchell said as he gestured back to his room.

"Well you can always come visit!" Paul replied, genuinely enthused.

"If I can survive my next boat trip," Mitchell replied, shaking the man's hand as the two made their way outside. Mitchell bid farewell to the guard and found that he had been the last of the group to be released, as Yumei and Roland were there to greet him outside of Central Station. Yumei had been discharged from Renji Hospital with the bullet successfully removed from her right shoulder and the cuts on her neck healing steadily. She still had to manage a hefty bandage underneath her collar, but explained to a concerned Mitchell that she was regaining range of motion, despite a persistent soreness. The two embraced and lingered in each other's arms for a long while upon reuniting, though Mitchell took care to be very gentle near the shoulder where Roland's bullet had struck her. "I threatened to slap him when I first saw him," she indicated to Mitchell by cocking her head in Roland's direction. "But I realized it probably would have been more painful for me, or tear the stitches of those clumsy physicians, so I restrained myself."

"Indeed, Mitchell and I can learn from your marksmanship," Roland said to Yumei, his expression grave. For his shin injury, he was supported by a crutch, but did not wear a cast. "But where my shooting failed, you may console yourself that I managed to expedite our release," he added as he reaffixed his disheveled formal hat. "And perhaps you perceived it, but the very air around McSweeney became distorted as my bullets approached. As for the prized book, it is lost, along with two of the tomb guardians." His tone grew heavier as he changed topics, and his silence that followed reflected the lowering hopes of the group at large. "But regarding our remaining tomb guardian, which surely would have been confiscated as cultural contraband, Captain Neal spirited the inconspicuous Russian doll to my associates in the city just in time. Captain Superintendent McEuen of the SMP seems like a reasonable fellow too, and I think that will be the end of our foreseeable troubles with the authorities, at least in Shanghai. But we must not delay any longer. Our detainment has given the Anshi Cult ample announcement of our arrival and time to organize a pursuit, or to block us."

"On the deck of the *Asia*, Shane McSweeney recognized you," Yumei added, studying him closely for his reaction.

"That he did, though regrettably I did not know him—but that's no surprise. There has long been something of a bounty on my head among Cthulhu's faithful, and that was my sole advantage in that madness," Roland explained calmly. "For a turncoat cultist such as myself to die of incidental violence on the deck of the *Asia* would not be nearly enough for a fanatic like McSweeney. I believe he was distracted with how exactly to drag me down to the depths of his greater kin, that I may be drowned a thousand times before my soul would be extinguished. But regarding the Irishman's fate, I had to press the superintendent considerably, and only yesterday did I at last learn that his body was never recovered from the water, nor was Louis Malcom's."

"I feel almost sorry for him," Yumei remarked, frowning. "I hope you can make your peace with that," she added to Mitchell.

"I would like to say he had it coming," Mitchell replied, adjusting his eyepatch as a dull pain resurfaced at the memory of his scuffle. "He always stuck his neck into dangerous partnerships, and it finally backfired on him. But no, I suppose no one deserves the fate that he suffered."

"Let us hope we are spared from it," Roland added, hailing for a coach.

They proceeded to Palace Hotel on Nanjing Road, an upscale establishment that catered primarily to Westerners. They rendezvoused with Roland's associates, who had secured accommodations for the three of them to also spend the night there. It was nothing short of glorious for Mitchell and Yumei, who bathed and refreshed themselves in the hotel's porcelain bath and tread barefoot upon plush, knotted carpeting. Even better was the promise of much more comfortable sleeping arrangements before setting out again.

In chairs wrought of fine rosewood, they discussed their plans and retrieved the remaining statue from Roland's associates. They were not connected to Mr. Hughes by cult membership, but instead to the Hughes family's global partnerships in various storefronts and enterprises. There was one local, Jing Zhao, an Australian named Anderson Blake, and a Spaniard, Rodrigo Valencia. Zhao coordinated the Hughes family's connections in China, while Anderson had recently arrived in the area having been summoned by Roland. Rodrigo had arrived by chance on a long business trip all the way from Spain via the Suez Canal and through the Indian Ocean, but was now available to assist the party.

It was decided that Rodrigo and Anderson would remain in Shanghai to monitor comings and goings, be prepared for the group's eventual return, and make any attempts to delay inquirers while Zhao would accompany them further inland.

On Monday, April 8th, Mitchell, Roland, Yumei, and Zhao departed in the afternoon via the canal, bearing for north-central China to reach their final destination of Luoyang, a distance of five hundred and seventy miles northwest, as the crow flies. Their path would mostly be across lowlands carved by the land's proud rivers, and the greatest threat would be the flooding that reportedly gripped the countryside. Zhao negotiated their passage aboard a canal barge that would take them from Shanghai up the Yangtze River until Zhenjiang. There, the course turned to take the Huitong section of the Grand Canal, the largest leg of the journey northwest until they reached the Wei River. Upon the Wei, they would go southwest, eventually arriving at the canal's terminal in Jiaozuo. Once they reached Jiaozuo, there would remain a relatively short overland journey to Luoyang, where the search for An Lushan's hidden sanctuary would begin in earnest. As it was uncommon for Chinese women to venture out into the public space, Mitchell and Yumei would pose as husband and wife when needed. The pretense fueled yet more playful conversations on Mitchell's part, which was increasingly tolerated and engaged with by Yumei. The two had grown close to the point that the part was not difficult to play for either of them.

The journey had also bought a moment's reprieve to inspect the remaining tomb guardian in their possession, which was revealed to have lost none of its original tricolor luster. This, of course, meant that its power had not yet been used and that Yumei had not perished on the deck of the *Asia* as she had claimed; even someone who had seen the statues a fraction as many times as Mitchell would be able to identify the distinction from the gray coat that the two expended statues had displayed. The discovery decisively indicated that it did not revive the Russian bodyguard because it was not directly touched by anyone in the encounter while in the container, even in one as crude as the Russian doll. It was impossible to determine how much time needed to pass to also prevent the resurrection, as the tomb guardian had been handled many times since, with no power passing from it.

As Mitchell pondered further, he also prepared to defend Yumei for her deception, yet Roland did not react with the incendiary mania that had seized him on the ship. Upon staring at the figure for a time, he merely shrugged and returned to his preferred spot on the barge. *He's either given up on the idea that all three statues will be needed,* Mitchell thought, *or he has decided to be diplomatic. Perhaps it is better to have one statue with its potency retained than three that are expended.* Mitchell saw no use in pressing Yumei about it either; he was most glad that she did not experience death aboard the ship, and furthermore, he did not embrace the idea of agitating her on the long journey. The statue's remaining power lent a degree of insurance to any further dangers and horrors they might face. But Mitchell was not wholly convinced of Roland's detachment toward Yumei's deception. As much as Roland had done to endear himself to the antiquarian, Mitchell felt obligated to be wary of his companion over the long and slow days on the canal.

There had been reports of catastrophic flooding that spring, which would spell dread for the harvest. Even within the posh Shanghai hotel, raised food prices already suggested the coming famine, which would be yet more pronounced in the countryside, causing the spring planting season to be abandoned in great swaths of territory. The group took as many food supplies as they could manage aboard their vessel, and as the canal boat took them further northwest, Mitchell observed that the flooding had created a new topography of floodplains extending on all horizons across the region. The worst rumors that they had heard proved astonishingly unexaggerated from their observations. Bamboo shoots rose above mires where upended rice plants mingled with debris from nearby villages. Oftentimes, bodies were found in the canal and in the flooded mires and marshes across the silent lowlands.

The journey would have been completely hopeless had they taken the roadways, and the canal was made more turbulent by the floodtide. Swamped fields at times formed one continuous body of water with the canal itself, threatening the direction of their passage and often prompting frenetic discussions between Yumei, Zhao, and the ferryman. "I hope we are not to think that . . . the missing statues . . . that *Cthulhu* himself is responsible for all of this," Mitchell whispered one evening, transgressing the usual stillness that had prevailed in the dead lands. He was also thinking about San Francisco the previous year, and he tried to stave off the belief that all recent natural disasters had their origins in these mysterious, dark gods and the portents of the missing tomb guardians.

"As much as I wish to share in your opinion, Mitchell, our whole mission rests on that premise," Roland replied. "It is despairing to think that such tragedies are ordained by the caprice or unintentional rumblings of such beings, but that does not negate the possibility. I cannot help but feel that when the earth itself has brought forth such death, the veil . . . the boundaries of the waking world grow thin. The madness, the unspeakable creatures that give fuel to nightmares and legends throughout history . . . they are always there, always ready to step from behind the curtain in areas touched by such death." A moaning sound from somewhere across a line of trees quieted further conversation, and Mitchell wondered if someone was stranded by the floodtide on some receding patch of island or floating rooftop, dying a slow death of starvation.

"Even after all you've witnessed, you doubt that the earthquake, this flood, that the disasters of this decade are not ripples from the Great Old Ones?" Yumei asked Mitchell, also not sharing his skepticism. "It is most certainly a sign of our lapsed vigilance, that the world will be given over to death if not saved by wretched souls like ours. The great flooded lands we are witnessing now . . . how easily could they spread throughout the lowlands of Asia, to connect to the world's oceans, with a few more earthquakes or monsoons?"

"That won't happen," Mitchell replied. "God promised He would not destroy the earth in a flood after He had preserved Noah and his family." Mitchell had applied his selective faith to find assurance in this tenant.

"I am aware," Yumei replied. "But that promise didn't extend that it will be spared from some other destruction." Mitchell had no retort to this.

Food remained scarce at the way-stops, even for the Westerners who offered whatever they could for bartering. Thousands, perhaps millions of farmers were dead as they passed by deserted villages with houses submerged to the rooftops. The three wayward travelers could not blame those they encountered at the waypoints for not exchanging what little they had salvaged. Three days out of Zhenjiang, when their supply from Shanghai had dwindled, they found a man who was willing to sell them a chicken and a bag of rice. They often went hungry, but avoided starvation by finding just enough farmers who valued the minted silver dollars of the Guangxu Emperor that Mitchell and Yumei had exchanged their remaining cash for in Shanghai. The most stupendous thing was that in all of the death and gloom, Mitchell still found a quiet contentedness in being this near to Yumei each day and night, regardless of the surroundings. He further understood that this feeling was amplified by how fleeting and fragile their time together would be before facing the unknown of An Lushan's tomb.

The midge population had exploded to a bumper population early that season. Approaching clouds of the pests became difficult for the party to discern against the frequent mists that accompanied the high tides of the rivers. For a time, the midges did not bite, but the constant presence of great swarms presented a risk of inhaling clumps of the buzzing flies and was turning the days perfectly miserable. "The boys do not bite," Yumei cautioned them regarding the midges. "But the girls do, and they will be out in much greater numbers within a month or so. By then, if we have not reached Luoyang, we will need to find a way to cover ourselves on the rivers." The sun was growing hotter each day, although that did not seem to quell the insect activity, and an unpleasant swell of vapors from the waterway always hung over them and turned cold at night.

"It is best to think of ourselves as such creatures," Roland managed with a didactic air as he gestured vaguely to a midge cloud above.

"Now there's a humility I wouldn't have expected of you," Mitchell managed, reaffixing a bundle of a shirt he had wrapped around his head like a turban to shield himself from the swarms.

"To the great cosmic forces that consume stars and turn bright, burning heat to cold oblivion, we are kindred with such gnats. Imperceptible, forgotten in a moment, the ripples we cast amount to little more than an itch that invites danger we cannot possibly perceive." Roland's tone was vacant to the point that it did not constitute a reply, but rather suggested an indifferent narration.

In the back of Mitchell's mind, he had prepared himself for one such moment from Roland. *He is still greatly unsettled. The very air is dangerous about him.* Mitchell tried to maintain a keen alertness, watching his companion closely. Apart from being disturbed by the words of lofty despair, it was difficult for Mitchell to square them. *If he has become so resigned to his fate . . . the grand insignificance of humanity . . . why continue this journey at all? Is there some hidden hope or desire he harbors?*

"I think too many of the midges have flown through your nostrils," Yumei offered in rebuke. "There is a benefit, though, to our new companions," she added, somehow noticing Mitchell's dread underneath layers of sweat, itch, and wrapped cloth.

"What could that possibly be?" Mitchell asked earnestly, swatting away the insects off his arm while his other hand batted them in the air.

"They will likely keep bandits off the rivers—any surviving ones in the area, I mean. I don't think we'd be worth the trouble!" Yumei's comment prompted one of the rare moments where all the members aboard the barge laughed, after she repeated it in Chinese. The ferryman was emphatic in his agreement and was prompted to share an account of his most recent run-in. For all of their trials, they fortunately encountered no outlaws upon that canal journey.

They reached the Wei River north of Liaocheng on April 13th, and it took them three more days to at last reach the canal terminal of Jiaozuo where they parted ways with the ferryman, who wished them well and did not conceal that he would miss their company. It would take another two days of hard travel to reach Luoyang via the roadways, as the paths had dried out just barely enough to be serviceable, at least in this part of the country. Being upon *terra firma* again renewed their energy, especially for Roland, who was curious to test his walking strength through the suctioning mud as his leg healed. He suggested continuing to Xian to view Xuanzang's sutras in the Giant Wild Goose Pagoda. Yumei dismissed the idea and overruled him, insisting that there was nothing once housed there not already known to her. There was nothing else to do then but press on and try to secure an accommodation in Luoyang.

Thus, nearly eleven days after setting out from Shanghai, they had journeyed through central China to reach Luoyang midge-bitten, hungry, and deathly weary. The city was situated amidst two rivers: between the southern bank of the Luohe River, which ran to the northwest, and the northern bank of the Yihe River, which ran nearly due north but bent westward as it neared the city to run nearly a parallel course with the Luohe, separated by a gap of about three miles which cradled the heart of the city center. Fortunately, none of the party had become ill from their sources of drinking water or from the oscillating exposure of sweltering heat and chilling mists on the canal. Zhao found them accommodations on the southern edge of the city, an area where their currency stretched an inch further and the floods had not been as extensive.

The time on the canal boat and ensuing days of walking had allowed Roland to finally discard his crutch, and Yumei no longer needed to reapply bandages—she could freely move her shoulder again. Conversely, Mitchell failed to notice any improvement in his vision and faced the prospect that he would never see more than a dark blur out of his left eye again. He knew of several optometrists in San Francisco, and the thought helped keep him moving that he one day might look upon San Francisco Bay again with both eyes clear. For now, he would continue wearing his eyepatch, which Yumei at least commented was not unhandsome on him.

In the waning sunlight of the evening of April 18th, they discussed their plans at the inn, the White Lotus. Mitchell proposed a solemn toast of remembrance for the first anniversary of the San Francisco earthquake, and the four each raised a glass. A musician was in attendance, playing a bamboo flute, and the long days of silence upon the canals amplified the instrument's effect, moving Mitchell rapidly between the emotions of the suffering around him and memories of his own city. "The world turns more gray," he said very quietly. No one disagreed.

Yumei was convinced from her ponderous research that the final piece of critical information was very likely somewhere in the nearby Longmen Grottoes, a splendid Buddhist site of antiquity. She insisted that somewhere amidst the sculptures was either an inscription on a cave wall or a stele left by the great monk Xuanzang, or perhaps a hidden cache containing writings that would be of use to them. "The earliest Longmen caves were already excavated by his lifetime. Xuanzang predated An Lushan by a century, but his knowledge may reveal some insights into assisting us with the curse of the guardians." No one had alternate proposals. Indeed, Luoyang had been chosen for its proximity to a number of Tang-era sites, and they agreed to set out for the grottoes early the next morning. Despite his tiredness, Mitchell found that he could not sleep that night as his mind constantly produced fantastic and bizarre shadow-figures in countless scenarios as he fretted about exploring the great cave network that awaited.

12

The morning mists were clearing by the time they left the White Lotus, which was only two miles from the Longmen Grottoes. Zhao guided them, but even in the flooded springtide, the amount of foot traffic in their direction would have made their course sure. As they approached, the view of the rising façade of the grottoes was obscured by the crowd in front of them. This necessitated that they approach closer until they could at last gaze at the majesty of the Longmen Grottoes. It was a most breathtaking sight. Set in proud cliffs of limestone, enormous and deftly carved rock reliefs of the Buddha and bodhisattvas adorned a landscape that stretched hundreds of feet to the viewers' left and right while also rising above them in the cliff wall. In addition to these, Yumei explained some of the other figures that were displayed: the honored disciples *Kasyapa* and *Ananda*; numerous images of the *lokapalas*, the heavenly kings; and depictions of the *dvarapala*s, the temple guards. Flying devas and other mythological creatures completed a panoply of wonder of the Buddhist faith.

The perfect serenity of the statues' expressions and the

ancient skill of the craftsmen gave such harmony to the display that Mitchell found himself greatly moved and full of an awed calm he had not expected this close to their journey's end. Even with the disastrous weather, many wayfarers had ventured to the site that day, so the four of them had to navigate past gazing onlookers and praying pilgrims as they approached the base of the cliff and paths up to the tunnels themselves. "It was started during the Northern Wei dynasty," Yumei reminded them. "But the great majority of the statues were commissioned and completed during the Tang period, though some additions were made after, but far fewer."

"What of the caves? Are they extensive?" Mitchell asked, recalling his listless mind from last night. He continued to imagine a great, penetrating network leading to the depths of the Longmen Mountains, with each looming statue representing great subterranean gates.

"All of the caves were man-made, so none are any larger than their designed purpose. I don't expect us to find any great passageways more than twenty paces long," Yumei responded with assurance, perhaps sensing Mitchell's dread.

"It is difficult for me to accept that An Lushan, the great traitor to the Tang who scorned the Buddhist faith, would be buried here, even covertly," Roland said. Mitchell noticed that although Roland had disagreed on their choice of destination, he too had been invigorated by the wondrous sight, standing with a new energy. "At the same time, it would be so very like the Anshi Cult, the Cthulhu Cult, to

subvert a proud monument of an opposing faith with some blasphemous shrine."

Some of the lowest caves closest to the Yihe River were flooded, but Yumei insisted on being exhaustive in her inspection of the grottoes. Of course, the entire search was for one specific stele, one message of forgotten and ancient lore from the scholar Xuanzang. As they approached closer so that they could move parallel to the cliff wall, Mitchell appreciated the sheer multitude of smaller alcoves that housed smaller shrines and lone statues. Some were nestled in such delicate recesses along narrow tracks of thin overhang that Mitchell deemed them completely inaccessible. For many of the other potential caves, he dreaded the prospect of investigating them across the stone paths, which had turned treacherously smooth in places.

The group ascended to a high row of caves that had piqued Yumei's curiosity. This formation was noticeably bereft of statues, and Yumei speculated that they could be among the oldest in the cave network. Roland and Mitchell caught each other from deadly falls on two occasions. The first incident was triggered by Roland's weakened legs, still finding their strength after his injury. They buckled under him while he was climbing, yet Mitchell and Zhao were there to steady him before he lost his entire foothold. Later that day, after the sun had lowered just below the horizon, Mitchell espied a ghastly creature within a cave not thirty feet away from their position. It was a shambling, half-formed creature colored of the same stone as the rock wall. It gave him such a start that he attempted to bolt away on instinct only for his feet to slip and scrape up a rush of falling pebbles. Roland caught him, pulling him back against the cliff wall with pained exertion. "You could not see it?" Mitchell asked in frenzied, uneven breaths. "I don't think it was the same manner of monster that stalked the *Asia*, but it was assuredly not human."

"Your peripheral vision is not to be trusted when your mind tires," Roland replied upon catching his own breath. "We are in the most peculiar vista in a land unknown to us. Your fears are ripe for suggestion. Besides, your diminished sight surely addles you all the more," he added, gesturing to Mitchell's eyepatch. He snorted, forming a wan smile. "The four of us are more than a match for any tunnel guardians, I'm sure."

Mitchell could not share his companion's confidence, and it was a bitter thought whenever he dwelled on his eyepatch, but Yumei drove them on. Aside from the danger of falling as they methodically ascended, the work of scanning the walls in translation was even more wearisome. Roland was conversant in the language, and Mitchell continued to pick up more phrases and words, but only Yumei could decipher the characters inscribed upon the stonework as Zhao was poor with his letters. Mitchell insisted upon being present wherever Yumei ventured. Roaming brigands made desperate by the flood and famine contributed to Mitchell's unceasing paranoia. Ultimately, the closer the party drew to An Lushan's burial chamber meant that Mitchell would at last face it in the waking world after viewing it countless times. *Will we beat the Anshi Cult there, or are they lying in wait?* He was powerless to dismiss the vague and persistent horrors that haunted his imagination.

The exploration of the tunnels proceeded slowly, but Mitchell could at least take careful notes of which sections they had already charted, which otherwise would have been enormously confusing. Methodically they navigated. He constantly marked directional notations or quick scribblings about the appearance of the closest statue at the entrances of tunnels they had inspected, then would rewrite them later, more neatly, that he would be able to make sense of them later. They had now separated themselves from the great crowds; they no longer enjoyed the vistas of the colossal Buddhas, but now squinted at smaller depictions and inscriptions in mostly derelict and echoing passageways that ran alongside the proud sculptures in the great limestone shelf. As Yumei promised, none of these tunnels penetrated to great depths. The curved paths were cut in very gentle bends running parallel to the cliff walls, and the tunnels that ran straight often terminated in dead ends after only about thirty feet at most.

The group carried on in this manner for two full days, as long as there was any daylight to creep into the tunnels. At the beginning and end of each day, when they made the small journey between the White Lotus and the grottoes themselves, they traveled in their full group of four. This was done as insurance against opportunistic brigands, and the subtlety of some of Luoyang's more desperate residents lessened on their return the second night. Mitchell saw one group of about half a dozen haunting their steps only twenty paces behind. They followed them all the way to the inn, and now knew both their route and where they were staying. Mitchell decided that they would need to adjust their routine the next day, or travel with a larger group to avoid disaster.

At the beginning of the third day of exploring the Longmen Grottoes, Roland awoke with a fever and decided to remain with Zhao at the inn. Mitchell understood that Yumei would not be dissuaded from venturing out just the two of them, and he prayed that they would avoid any encounters. Yumei followed his lead as they joined in with the largest throng setting out that day, whom they had waited for at the expense of starting later in the day. As Yumei set to work, Mitchell noticed that he too felt weary and drawn by days of squinting in half-lit tunnels, now exacerbated by looking over his shoulder for unscrupulous types. Since setting out from Shanghai, Mitchell always carried the tomb guardian on his person in a backpack and suspected the long custody was wearing on him. "Yumei, I understand we are looking for Xuanzang's inscription, but what of finding An Lushan's burial chamber?"

"We will surely stumble upon it in due time," she replied vacantly, scanning the walls of the cave with an infinite reservoir of focus.

"At some point, we must accept the possibility that no such inscription exists," Mitchell offered. At that moment, he felt a sapping weakness, but the worst had been a growing hunger. "My belt loop is as tight as I can fasten it, and my trousers are barely staying upright as it is. I don't know how much longer we can stretch our resources . . . *ourselves*, here."

Yumei now fully broke her attention away from the inscriptions. She nodded and looked much more exhausted than Mitchell had ever seen her. "Then this day shall be the last," she conceded. "I will adjust my method and move more swiftly in the remaining sections."

"Thank you. I know it's not easy . . . with such an opportunity as this," Mitchell replied as the two shared in a weary smile. "Have you learned anything interesting along the way? I've noticed you have taken some considerable notes."

"There have certainly been some intriguing fragments and references. I will be able to update the scholarship on the grottoes, should I have the opportunity."

Just past midday, they entered a half-flooded tunnel near the southwest gate, which neighbored the western shore of the Yihe. The tunnel sloped gently downward, and Mitchell anticipated it would be difficult to return out along the wet rock. The portents were more promising for Yumei, who uttered the name *Xuanzang* with elation as she pressed close to the wall, taking care that her notebook did not become submerged as the water came above her knees. Mitchell could not properly understand the characters upon the wall, but did note the prevalence of a certain star pattern that prevailed in numerous places, looking something like a rotated and stretched Star of David. "The *Biāozhì* . . ." Yumei whispered. "The Elder Sign."

Mitchell took a lingering glance at the symbol, then used his sleeve to wipe down the coat of moisture along the inscribed calligraphy and eventually managed to get the lantern lit as he raised it aloft for her. "Much better," she exclaimed, and her renewed enthusiasm had a contagious effect on Mitchell, who found the lamp lighter in his grasp. "I have finished," Yumei said surprisingly quickly after the discovery. "And if my observations are correct, there is yet one other treasure in this tunnel. We must wade further in."

The two did so, coming to the dead end of the passage at the far end of the interior. Yumei had left her notebook behind, securing it in a high nook she had spotted. Water now came up above Mitchell's waist and just below Yumei's neck. It was chilling, and Mitchell would count himself lucky if he did not catch pneumonia if he lingered much longer. "There should be a hidden chimney of some kind, a shaft in the roof of the tunnel," Yumei explained, her teeth beginning to chatter.

"Yes, I see it!" Mitchell exclaimed, pointing out a circular hollow above. "Rather narrow . . ."

"Let me get on your shoulders," Yumei said.

Mitchell lowered himself, closing his eyes and submerging his head beneath the water so that Yumei could get her feet up. When he could feel her hands steadying just above his neck, Mitchell slowly brought himself back up. The feat was not difficult; Yumei was light, almost weightless as Mitchell straightened himself to his full height, his head and shoulders cresting above the water again. Yumei grasped upwards into the shaft, pulling herself up and disappearing into it. *There must be a type of crawl space or landing*, Mitchell thought. "Please be careful, Yumei!"

Less than a minute later, Mitchell heard faint movement above. "I'm coming down!" Yumei's muffled voice called out, and Mitchell saw her legs begin dangling out of the concealed chimney. She pushed off and fell clear through the small opening, her arms and legs straight as an arrow to buy her the essential space to clear the shaft. Mitchell was ready. He caught her, lowering her gently to her own feet. They shared a kiss, and to Mitchell's amazement, Yumei produced another tomb guardian which had been cradled alongside her body in her right arm. "One of the areas Emperor Gaozong deposited a guardian," Yumei explained. "Rather convenient for us, I was able to piece together a few inscriptions and at last understand the hiding place."

"You are a wonder," Mitchell offered.

"Let us keep this one a secret," Yumei responded while the two backtracked down the tunnel. "I still do not entirely trust Mr. Hughes, and I doubt I ever will completely."

"I understand he was quite possessed by his own convictions on the ship," Mitchell replied. "But I think we all have been touched by the death that has surrounded us since coming here."

"It is not because of that. I think it's admirable that he has attempted to leave the worship of Cthulhu, but I am unconvinced anyone can leave the cult of a Great Old One with a fully intact mind. We may have caught a small glimpse of instability in our last hour aboard the *Asia*, yes, but I fear he may harbor something much darker before all this is over. He has much to be bitter about, and I feel his motivations remain clouded. Having an added statue may provide us with leverage I hope we will not need."

Mitchell had nearly gotten over the apprehension he felt towards Roland, yet he found Yumei's suggestion prudent. He would continue to carry the tomb guardian as always in his backpack, and Yumei would also bear the newly discovered one in her case, which did not noticeably bulge further once she rearranged her writing materials. "I will need fresh parchment, lots of it," she mentioned as they left the caves. They wrung their sleeves and rubbed themselves, and the sun emerged to help dry them. "It's possible I found something very useful from Xuanzang's inscription, but it will involve extensive practice in my calligraphy. I must return to the inn after getting the paper and find someplace quiet to work. I entrust finding An Lushan's tomb to you and Roland."

"That's more than a little abrupt!" Mitchell protested. "How are we—"

"If you had concerned yourself so chiefly with the paralyzing question of *how* up to this point, would you have made it this far? Surely you will discover some method."

The point was well taken, but Mitchell was more preoccupied with how to return safely to the inn that day. It had not rained heavily since their arrival, but an afternoon storm had swept in over the mountains from the west, covering the sun just as the two were getting dry. They took shelter again in an adjacent cave as sheets of rain washed over the cliffs and colossi. From his perspective at the mouth of the cave, Mitchell discerned that most of the visitors had been driven away by the change in weather. Alarmingly, the receding floodwaters of the Yihe began to rise again. Two choices presented themselves to Mitchell—to hide in the cave and wait for the rain to pass, or to attempt back for Luoyang in the storm. Yumei made the decision for them, sprinting ahead with an uncanny burst.

It was a miserable trek. The pair had just made themselves somewhat dry from the flooded cave but again became drenched by a hard and cold rain. It was a disorienting frenzy, but fortunately they could follow the path of the river north back to the town, often having to mind their steps as mudbanks began to give way and slope dangerously down to the rushing river. Mitchell later wondered how he had maintained the energy for their flight across the deepening muds, then realized he had been spurred on by the thought that they would be spared a vigil of darkness in the caves, waiting long into the night until the threat of bandits would pass. Finally, later that evening, what money remained between Roland, Mitchell, and Yumei was consolidated to secure a less scanty lunch that day of cooked fish with steamed rice and broccoli and fresh, blessedly hot tea. "There are plenty of trinkets I can pawn on the way back to Shanghai," Roland expressed through congested dismissal. "Let's hope the two of you don't end up worse off than me after today. But might we learn what exactly you discovered in the grottoes, or would you consider it above our understanding?" he asked Yumei.

"In essence, through perfect calligraphy and arrangement of about a dozen ancient seals and signs, the protective ward of the burial chamber may be removed for us to access it. Xuanzang described it as a pillar of silver, possibly mercury, that must be passed through. Otherwise it is quite unreachable. I need to practice the inscription, but I obtained adequate copies from the instructions at the grottoes."

"And that is in addition to the challenge of finding the tomb in the first place," Mitchell added, conveying to Roland what the men's task would be.

"Something we can manage. Something we must manage," Roland responded, resolute. "Very well done, Yumei. Mitchell, we must not allow ourselves to be outdone. We've enjoyed a small peace here while Yumei carried out her research, but I promise you it will not last. The Anshi Cult is here, and perhaps a greater presence will be arriving soon. I think the time we have has been purchased by the floods. We must find the tomb before any pursuit reaches us, or this entire effort will be wasted."

Despite Roland's words, he was in no fit condition to leave the inn while he languished from his fever, though he did promise to hold the fort, keep his ear to the ground to overhear anything said in the inn's common room, and guard Yumei while she worked. It would primarily be up to Mitchell to ascertain where An Lushan's burial chamber could be located, and he granted himself only a few hours' rest before he would resume the search that same night. Fortunately, he would have Zhao's assistance as a translator, and the two set out that evening to ask the locals. Mitchell could not avoid the risk that he might broach the question to a cultist and immediately betray his own cause, but he did not have the luxury of more patient tactics.

Mitchell focused on the area south of the city center and north of the grottoes, hailing travelers, farmers, and fishermen making their way along the road. He did not dare venture too far from the inn and made note of where he had noticed their party first being followed. Of the passers-by that Mitchell spoke with, he was often rebuffed as a *gweilo*, despite being accompanied by the native Zhao. Yet for as many who ignored him in this way, an equal number stopped to converse with him out of curiosity. Mitchell framed his questions as searching for a very particular pagoda or temple, claiming that he was unfamiliar as a new convert and aspiring pilgrim to Buddhism, discovering its enlightenment in relation to the decadence of the West. This small deception went a long way in some very earnest townsfolk giving him detailed directions to the local pagodas and shrines. Mitchell and Zhao dismissed the most commonly mentioned examples and narrowed their following questions to the ones that were only spoken of by few or were accompanied with less consistent and hazier directions.

By nightfall, they had discerned that one pagoda greatly troubled the crew of a fishing skiff as they regularly passed up and down the Yihe River between Luoyang and Yichuan.

Mitchell pressed the man for more details, but to get anything more, he had to surrender the very last of the silver coins shared between the group. Upon gently biting down on the silver coins, the fisherman related that his crew collectively referred to the place as the *Hēi Tǎ*, the Black Pagoda. He explained that it was not always visible as they made their pass, and they were glad when there was no sight of it. Yet when generous moonlight and clear skies prevailed, the foreboding tower could always be spotted, a pillar of black camouflaged amongst tree trunks nestled in the foothills of the Longmen range. Just looking at the place inspired dread, and the crew had made a practice of releasing a portion of their catch back to the river in supplication, that they might avoid any curse of its power. The fisherman muttered something, and Mitchell caught *Dúyǎn de* at the end of the man's breath, and he took his leave of them. "What did he say?" he prompted Zhao as they made their way back to the inn.

"He said . . ." Zhao paused, considering a polite construction. "He said that he felt the same discomfort when looking at you, the one-eyed, as when he would look at the tower."

Mitchell sighed, and the statue weighed heavily on his shoulders for the rest of the walk back. He had gambled with the remnant of their precious wealth on this information. Yumei and Roland had both retired by the time Mitchell and Zhao returned, and Mitchell would do the same before bringing it to their attention. *Generous moonlight,* he pondered. *Tomorrow is April 22nd. The full moon is due on the*

28th, or perhaps the 29th by reckoning the date on this end of the world. We have time yet, if this is the key to finding the place.

The group all enjoyed a more generous measure of sleep that next morning, at last assembling for lunch an hour before noon. Mitchell and Yumei had recovered from the day before, and Roland also looked much the better for it; resting in the inn had proved much more productive than probing the damp and miserable grotto tunnels. Mitchell shared the information that he and Zhao had extracted from the shaken fisherman, as well as the unfortunate announcement of their bankruptcy. "I shall check my luggage," Mitchell began. "I'm sure I can find something else of value—"

"There is one man, a monk from his clothing, who had been going on and on about a *Hēi Tǎ*," Roland interrupted excitedly, remembering the phrase. "I too thought it promising at the time, but Yumei then explained that there is one such place in India, near Puri down the coast of the Bay of Bengal. We both assumed he must have been speaking of that place . . ."

"Is that man still here?" Mitchell pressed him.

Roland and Yumei scanned the room. Without finding the man from the initial inspection, Yumei spoke with the innkeeper and several others, inquiring if anyone knew him. Some minutes later, she returned to the table. As it turned out, while almost everyone presently assembled in the inn's common room recalled the man as well as the party did, no one knew his name. He was not from Luoyang, but made appearances often enough. The innkeeper believed that the man was once an itinerant Buddhist monk; he had been defrocked but retained a wandering lifestyle. When given payment from Roland for rented rooms for another week, the keeper also shared that the monk was Japanese, despite speaking perfect Mandarin. "Itinerant," Yumei mouthed through a grimace. "Piss on our luck," she added, bringing her head into her hands as her elbows rested on the table. "Perhaps we've missed our only chance."

"I wonder why he was expelled, or if he chose to leave the order?" Roland muttered lethargically to no one in particular.

"Let's not resign to defeat just yet," Mitchell offered, which surprised the others as much as himself. Mitchell was usually the one who required encouragement, but now seemed to retain the most willpower as he rose from his chair. "My God, we are in Luoyang, China, not a café on Geary Boulevard! I didn't endure such trials to get here, engineered by your scheming," he added to Roland, "to fall into despair when one potential lead slips by!" Some of the Chinese patrons were now staring at him. "We get out there, and we find him!"

Yumei smiled. "Your friend Roger would be proud. Now I see in you some of that same cold-blooded resolve that he displayed that night in Chinatown."

"I must be letting the malaise of these floods and insects get to me," Roland said as he rubbed his fingers over his growing stubble. "You are right, of course, but I have no thought as to the method of any search. You did have some luck accosting travelers on the road with Zhao, I suppose."

"You said the fisherman described the pagoda as visible in generous moonlight," Yumei said, which Mitchell nodded at. "Then perhaps we require no further guide and simply follow the vague directions and trace the Yihe."

They continued discussing their options. It was the 22nd of April, and Roland and Zhao eventually decided to look for the former monk on foot by taking the road to Sanmenxia, a location that had been muttered by the man nearly as much as the *Hēi Tǎ*. The town was one hundred miles to the west, so if they had not caught up to him within two days of departing, they would return to be ready in time for the 28th: the full moon. It was a gambit; the lapsed monk may have taken another way entirely or would outpace them if he moved quickly. Yet there was little else to be done in the span of days, and it was as good a guess as any. Yumei insisted on staying in Luoyang to make a final appraisal of the grottoes and her research, and Mitchell would remain with her. Realizing that these may represent the final nights of being with Yumei, Mitchell savored every moment, often staying awake for an hour or more after she had fallen asleep, her head resting on his chest.

Roland and Zhao returned the morning of the 26th and had been successful in tracking the former monk down, although he had not returned with them. The monk, who simply went by the name "Kenko," claimed to know of the Black Pagoda's location and to have visited it on several occasions. "He seems half-insane himself," Roland explained through partial congestion, getting over the final symptoms of his clinging illness. "He refused to lead us there personally, not without outrageous payment. Just in getting him to say anything of the place I had to surrender a pair of cufflinks as well as the golden chain for my watch."

"Then we are all broke," Mitchell offered after a sigh. "However fruitful our final investigation proves, we can't be accused of holding anything back. I hope he had some more interesting things to say?"

"Naturally, and his description was convincing enough," Roland replied. "Apart from his clear dislike of the place, he took great pride in his secret knowledge of its location. He provided us instructions for how to reach it when leaving from the southwest gate of the Longmen Grottoes. This information had to be carefully sifted from his cautionary ramblings about the Anshi Cult. It is a place that is utterly shunned by locals, and the moonlight is the only hope of identifying it amongst the terrain itself, having almost been swallowed up by the forest. Even after centuries of neglect, the building's structure has a resiliency." Roland finished his drink and sighed, clearly dreading the next part of Kenko's account. "He complained that on his last visit, he sighted a number of strange, grotesque, man-like figures in the river. I tried to explain to him that with the floods they may have been floating corpses or bunches of debris, but he insisted that the forms were living, horrid creatures that glide through the water. Not unlike what we have already encountered."

"There was a boatman at the inn last night," Yumei

began, "who observed the Yihe flowing in entirely the wrong direction and glimpses of pale monstrosities coursing through the water. He said further that they had a certain stink, an *ocean* stink."

"This far inland?" Mitchell asked, his heart racing, his memory as vivid as burning coals of the Deep Ones astern the *Asia* during the deadly confrontation.

"Oh yes," Yumei said, her expression distant. "It's true that our path along the canal had a number of transfers, but the Yihe flows to the northeast, connecting to the Luo, which in turn flows to join up with the Yellow, which empties into the sea north of Weifang."

Mitchell hesitated, leaving his thoughts unspoken, but Roland did not hold the silence. "They've been racing us here . . . hugging the coastline north from Shanghai. Not just the cultists themselves, but their ascended brethren as well. Walking . . . or more likely swimming along the coastal shallows and the riverbeds. I cannot guess their speed; even if we had beaten them to Luoyang, we have tarried in the area for almost a week."

"Then there's no time. We must attempt to find and enter the *Hēi Tǎ* tonight," Mitchell said.

"It's possible that we've already been beaten there," Roland supplied calmly, studying Mitchell's reaction. "If they recovered the other statues from the depths, then we have done much in reviving the old dream for them of having all of the statues assembled. We may face great horrors should we ever find the *Hēi Tǎ*."

"Are you spouting this to simply test my resolve?" Mitchell asked. "It's not like you to be indecisive."

Roland could not conceal his surprise, then grinned. "You certainly have a fire inside of you, Mitchell Bernheim. I have known you for not even a month, but as our danger grows, only your determination seems to outpace it."

"I am more than ready to be rid of the statues, forever," Mitchell replied. "To be able to rest peacefully each night, to return to my shop on Van Ness, that's all I want. But I know too much now that the burden of turning away would be even worse, knowing what evils we risk upon the world by not acting."

"Are you not a Jewish man?" Roland asked. "I recall a verse from the book of Proverbs about towers . . . 'The name of the Lord is a strong tower: the righteous runs into it, and is safe.'" He then laughed dryly. "The tower we seek is of quite a different nature. Perhaps you can summon some angels to our side."

"I think you'd want my father for such business. I am not so upstanding," Mitchell responded. "It's true that great stock is placed in angels in our faith. There are of course many different categories," he began, remembering the old lessons. "The great named archangels, warrior angels, interceding angels, messengers, teachers . . . I do not doubt we could benefit from all of them in our situation."

The group began making ready. Yumei and Mitchell exchanged a glance, and she raised up her satchel just before slinging it over her shoulder, indicating that the tomb guardian recovered from the caves was within. They left the White Lotus, walking along the road towards the grottoes in the dusk. "Although my father insisted on not relying on angels, or any such creatures, and seeing God's blessings in our own talents and energies," Mitchell resumed, "in a sense, 'we become angels to others,' he is fond of saying. 'When we fulfill God's promises to us in our service to each other, we become angels of His promises. It is in this way that we may stand shoulder to shoulder with Abraham, Moses, and Solomon . . .'"

"How lofty," Yumei remarked.

"Not to him," Mitchell responded, and he suddenly turned at a splash he heard in the water as they walked along the bank of the Yihe. There was nothing.

13

The group risked one lantern so that Roland could read the instructions he recorded from Kenko. They seemed ill-favored to find the *Hēi Tǎ* that night; it would have nearly been a full moon, but heavy overcast obscured things so that they also made use of the lantern to guide their uncertain steps. The woods were dense with cypress trees and pines on the foothills that crowned the grottoes. It was disorienting, save if one retraced their steps down the hill to return to the bank of the Yihe. Zhao, who was familiar with countless tales of such haunted places within China, proved the most hesitant to undertake the journey. In the end, Roland did not compel the man to go, yet this mercy seemed to shame the man to the point that he ultimately accompanied them on the haunted way.

They had left at dusk, taking care to attract as little attention as possible both in town and when skirting past the Longmen Grottoes. If anyone was following them, it was difficult for Mitchell to imagine how their pursuit would not have been frustrated by the maze of close-packed trees on the slopes just beyond the great sculptures. Rather, it would have granted cover if they did not have to keep their lantern lit, but Mitchell could picture the flickering of the lantern as a ghostly orb to those who would look up into the forest from the path that ran to the southwest gate. It would surely betray their location, perhaps for over one hundred yards. "Roland, can't you manage without the blasted lantern for a while?" Mitchell whispered. "We've been at this for some time now, and I would think you would have committed some of Kenko's advice to memory."

"His directions were all landmarks, and they are damned confusing," Roland spat back, clearly agitated, squinting at a cluster of peculiarly bent cypress trees. "Ah, but what's that now?" he said vacantly, looking up. His face was illuminated as the moon at last cracked through a breaking in the clouds. "There, that's a marked improvement, if it can last. Yes . . . from this cluster, we need to look for where the ground begins sloping downward—on the western side, leading away from the river. That's the real difficulty. The Black Pagoda is not atop one of the foothills, as one would expect, but at a low point in a vale. The top of the pagoda itself will be in line with the treetops of some venerable pines rather than rising far above them."

The moonlight did not stay out evenly, but the clouds were breaking to the extent that there were enough pockets for them to continue following Kenko's directions. At the very least, to Mitchell's considerable relief, they could get by without the lantern, albeit slowly. They found the valley and, just minutes later, as described both by the Luoyang fisherman and the wandering Kenko, a pillar of black. The small tower was darker than the pine needles and cypress leaves and greedily absorbed the lunar radiation. After a journey of thousands of miles by land and sea, they had found the resting place of the usurper Emperor An Lushan. They had found the *Hēi Tǎ*.

The Black Pagoda was modest in stature to some of its greater kindred in the region. It was about three stories high with eight distinct levels in its outer design, very much in the manner of the Wild Goose Pagoda in Xi'an, but on a smaller scale. None of the four could guess the construction materials used by the original builders to achieve the perfect blackness of coloration on the outer edifice. "Could they have hauled obsidian from some volcanic slope?" Mitchell muttered to himself. There were scattered remnants of a ruined courtyard wall that enclosed the tower on all sides and an open arched gate to approach the temple itself.

"*Hēi Tǎ* . . ." Zhao whispered, frequently checking behind his shoulder toward the river, though their view was now very limited in the valley.

"Yes, we have found it at last," Roland responded, placing an arm on his associate's shoulder. "Next, the burial chamber."

The investigators crept forward, passing through the moss-grown outer wall into the inner courtyard. Although it was nearly May, the soil surrounding the Black Pagoda was barren. Roland, to spare his man from any madness within, had Zhao posted at the gate as a sentry to alert the group if others were coming. The doors to the *Hēi Tǎ* itself appeared to be cypress and were carved with dreadful depictions of Deep Ones and greater beings of which Mitchell had no name congregated around a large, winged octopian mass that must have been Cthulhu himself. The doors, perhaps twelve hundred years old, creaked and yielded as Mitchell and Roland pushed. Stale air rushed forth with a moaning sigh. Roland relit his lamp as they entered the utterly silent and dark space. There was one central chamber that comprised the interior, with a high ceiling that rose uninterrupted to the top of the structure. There was an altar caked a brownish-red color, which evoked a murmur from Roland about the deathly rites and sacrifices to Cthulhu. There was also a strange pool in the very center enclosed in a brick edifice, much like a well. The liquid had a thick, shining complexion. "Could it be?" Mitchell asked vacantly, leaning precariously toward the pool. "Liquid mercury?"

"Stay back!" Roland warned, and Mitchell regained his senses.

"Mercury of course has a long connection to immortality in Chinese culture," Yumei reminded them didactically. "Qin Shi Huang, the first emperor of unified China, fatally poisoned himself by taking mercury pills to obtain everlasting life. It also appears to be Emperor Gaozong's method of preventing anyone who would dare enter the burial chamber. But I have prepared for this," she added, taking out her large bolts of parchment that had been huddled beneath her arms. She placed the eight scrolls in an octagonal pattern around the well of mercury in the center of the room. Yumei explained that these corresponded to the eight corners of any proper pagoda. The scrolls already had fastidious and intricate calligraphy and diagrams inscribed on them—the product of months of Yumei's strenuous research into the esoteric and occult and recent days of frenetic inscription. "Xuanzang had indeed documented a certain incantation, titled *Tígāo Shuǐ*, Raising Water. The ritual predates the Xia dynasty. It is older than all of China," she added while delicately unrolling each bolt to her satisfaction. "Xuanzang postulated that it was used by the Priest King of Mohenjo-Daro to revive a noblewoman's drowned daughter. For our purposes here, it should remove the mercury to allow descent into the burial chamber."

Roland and Mitchell watched while Yumei saw that everything was prepared. Eventually she nodded to herself, then drew a small silver cup from her satchel. She carefully stooped over the well of mercury, securing a small amount in the vessel. She stepped back over the ring of scrolls and carefully turned over the cup while drawing it towards her in one smooth motion. Mitchell gasped, expecting to see the poisonous element splash about her. Instead, it floated in place, then slowly began rising like bubbles in an upward draft. The lines of careful script began to shine with a luminescent, cyan radiance, painting the chamber with a glowing aura. The mercury in the well also began rising up in larger particles until a pillar of the silverite element ascended and stretched up to the pagoda's lofty ceiling. During the mesmerizing display, Mitchell became aware that Yumei slipped him the tomb guardian she had been concealing, and he quickly placed it in the interior of his heavy jacket while Roland continued to observe the ascending mercury. Zhao ran into the chamber, temporarily stunned by the arcane display. "Mr. Hughes!" he managed at last. "There are men coming! We've been followed!"

"How long will this last?" Mitchell asked Yumei, pointing up to the raised pillar of mercury. "We could all enter the tomb chamber now!"

"I . . . I do not know," Yumei replied with a rare uncertainty. "Anyone who descends below may become trapped!"

"I'll be the one to do it then," Mitchell offered immediately. His memory of Yumei mortally ill at his bedside in his previous life instilled a spark of the protective courage that roused the highest forms of heroism. "I've already been granted more than my share of extra time. You both have too much work yet before you."

"I should be the one," Yumei rebuked, her voice trembling. "I may be able to devise some way to escape the chamber after seeing to what needs to be done."

"We cannot debate—" Roland began.

"I'm sorry, but I will not defer, as a gentleman should," Mitchell said, pulling Yumei close and kissing her. "I acquired the statues, and the burden is mine to put to rest. Please keep an eye on her for me, Roland," he added, and his companion nodded back to him.

Yumei held Mitchell close a moment longer, but then indicated with the slightest of nods that she would abide by Mitchell's determination. "Remember the Elder Sign," she cautioned him sadly, and Mitchell recalled the strange symbol from the grottoes. "Quickly then!" she added with alarm, and they all could discern that the raised mercury was vibrating and now slowly descending, as if a fan was blowing air across it. Roland drew his pistol but accompanied Mitchell to the well's edge to steady him. Mitchell steeled himself and squinted into the now empty shaft, furtively feeling his pocket to ensure that the tomb guardian was secure while readjusting the straps of his backpack, which held the other. Peering down, he could not discern the depth of the shaft, and fighting his instincts and reason, he heaved his legs over the ledge and allowed himself to fall.

Things went awry immediately. The fall itself was not deadly; Mitchell could feel the narrow confines of the earthen shaft slide against him as he thudded into the earth of the burial chamber. The pain from the fall was quickly overcome by surprise as a second body thudded against his from above. "What the—Roland? What the hell are you doing down here?"

"Give me just a moment," Roland groaned back to him, and the two untangled themselves and moved away from the shaft. The mercury descended in their wake but did not fill the chamber—there was a landing that dropped lower, separated by a ledge from the room itself, which Roland and Mitchell had to step over to enter the burial chamber.

Additionally, there were shaped inlets that diverted the excess mercury into compartments inside the walls. Mitchell immediately recognized the room from his dreams; there were eight alcoves in the wall to house the tomb guardians, all corresponding to a point in the pagoda, and each alcove was surrounded by wheels of Chinese characters.

Only two of the eight niches were occupied by lustrous tomb guardians, which likely had remained undisturbed since the time of Emperor Gaozong's raid. The walls pulsated with a glowing light at these areas while the other recesses were barren, and the very air felt tense and unstable, ready to burst from hidden pressure. In the center of the room in a slight depression was a jade sarcophagus, no doubt An Lushan's, set with onyx and rubies. The shining mercury from the shaft, which blocked their return to the ground floor, at least provided a very faint light source. The room's decoration was saturated by rock-cut reliefs of An Lushan's short-lived dynasty and devotional images to Cthulhu as well as the same kindred race of octopus-like beings and corpulent dragons that Mitchell had seen in the main chamber. "Not Deep Ones," Roland said, noticing Mitchell peering at the strange creatures. "They are much greater, more akin to Cthulhu himself. The Star Spawn . . ."

"You should be protecting Yumei!" Mitchell interrupted Roland, grabbing him just beneath his collar. "Why did you trap yourself down here with me?"

Roland emotionlessly waited for Mitchell to finish, then brushed off his shoulders when the man released him. He gestured as if to speak, but then aimed and quickly fired his pistol twice, hitting both of Mitchell's kneecaps with his cold, signature accuracy. Mitchell folded over to the ground, breathless at the pain, until he managed a type of croaking agony. "I don't believe that Yumei is in any immediate danger," Roland resumed while carefully removing the tomb guardian from Mitchell's backpack. "There are no cultists—no one at all is coming, although I instructed Mr. Zhao to give that warning. I imagine he and Miss Han may make their way back to Luoyang in what time remains for this world. But we are quite alone here. The last of the Anshi Cult was eradicated in China some years ago, though the Cult of Cthulhu lingers in disunified pockets across the earth, save for the brethren who live below the sea. Although there is a resilient community in New England, if a bit primitive."

The horror of the cold betrayal seized Mitchell's spirit and left him wordless for lingering and painful breaths. He had expected to see a new ghoulish light in his companion's eyes, or some ghastly new expression that illuminated the treacherous madness. Instead, what was disturbing about the display was the perfect continuance of a placid, almost bored look on Roland's face. The man had perfected his mask, or perhaps had totally succumbed to insanity so that no frenzies or even residual emotion could be stirred in him. "You left the cult," Mitchell managed through pain that threatened to overcome his consciousness. "You, out of all of us, were the most determined to stop them!"

"Indeed I did, and indeed I am!" Roland replied earnestly,

clearly finding it important that Mitchell understood. "I am no longer a disciple of Cthulhu. No Great Old One will ever claim my allegiance again. I am of poor birth by their reckoning and was of meager rank in their fellowship; neither of my parents were of the blood of R'lyeh themselves. Damn them, damn all who consort with such creatures." He bent his knees to stoop down close to where Mitchell's head rested. "The cult took everything from me, you understand. My childhood, my sanity, my brother Matthew, who I swore would never follow the rites and my path. But when I executed my resignation . . . my betrayal . . . it was ever so slightly premature. I had not accounted for all the possible risks, the counterattacks. They tried to kill me and failed, but they did succeed in murdering my brother. As this journey progressed, as we lost two tomb guardians already to them . . . I finally understood that the best revenge and our only remaining option was to give them their fondest wish. I will give them the awakened Cthulhu so that they may find the oblivion they court so carelessly. Such damned fools! All of these cults and many of the world's religions as well! Their longing for the End of Days, their pornographic view of eschatology . . . it will not purchase life, only death."

"Exactly what you are imposing upon me," Mitchell hoarsely rebuked.

"I apologize in keeping this final purpose from you. I am not fond of deception of that kind, nor of the added, momentary pain I've caused you once again. But clearly you would not have brought me here with the statues otherwise, and I had to keep you from sabotaging this critical moment." He brushed some of the dust off Mitchell's shoulders. "I'm not going to kill you, Mitchell, though of course you knew that. Don't convince yourself out of your pain or self-pity that I have malice toward you. You alone will get to witness as I destroy the guardians and send clanging symbols that will be heard in R'lyeh."

"I'm sorry for your brother," Mitchell replied, his breaths becoming more calmed. Adrenaline and cold logic demanded that he try to persuade the fanatical Hughes. "Perhaps . . . perhaps he is still alive? Did you ever confirm his death? You may be condemning him, and your world isn't nearly so dark—"

"Do not speak of things you have no knowledge of," Roland replied evasively.

"But your pain doesn't give you the right to doom everyone on the earth for your vendetta. Such is the action of a cultist, not of a liberated mind."

"The *right*," Roland scoffed. "The right to do anything is simply a subjective designation, defined by a feeble-minded church or despotic government, institutions that always fail in their promises of protection, failed concepts to the core. The only rights that mean anything are the ones we can claim for ourselves. It's our most primal link to existence itself, natural law, the evolution of eons." He moved away from Mitchell, no longer regarding him. "Throughout my life, I've only further confirmed my disgust of our planet and those who inhabit it."

"You're a fool for thinking that Yumei won't devise a way to stop whatever it is you're planning," Mitchell called out, trying to keep Roland's attention fixed on him.

Roland gave a mirthless laugh and set the tomb guardian he had taken from Mitchell on the floor. He leveled his pistol at it, then fired. The pistol's bullet ricocheted off, only chipping the vibrant guardian while the bullet buried itself somewhere in the dirt floor. "Do I need to alter them first?" he asked himself, curious. "I suppose if I simply died three times, all three would be bereft of their magic . . ."

"An excellent idea," Mitchell suggested.

"That's enough!" Roland spat, although he now seemed to regard the idea with suspicion, trying to interpret Mitchell's provocation. "Ah, perhaps simply removing the remaining two from the alcoves will suffice. Yes, of course, perfectly simple. I could toss them all into the mercury, if needed." Roland strode to the side of the chamber where the statues remained, and Mitchell knew he only had seconds to take action. Mitchell could not move his right leg whatsoever, although perhaps Roland's shot to his left knee had just missed the mark, as the antique seller could assist his crawling with slight exertions from this leg.

Mitchell had no chance of reaching his statue on the floor, nor could he reach the entry shaft of mercury. He had a concealed tomb guardian within his jacket, but that would mean nothing if the remaining two were seized from the alcoves. He crawled to the jade sarcophagus and was able to reach up and grip around the lid. He tried to pull himself up with the strength of his arms, but faltered. He thought of Yumei and tried again, his teeth locked. The exertion brought forth blood and sweat. Mitchell had lost some thirty pounds since arriving in China due to the famine, though his arm muscles had been strengthened out of necessity in assisting the operation of the canal ship. He was able to hoist his body up, which prompted Roland to turn and regard him. He held one statue in his hand, leaving only one to yet be removed from the alcove. "Impressive!" he remarked. "But your heroism would be better spent in calm acceptance."

The lid to the sarcophagus was not perfectly sealed, and even with his overworked arm muscles near the point of tearing, Mitchell was able to push the lid to the side. The skeleton of An Lushan was revealed to be inside, strange in its physiology. It was stoutly shaped, and the skull structure had broadened, suggesting that a change had indeed occurred over the usurper general. A shroud concealed his face, which contained inscriptions in heavily faded ink and bizarre symbols of a similar kind to what Yumei had written on the scrolls. "What are you—stop!" Roland commanded.

Mitchell leaned forward and was vaguely aware of his shoulder being struck by another bullet or two. The pain was relegated to nothing from the constant pain of his knees, and he removed the veil from the usurper emperor, the Göktürk barbarian's face.

It is difficult for Mitchell to describe what happened next. There was a moment of perfect, arresting terror at seeing the horrifying and shriveled visage, which still retained a layer of oily flesh. To look upon the eyeless pits was to be locked in perception of it; one's whole universe only had room to contemplate the horror of the undead mask. Such was the effect that Mitchell felt struck dead on the spot, yet he remained somehow dimly aware and his body remained upright. Without control, his body danced in staggering motions, lifeless marionetted lurches toward Roland Hughes. Independent of severed muscles or the cessation of heartbeat, Mitchell's body would not stop its unnatural dance of halting movement. Roland immediately abandoned his reservation of killing Mitchell and risking triggering the magic of the tomb guardians, but it did not matter—bullets passed through heart, head, and limb without effect in the final barrage of muzzle flashes that dazzled the cramped chamber in dark silhouettes. Mitchell saw his hands lunge forward toward the horrified man, who lamely tried to ward the attack away by shoving out his elbow. Mitchell's fingertips passed through Roland's chest as if they were titanium-edged. They continued in a savage flurry that rent the man's flesh in great cuts. Roland, in his death throes, attempted to shield himself by raising the tomb guardian he had seized.

When Mitchell's hand touched the guardian, his spirit return to his own crumbling body, ending his possession by An Lushan's spirit. The skeleton of Lushan had sublimated into an aura of dust that still lingered in a cloud above the sarcophagus, but it seemed momentarily unable to take flight or enter a new host after coming into contact with the tomb guardian. The chamber itself had begun trembling, shaking violently as only one tomb guardian remained in its proper place. Roland Hughes wheezed weakly, incapacitated, and Mitchell found himself numb, his body no longer a thing of the mortal realm but an energized husk rapidly decaying. His limbs were stiff as boards and growing impossible to move, yet he spent these final moments shambling to place all of the assembled statues in their alcoves. The task was impossible; Mitchell's legs began to shatter in their petrified frailty, and all that his stiffening fingers could manage were to close in on the statue he already clutched.

The final tomb guardian was knocked from the alcove by the earthquake. When this happened, all that remained of Mitchell's flesh, blood, and bones evaporated, and in an instant, he was in the presence of the great city from his dreams. The Black Pagoda revealed itself as a conduit to the very center of the accursed R'lyeh. He beheld the form of the Great Cthulhu, a gigantic, ageless, winged octopian mass that shrank the spirit of the beholder. Only in that brief instant could Mitchell understand the terrible being's immeasurable power, and the scalding presence of the abominable form peeled back any remnant of his sanity. His mind vaporized in the same degree as body, shattered in exponential fractions to flee and dissociate the temple of his spirit from that paralyzing madness.

Yet Mitchell had not ceased to exist. He remained as a dark and closed-in awareness, only partially sundered from his memories. Thought came slowly, but when one has an eternity, thought may materialize in oscillating primordial ripples even without a mind. His mind absorbed not only his own memories, but countless other pockets of satellite thoughts and consciousnesses, occasional intersections in endless space. It was a state of utter darkness with the crushing oblivion that a light would never come, that one's vision could not adjust without eyes or without some outside flare to latch onto. In the crude form of bat and octopus, a tricolor facsimile of shaped earth, Mitchell joined his fellow tomb guardians in their failed vigil of dust, deep in the forgotten chamber.

At some point in those eons or seconds of indistinguishable time, Mitchell recalled a familiarity of this peculiar sensation, even a moment of recall. This existence was defined by the same inertia and perception as when he used to dream of this place. A humorless revelation eventually surfaced. Mitchell came to regard himself as an antique with a purpose never fulfilled, a drop in the emotionless river that he floated in. The stars had become right, and Cthulhu awoke along with the race of the Star Spawn, populating the sky like drifting *Scyphozoa* and subjugating the world once again. There was a rebirth of gargantuan warfare within this pocket of the universe with other Great Old Ones. Only this final apocalypse that rent the foundations of earth and space itself finally extinguished the spirit of Mitchell Bernheim, obliterating the guardian and very chamber he occupied. But the statue's enchantment was woven of that same eternity, and for the third time, he crossed back through the iron gate of death.

Mitchell thumped down into the burial chamber. He would have moved himself out of the way of Roland dropping in after him, but he could do nothing but tremble and claw at the dirt of the chamber, his one good eye welling with moisture while saliva spilled out of his mouth. His soul inhabited a body again. It was infinitely better than the paralyzing and eternal oblivion he had emerged from. As far as his natural anatomy was concerned, he again possessed a perfectly healthy brain, but his state of being was far from this. In witnessing eons of time, his sanity had been stripped from him, knowledge of the ages and the memories of his own lifetime overwhelmed his waking thought. The antiquarian's consciousness was now thousands, perhaps tens of thousands of years old from his existence as a tomb guardian from a doomed earth, and it is no simple thing to come back from that.

"Mitchell, mind yourself!" Roland exclaimed, pulling the man from the bottom of the shaft just as the pillar of mercury returned and flooded the small landing. "What . . . what has happened to you?" he asked curiously, closely observing Mitchell's face.

Still, Mitchell could not rouse any alacrity of mind or body. In a dark corner of his memory, he might have known of Roland's impending treachery and the same path of doom so perilously close to resuming. But Roland's features and echoing words were as pronounced as every grain of dirt in the dim chamber: an indistinguishable blur meshing with patches of darkness. To Mitchell's one good eye and addled senses, all sensory stimulation was a river of indiscernible impulses. Roland laid him down, removing his backpack with the tomb guardian. He continued inspecting his companion, discovering inside his jacket the concealed tomb guardian now defined by gray petrification, its power exhausted. Confused, Roland took up this statue, and the moment he did, in a wash of pain and overpowering return of cognition, Mitchell regained true consciousness. "God! God!" he exclaimed, lunging forward, heaving nauseous and difficult breaths.

"Ah, there you are," Roland replied cautiously. "I see you've smuggled in another statue."

"I . . . yes, I did," Mitchell managed. "Roland, if you would follow an ounce of the heroism of the legendary knight from the *Chanson*, don't go through with this evil." Mitchell's mind was flooded with detained thought, and his speech could not match the pace of conscious output.

"*Chanson?* Evil?" he asked, ambushed by the accusation. "What are you talking about?"

"We've been here before . . . as you might have guessed. I've been brought back once again by the tomb guardian's timeless magic. I witnessed your pain, your despair . . . you managed to nearly kill me and succeeded in bringing doom to yourself and to all the earth. Your brother's death—Matthew's death—was your principal grief and inspiration," Mitchell added, his breaths slowly becoming more even. "But I was brought back, indeed, I have returned!" He paused, feeling stable enough to stand at full height, though

284

he still braced himself with one arm on the chamber well. "But in this instance, my death was not realized until many millennia had passed in slow torture, until the stars signaled the final destruction of the earth. My death from the plague was but a blink compared to that cold, endless horror."

Roland fell to his knees, and for the first time, Mitchell observed the man weep. It seemed that Mitchell had been convincing, convincing in the way that only someone also touched by such eldritch magic, whose mind had been similarly assailed by certain madness, could believe. "Why . . ." Roland finally asked, his tone altogether different than Mitchell had ever observed. "I never would have wished such a fate on you, on any man! Though I won't deny that I wronged you—what use would it be? But how could you not immediately take your vengeance on me? You could have gained the upper hand before revealing all of this to me, used my gun or some implement to kill me. I condemned you to a hell before death! Why would you make any such appeal to me?"

"Because, Roland Hughes, killing you would be taking your path, and An Lushan himself had already seen to your demise before all things went dark." Mitchell looked down to the sarcophagus, safely covered. "I would be bringing an easy end to things, for pleasure's sake, for convenience' sake. Hopefully you can understand I see no use in that in my current state. As far as revenge goes . . . forgive my grimness, but it would be hard to be satisfied; I cannot conceive how I could exact a punishment as great as what I've suffered." Mitchell sat back down with his back to the wall of the chamber. He felt a hollow and numb tiredness. It was very exerting to maintain his presence of mind, which always threatened to jump to an unrelated memory of his great score of knowledge. "With these options being unacceptable, I aimed for a loftier purpose in place of your all-encompassing justice," he explained with a wan smile. "And how could I possibly convince you to turn from your course if I had not managed to somehow convince myself first? I am a tortured immortal now, but one uniquely equipped to take up the old efforts of preserving humanity. I've given you my reasons, but I still can do nothing without your help." Mitchell rose and approached Roland, placing his hands on his shoulders. "Should all the world be filled with devils and debased souls of the worst kind, I will still attempt to set aside what our nature invites us to do. I fear if we do not, then no one else will."

Roland's face was downcast and obscured, and Mitchell could scarce perceive the man breathing. Yet then he lifted up his head and reciprocated by placing his hand on Mitchell's shoulder. Roland began to speak in a strange fashion, and Mitchell quickly realized that he was quoting from memory. "Then Abraham said, 'May the Lord not be angry, but let me speak just once more. What if only ten righteous can be found there?' He answered, 'For the sake of ten, I will not destroy it.'" Roland smiled, a tired, but wholesome and unburdened smile that Mitchell had not before witnessed in him. "In other circumstances, I would take great interest in asking many things of you, who is likely the oldest soul now to have ever existed. But what must we do to stop Cthulhu's awakening?"

Mitchell brought his hand across his face, rubbing it tiredly while avoiding his eyepatch. He had been granted understanding of the mechanics of the chamber in his recent eternity, and naturally it involved the tomb guardians. Mitchell and Roland had four statues between them: the two that had remained undisturbed in the tomb's alcoves for many centuries and the two that Mitchell had brought into the chamber, one of which had turned the lifeless gray in reviving him. "Neighboring statues may draw strength if an unharnessed guardian is placed between them," Mitchell instructed. They placed them accordingly so that the two tricolor statues were separated from each other, first by the gray guardians, and then by empty spaces.

"But that still leaves four empty spaces," Roland said, then cursed. "Would that we still had the two others from Yong's collection, although that would still leave two short, and we'd need another tricolor one. Will this be enough?"

Mitchell did not answer immediately, finding that he could now read the inscriptions of the burial chamber's walls. He could see a new universality in the meaning of all scripts, being touched by the unknown essences and minds he encountered in his millennia of astral exile. "With these many statues present, we can in fact create more, which will serve in containing and sealing the magic of the Black Pagoda to the effect that it will likely never be found by anyone again. But it is not without cost."

"Name it," Roland immediately replied.

"We can create the remaining statues . . . with the forfeiture of our bodies and spirits. By sacrificing one's body, it is sufficient to produce a gray statue, while a spirit sacrificed will produce a radiant one of tricolor design. Between the two of us, it will be enough to complete the effect, to seal the chamber. In a way, it is like restoring an electrical circuit. Do not misunderstand; we would be consigned to the existence that I just escaped from."

For Roland Hughes, the news seemed to lend him a new energy, that he may be a participant of some higher form of miracle than his most recent plan, a crucial role that had never been obtainable in the course of his life. "This is the only recourse?" he asked.

"Yes, short of trusting that the four we have placed here will be enough."

"Which it will not be," Roland replied knowingly. "Not forever."

"Sooner or later, it will be rediscovered, or the current guardians will be removed or fail," Mitchell agreed.

Roland straightened his shirt and jacket and stood tall, brushing the dirt from himself in the manner one does before presenting oneself for a date. "I am ready," he said sternly. "I was prepared for my life to end, and now from your insights, I can be sure of its meaning."

Mitchell himself needed no time; it was difficult for him to arouse much of any emotion as he was still under the stupor of his drifting eternity. They wasted not a moment.

Mitchell and Roland positioned themselves in preparation to reconnect the circuit of ancient magic in harmony with the pagoda's octagonal shape. While they only had two unharnessed statues between them, they could offer their own life forces to connect the gaps and utilize the ashen gray statues. The overall shape where the men and statues stood perfectly traced the points of the stretched star shape that Mitchell had observed in the one grotto tunnel where they had discovered Xuanzang's verse and the one tomb guardian.

"We will be channeling the sigil of the Elder Sign in our positioning and will make use of the spell that lies over Lushan's tomb." Mitchell did not ask for further confirmations that Roland was ready; he hoped that Roland's single-mindedness would remain on the task at hand before oscillating back to a new inspired plan or madness. "On my count, and not sooner, place your hands firmly onto the base of the alcove in front of you, Roland," Mitchell instructed. "Three, two, one." The men placed their hands down in unison, and a surge of energy channeled through the walls of the tomb. The circuit of ancient magic was reconnected by the living conduits, who offered their matter and essence as new statues immediately began to convalesce in the alcoves where their hands were placed. Their flesh, down to the bone, disintegrated in protoplasmic, silver flakes that cast a pale light to the mercury pool. It was over in moments. The bodies of Roland Hughes and Mitchell Bernheim ceased to exist.

Mitchell's spirit lingered even as he felt the consuming pull of the tomb's magic. He perceived all of the tomb guardians set in the walls but somehow had been afforded a moment before his spirit would be forever trapped inside. The antiquarian had not expected this; he later thought that his soul had gained a degree of resilience, either from the many thousands of years his spirit had been dragged across the stars or from a lingering energy of the guardians that had brought him back three times. He thought that his weightless form might escape up the shaft of mercury, and with this thought, it was so. Mitchell's spirit was there, perceiving the main chamber of the Black Pagoda. Yumei and Zhao had either already gone, or he could not perceive them. He continued coursing through the airs above Luoyang, a ghost given flight. The spirit flew over the waters of the Yihe River, and Mitchell beheld a wispy, silver trace of his appearance, as if his features had been skeletally traced with stardust by one mapping a constellation. He dipped his hand into the water. The surface was not disturbed. No amount of movement would cast a ripple.

Mitchell Bernheim thought himself an angel of the promise, his investigation at last concluded by forestalling great floods, earthquakes, and an awakened Great Old One to drown the world. A being of residual energy, not corporeal nor a formless ghost, he would begin yet another watch. Instantly transporting his spectral form over many miles, commanding the particles of dark matter through sheer will, he would oversee the tenuous existence of humanity on earth—as long as he could remain. Thinned, but reinforced by the preceding existence of millennia, he had obtained astral knowledge of millennial shifts and felt the death and birth of stars across the firmament. He longed for the comforts of a human existence again and would gladly exchange for it. His essence would surely unravel to give himself over to such yearning, and he would have to fight this desire, knowing it only hearkened him to his final rest. For as long as he remained, he continued in the habit of watching over those who had guided his first steps in confronting the cold darkness, of which life itself is a momentary and flickering candle.

Epilogue:

The Incident on Russian Hill

J.R. Longstreet rubbed his temples. Being appointed the executor of Mitchell Bernheim's will seemed a simple matter from the outset. Mitchell was some fifteen years Longstreet's junior, and the lawyer anticipated reaching retirement age before the matter would ever reach his desk. To his surprise and distress, Mitchell Bernheim had been reported dead in China, one of the countless victims of the historic outbreak of flood and famine that still reportedly gripped the country.

There had been troubling news in San Francisco as well. In early May, a particularly bitter streetcar strike had commenced, and on the seventh of that month, a shootout on Turk Street left two dead and nearly two dozen injured. Armed 'strikebreakers' brought in by ship now worked the various lines throughout the city, and even the city's mayor, Eugene Schmitz, had been found guilty of corruption and was replaced. The specter of further incidents and violence loomed while the strike continued, and as a result, sifting through the newspaper had become a more difficult business. Yet, when reflecting back on Mitchell, Longstreet also noted the recent disappearance of another upstanding Jewish resident, Herschel Graf. He still remembered the day very clearly when the antique salesman had visited him five months ago in March. *What dark business drew him to China?* Longstreet wondered. *He seemed to understand the danger, even then . . .*

Longstreet was first informed of Mitchell's death in mid-June by a Miss Yumei Han, who had presented the lawyer with the news and death certificate. She was a signatory, along with two others, a Spaniard named Rodrigo Valencia and an Australian, Anderson Blake. The stationery of the death certificate was of the Shanghai International Settlement. Mitchell's body had been lost in the flooding and had not returned with Miss Han across the Pacific. As grim as the news was, Longstreet had all he needed to proceed with the will. Before Miss Han had left his office, he examined the file left for him by Mitchell. "You are included in the will, Miss Han." Longstreet cleared his throat. "Listed right at the top, in fact!"

"He didn't need to give me anything," Yumei replied. "I won't be attending the distribution."

"No, please wait, Miss Han!" Longstreet called to her as she reached the door. "Mr. Bernheim was quite clear that you were to receive just one thing, a very modest folder of documents. In fact, I have it here with me. He entrusted me with them at the same time the will was finalized," he added. "It's clearly important to him."

Yumei halted, but sighed, shaking her head. "Even still, my presence will only be a—"

"Ah, I think I'm beginning to understand," Longstreet offered, rising from his desk and shuffling towards her. "My dear, these situations may be a bit sensitive between the respective parties . . . tell you what, Miss Han, it's a small allotment really, nothing monetary. How about you just take it now, and the rest of the beneficiaries needn't know about you ever having been represented in the will."

Yumei crossed back to the man, a small smile forming. "How could I decline such an offer, Mr. Longstreet? I see why Mitchell chose you." She accepted the folder and opened it to inspect its contents.

"Ah! Well, you are very kind to say so, Miss Han. I try to do right on the rare occurrences where my profession allows it . . . it appears that you have found the contents intriguing?"

Yumei looked surprised after her inspection, then laughed quietly to herself, closing the folder. "Yes, thank you, sir, for convincing me as well." With a courteous nod, she turned and left, and that was the last time Longstreet had seen the woman.

Presently assembled in Longstreet's office on a rainy August afternoon were the will's beneficiaries. These included Elazar, Miriam, and Isaac Bernheim: Mitchell's parents and only sibling. Roger Merrick, an out-of-towner, and a woman named Wanda Silverman were also invited, rounding out the party. "Well then, I believe that we are ready to proceed," Longstreet said at last, grabbing a glass of water for a sip. He was not interrupted as he recited each line, and the business was done rather quickly; the parties nodded or murmured their assent as Longstreet addressed the various items. There appeared to be a consensus and approval of the will's intentions; the antiques business and most of Mitchell's remaining capital was willed to Isaac, while the others received specifically designated items from Mitchell's inventory—personal effects or valuable trinkets. "Well, that went very smoothly. My secretary is procuring a final set of forms," Longstreet explained. "It should just be a few more minutes."

"No body . . ." Elazar mouthed. "And no burial. He is truly lost to us, to God."

"Elazar," Miriam rebuked. "Come, we don't know all the details."

"It would seem that no one does!" the rabbi responded hysterically, beginning to lose his grip of the situation. Longstreet thought to offer a consolation, but then took another sip of water. "Roger." Elazar turned to the journalist. "What did you know of my son's voyage to China? You seemed to have become fast friends with him in a very short time."

"It was an excavation of tremendous significance," Roger offered. "I'm sure the floods over there accelerated the timetable, such that Mitchell risked . . . and lost his life."

"He was under the spell of that woman, Miss Han," Elazar continued through a frown. "She was one of the witnesses to the death notice. I wonder if she thought to gain his wealth by charming him and leading him to some doom."

Wanda nodded in agreement and placed a comforting hand on Elazar's shoulder.

"That was not the case," Roger insisted. "Yumei would have wished no more harm on him than any of us here. I think they both became very committed to each other."

"Are you saying that she loved him?" Wanda asked, scoffing.

"No, I can't speculate on that . . . but they both were very much dedicated to the same goals," Roger said. "I think we will have to make our peace not knowing all of the details of what transpired there. I, for one, was very fortunate to know Mitchell, brief as our friendship was, and I think his memory is worth honoring."

"Mr. Longstreet, perhaps Miss Han should be compelled to appear. You could file the proceedings," Elazar suggested. "I just feel there's something she hasn't shared about what happened."

"No, I cannot compel her to do any such thing," Longstreet spoke, shaking his head. "She has fulfilled her legal responsibility."

"Mr. Bernheim," Roger addressed Elazar cordially. "I know where her apartment is in Chinatown. Perhaps when we are finished here, we may go together and talk with her— as long as she is comfortable with it," he emphasized. "You must understand that she too has suffered, not just on account of mourning Mitchell, but also remains traumatized and exhausted by the journey. We must not be so quick to call her a scapegoat, to place the value of her emotions below ours."

"That's . . . how perfectly decent of you, Roger," Elazar replied, brightening. "I would like that very much. You do have my word that I will act . . . with respect to her. But you may also keep me . . . *in check*, should the need arise."

"When it comes to my father, you'd best take my assistance in that. I too would be very interested in hearing whatever else there is," Isaac spoke for the first time, his passive solemnity turning to a smile. "You must be from the Midwest," he offered at Roger's inflection, triggering a friendly conversation between the two about cities and towns along the Great Lakes. Isaac resembled his brother but took more after Elazar than Miriam in appearance. There was a quiet contemplation to his expression, though he was of larger build than his brother Mitchell. The three men all seemed to be lifted in spirit and agreed that they would set out for Chinatown after the distribution. "Are you on the ten-thirty train tomorrow?" Isaac continued, asking Roger. "Have you seen the Mizpah Arch at the Denver Station?"

"Surely you are not leaving so soon!" Miriam gasped to her son, her expression wounded. "It has been so nice to see you again, and you've only been in town for two days!"

"Of course he's leaving," Elazar offered, his sour mood returning instantly. "Did you hope for him to take up the business here? I'm sure he is none too eager to escape from us."

Isaac sighed. "No, I thought I had mentioned . . . I can only take so much time off of work during the warm months. The Great Lakes freeze during the winter—"

"Yes, we know," Elazar supplied wearily. "And then, of

course, travelling becomes much more difficult when the trains are snowed in."

"You are welcome to move closer," Isaac replied earnestly.

With hushed words, a more private deliberation between Isaac and his parents ensued. Wanda Silverman crossed her legs, looking supremely uncomfortable. Roger straightened in his chair. The door to Longstreet's office opened, and his secretary stepped in, holding papers and looking as uncomfortable as Wanda. "Mr. Longstreet, I have the forms ready, but there's a German gentleman insisting on seeing you."

"Dolores, I'm quite sure you must have told the man that I'm indisposed. Did you say German?" Longstreet asked vacantly, thinking back to the documents he had provided to Miss Han. "Well, it would seem you have the final forms ready! We can send you good people on your way now." Longstreet excused himself, wiped his brow with a handkerchief, and crossed back into his office's reception area with the others.

Sure enough, a very tall, broad-shouldered gentleman was standing there, waiting. His coat and hat still shined with moisture from the rain, indicating he had not been there all that long. Through piercing amber eyes, the stranger carefully scanned the faces of all who emerged from the office. "You are Herr Longstreet?" he asked in a deep voice, looking straight at the lawyer. His face betrayed no emotion of any sort.

Longstreet had an uncanny yet pronounced feeling of dread at the question. "What—what's this about?" he managed in response.

The stranger smiled unpleasantly. "The matter of a certain *verfügen*, will. I am trying to determine the whereabouts of a *liste*, a roster from China that I understand you may have . . . forwarded?"

By this time, Wanda had already excused herself, and it seemed that Mrs. Bernheim was being escorted back to accommodations by her son Isaac. "Shall we be on our way, Roger?" Elazar asked, prompting the two to leave. The rabbi checked his umbrella, then carefully guided it through the door and back out into the street with Roger following after him. From their drifting conversation out the door, a later meeting at a "Lucky Li's Club" and the name "Miss Han" could be discerned among other mumblings.

To Longstreet, it was as if the very air in the room had shifted. The German gentleman's eyes could not resist a flickering animation at the mention of the name. *He knows I gave her the list*, Longstreet acknowledged to himself. *That is the very nature of his visit. What an uncomfortable presence the man has!*

Longstreet had moved over to Dolores's desk as casually as he could, where under a stack of papers in the bottom drawer, a Colt 1900 pistol could be accessed. The German gentleman hesitated, giving Longstreet a wary glance, then cocked his head with a thin smile. "It would seem that I was in error, Herr Longstreet. I believe I mistook you for another solicitor." He strode back out into the street with purpose.

Dolores was confused as to why her employer was keen to close the office early that day, and Longstreet attributed it to his desire to spare them both from taking a later line than necessary with the more dangerous climate brought about by the streetcar strike. He offered full payment to the grateful secretary for the missed hours that afternoon since they had no further appointments that day. In truth, Longstreet wished to intercept Mr. Merrick and warn him of what he perceived as the immediate danger the strange German posed to him and Miss Han.

Longstreet's office was in Russian Hill, and it was his intention to hurry to the nearest streetcar stop on the Hyde Line, for the moment overcoming his trepidation of both the stranger and the situation with the streetcars. This line was still cable-operated, owing to the gradient of the hill being more difficult for the city's rapidly expanding network of electric cars. The afternoon thunderstorm persisted, and the lawyer was able to step aboard before it commenced its route down the hill toward Washington Street. He had guessed correctly that this was the car that Roger Merrick would take toward Chinatown, and his suspicions were confirmed as he saw the German, who had taken a seat nearly across from the Chicagoan. Apart from the two of them, the car was empty, unusual even with the strike. Longstreet offered his fare to the operator, a grim man who merely grunted in reply. The lawyer nervously readjusted his hat as he stooped to take a seat to Roger's left, putting him at a diagonal from the German.

"I've heard it is quite an adventure, taking these cable cars," the German spoke, surprising Longstreet. "Reports of sabotage and violence—what is the world coming to?"

He paused as the line began moving, and stunningly, the operator abruptly stepped out through a door and closed it behind him with fumbling hands, isolating the three of them. Moments later, the streetcar grew quite louder than Longstreet was accustomed; there was a sharp grating sound and a vibration in the undercarriage. Something was wrong.

"You mean to trap us here," Roger spoke, maintaining his calm while rain continued to patter against the cabin roof and windows. "Then you must already know that Miss Han—"

"Is out of country, *ja*," the man finished with an air of disappointment, unable to resist flaunting his knowledge. "She will be more . . . *difficult*. Yet disposing of you removes the loose ends on this coast."

Longstreet had no intention of being a loose end and rose from his seat, making for the nearest door, but was knocked over just as quickly. He was just able to keep himself from falling flat on his face by gripping a nearby seat at a sudden lurch. The streetcar was now being carried down the hill by gravity alone and rapidly accelerated. The vehicle seemed to be separated from the cable itself, and the entire car was off balance, beginning to rock to each side more violently, threatening to topple over in a spectacular derailment. The German rose from his seat and grinned. He grasped the ceiling's handlebars within the cabin in a wide stance, blocking the exits save for those who would attempt to pass him. His perfect relaxation suggested that he possessed no fear of his impending fate. "Longstreet! I can get us out of this, but you need to keep him busy!" Roger exhorted.

The stranger's expression shifted as Roger staggered to the rear of the vehicle, and for a second time, Longstreet rose, this time accounting for the leaning force of their descent. Being trapped in a steel box of sure death, he was forced into courage as he put his hands out to grapple with the German, who lunged at him. Longstreet had wrestled during his schooling years and was by all accounts an athlete. Years of marriage, fatherhood, and career had softened his frame to a degree, but with his life on the line and an expanding mystery that taunted his self-dignity, he would offer his opponent all he had.

The German had the momentum of the car against him, yet Longstreet allowed himself to yield ground as the man slammed into him. The tactic lessened the effectiveness of the charge, but still Longstreet reeled back and thought that he would certainly collapse. But his fingers found an old strength. He connected with a grapple, finding his footing much surer when joined with the tangled and anchoring weight of his adversary. Longstreet heaved forward, reawakening all manner of muscle memory and faded instinct. He could smell the man's breath and gaze into the great amber pits that were his eyes. The German's skin radiated a strange sheen; indeed, an oily coating persisted over both clothes and flesh, but Longstreet felt no moisture in his grip. After long seconds of the struggle, Longstreet's entire body was in pain. The German was younger, stronger, and larger, and the lawyer was near the point of breaking. "Get yourself away from him!" Roger shouted.

Longstreet disengaged, releasing the man and allowing himself to fall back. The German intercepted, catching the lawyer's forearm, but with a quick hook, Longstreet was able to punch away the man's lingering grip. Longstreet careened back, and Roger did the best he could to steady the man as he slammed against the cabin's rear. A chalky, sapphire line had been drawn along the eight-foot width of the cabin floor, presumably by Roger. The odd trail was only about four feet from the rear wall itself. Longstreet instinctually drew his body away from it, and he saw Roger hold aloft a large silver coin in his hand, not a silver dollar, but older, perhaps from Roman times. The coin began to glow with the same azurite radiance of the line of dust. No sooner had he wrenched back his leg than the traced line grew exceptionally bright, flashing like a blue flame. Astonishingly, the metal moldered in a pungent plume of dark smoke, and the blinding line burned through the metal frame of the cable car. This cleaved the very streetcar, creating a rapidly expanding area between their tight space and the twenty-two-foot front section. The disconnected section of the cable car rotated and fell backward, no longer contacting the pavement with its underbody but instead with its enclosed rear scraping along the ground. The two clung for dear life to the sides of their overlarge, makeshift sled. The cage of sundered steel veered and slammed against a lamppost, then scraped and bumped along sidewalks, gardens, and mailboxes before it finally stopped.

They were afforded a last glimpse of the fate of the cable car's front; it had continued speeding down the hill and flipped on itself nearly a dozen times in a tremendous thunder of crashing steel. Longstreet and Roger found that they could both still move and collected themselves in silent gratitude as they regarded the twisted wreckage of the front section, which had become so mangled from the impact that Longstreet breathed relief that no human within could survive such calamity. "I would have been dead without your intervention," Roger said to Longstreet. "Thank you."

"I'm obliged to say the same!" Longstreet replied in wonder and earnestness. He noticed that Roger must have either stowed away his odd coin or it was lost or otherwise destroyed in the ensuing chaos. Any further talk between the pair was stifled as the rain continued to pelt them. They began moving towards the wreckage, spotting odd bits of chairs and components of the cable car's interior on the oddly silent street, though murmurings and marshalled footsteps could already be heard in points unseen. Longstreet had made acquaintances with enough strange company of late that he understood that now was not the time for explanations, and he would follow the lead of the man who seemed his ally. His interactions with Mitchell Bernheim had suggested that the antiquarian had taken on a doomed aura, a resignation from being caught in the vortex of a world both more real and dark. Longstreet felt that sensation in his own steps toward the cleaved cable car.

The body of the German had been thrown clear to the point that the two did not need to attempt to enter the wreckage itself to confirm it. To Longstreet's great astonishment, the body appeared intact, though only paltry tatters of clothing clung to the corpse, which was bloodied, and most of his face had been torn away by the pavement. *His bones ought to have been crushed, any flesh completely shredded . . . how is it that his body remains in one piece?*

The shock of the discovery increased as the man wheezed a broken cough, gazing through one remaining bloodshot, amber eye at the pair. "Obwohl ich sterbe, wird die Bruderschaft leben," he rasped in the moments before death glazed over his eye. The man's collared shirt was all but gone, but a medallion remained around his neck that had been spared from destruction. The chain was gold and adorned by a single ruby set in a finely wrought pattern much like a pyramid. The murmur of voices and startled yells loudened, and on impulse, Longstreet snatched the medallion as Roger nodded for them to leave the scene.

"Die Bruderschaft . . . the Brotherhood?" Longstreet asked Roger, rubbing his side. People were shouting on the street, pointing at the wreckage, and the two of them limped away from the bisected streetcar while police and onlookers began to surround it.

"Keep an eye out for that operator," Roger replied, warily scanning the way back up the hill. "I don't think he was with the strikebreakers."

There was a great gasp from the crowd. The two checked their movement, taking cover around the corner of Jackson Street. "A survivor!" someone shouted. "He needs medical attention!"

In disbelief, Longstreet forced his weary steps forward, haunted with the thought of a conspiracy of immortal men. In their continued retreat, there was no sight of the operator. Longstreet thought that if they had lingered a moment longer, they would have been intercepted as witnesses, and he was already preparing his account if he were to be identified at a later time. "Do you know what he's going on about?" Longstreet asked again once they were further away. The journalist remained silent, staring at the amulet in Longstreet's hands with a lingering wonder. "Who . . . what is the Brotherhood?" Longstreet repeated, limping to within inches of his companion. "Roger?"

"I cannot say," Roger replied at last, wrenched back from the magnetic enchantment of the trinket, looking back at Longstreet with a moonstruck glance. "But I expect all the world shall know soon enough."

Sean Michael Malone is a native and lifelong resident of Wisconsin. He studied European and Medieval History at Concordia and Marquette universities and is also the author of *Spring City Terror 1903*. A student of historical, Lovecraftian, and fantasy literature, he enjoys seeking further inspiration abroad with his wife, Athena.